Thoroughbred Legacy

The stakes are high.

Scandal has hit the Australian branch
of the Preston family. Find out what it will take
to return this horse-racing dynasty to the winner's circle!

Available December 2008

#9 *Darci's Pride* by Jenna Mills
Six years ago, Tyler Preston's passion nearly cost him everything.
Now he's rebuilt his stables *and* his reputation, only to find the
woman he once loved walking back into his life.

#10 *Breaking Free* by Loreth Anne White
Aussie cop Dylan Hastings believes in things that are *real*.
Family. Integrity. Justice. In his experience, the wrong woman
can destroy it all. So when Megan Stafford comes to town,
he knows trouble's not far behind.

#11 *An Indecent Proposal* by Margot Early
Widowed, penniless and desperate,
Bronwyn Davies came to Fairchild Acres looking for work—and
to confront her son's real father. This time she'll show her lover
exactly what she's made of…and what he's been missing!

#12 *The Secret Heiress* by Bethany Campbell
After her mother's dying confession,
Marie walks away from her life and her career…only to
find herself next door to racing-world royalty. Wealthy
Andrew Preston may make Marie feel like Cinderella, but
she knows men like Andrew don't fall for women like her….

Available as ebooks at www.eHarlequin.com
#1 *Flirting with Trouble* by Elizabeth Bevarly
#2 *Biding Her Time* by Wendy Warren
#3 *Picture of Perfection* by Kristin Gabriel
#4 *Something to Talk About* by Joanne Rock
#5 *Millions to Spare* by Barbara Dunlop
#6 *Courting Disaster* by Kathleen O'Reilly
#7 *Who's Cheatin' Who?* by Maggie Price
#8 *A Lady's Luck* by Ken Casper

Dear Reader,

Like many little girls growing up, I loved horses, though I knew I would probably never own one. So my relatives, bless them, gave me horse books!

My beloved Aunt Charlotte gave me a special book on great racehorses.

The story that most haunted me was of Black Gold, a great little horse that won the fiftieth Kentucky Derby. Run for too many years, he finished his last race—but broke a leg. He crossed the finish line on three legs—but he crossed it. And then was put down.

I thought of Black Gold when writing about Andrew, the quiet and serious hero in this book. He is a man who loves horses and is passionately devoted to both keeping the sport fair—and free of tragic endings like those that befell Black Gold, Ruffian, Barbaro and Eight Belles.

We need more like him.

Bethany Campbell

Thoroughbred Legacy

THE SECRET HEIRESS

Bethany Campbell

Silhouette Books

Published by Silhouette Books

America's Publisher of Contemporary Romance

If you purchased this book without a cover you should be aware that this book is stolen property. It was reported as "unsold and destroyed" to the publisher, and neither the author nor the publisher has received any payment for this "stripped book."

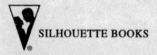

SILHOUETTE BOOKS

ISBN-13: 978-0-373-19937-2
ISBN-10:   0-373-19937-6

THE SECRET HEIRESS

Special thanks and acknowledgment are given to Bethany Campbell for her contribution to the Thoroughbred Legacy series.

Copyright © 2008 by Harlequin Books S.A.

All rights reserved. Except for use in any review, the reproduction or utilization of this work in whole or in part in any form by any electronic, mechanical or other means, now known or hereafter invented, including xerography, photocopying and recording, or in any information storage or retrieval system, is forbidden without the written permission of the editorial office, Silhouette Books, 233 Broadway, New York, NY 10279 U.S.A.

This is a work of fiction. Names, characters, places and incidents are either the product of the author's imagination or are used fictitiously, and any resemblance to actual persons, living or dead, business establishments, events or locales is entirely coincidental.

This edition published by arrangement with Harlequin Books S.A.

® and TM are trademarks of Harlequin Books S.A., used under license. Trademarks indicated with ® are registered in the United States Patent and Trademark Office, the Canadian Trade Marks Office and in other countries.

Visit Silhouette Special Edition and Thoroughbred Legacy at www.eHarlequin.com.

Printed in U.S.A.

BETHANY CAMPBELL

has written forty-eight novels and novellas of romance and romantic suspense. An eight-time finalist for the RITA® Award, she has won three, as well as three Reviewers' Choice Awards, a Maggie Award and a Daphne du Maurier Award.

Under another name, she has published articles, short stories and poetry. Her proudest moments outside of romance were doing a poetry workshop with Maya Angelou, and being presented two poetry awards in one evening by Gwendolyn Brooks.

She won the 2005 Cape Fear Screen Writing Award, and her film script, *Three Apples Fall,* has just been shot and edited by LCW productions.

Her husband, Dan, has written science fiction, a syndicated humor column and a number of short plays and screenplays. The couple lives in northwest Arkansas with three cats and a garden that's been out of control for fourteen years. Their favorite pastime is watching movies and videos. They plan, someday, to clean their office.

To the memory of Charlotte and Jesse Hall
and to their children, John and my dear Mary Ann

PART ONE

Australia, the Northern Territory
February

Chapter One

The tall Kentuckian, Andrew Preston, was new to Australia.

And he'd come to the Northern Territory for a practical reason. He'd meant, with the help of his old friend Mick, to test the Territory's political waters. He needed support in his run for the presidency of the International Thoroughbred Racing Federation.

At the moment, though, the political waters were icy cold.

"Listen, Yank," the big man, Francis Bleak said. "Australian leadership should come from Oz. Reforms? We don't need none. We're doing fine as we are. Now I got work to do."

The Thoroughbred breeder turned his broad back and walked into the stable. The three men who'd stood by him, listening stony-faced, cast cold glances at Andrew and silently followed Bleak inside.

Andrew looked at Mick and Mick looked at Andrew.

Straight-faced, Andrew said, "This is starting out really well, eh?"

Mick, a breeder himself, ruddy and red-haired, shrugged.

"You told me to introduce you to some tough ones. I just did. It could have been worse. He could have shot you." Mick started toward his Jeep.

"Be quiet," Andrew cautioned. "We're not out of range yet. I take it he'll vote for Bullock."

"Righto," Mick said with a nod. "But I warned you about Bleak. Hey, I've known him all my life. He may raise horses, but he's an ass."

Mick and Andrew, both thirty-five, had once been roommates in grad school in Kentucky. Mick, squarely built and freckled, had returned to Australia, where he now was president of the Northern Territory Thoroughbred Association.

In Kentucky, Andrew had served two terms as executive director of the Thoroughbred Association of the Americas, Southern Region. He was a tall, lean and broad-shouldered man. His dark hair was thick and wavy, his features finely carved. For generations, his family had bred and raced Thoroughbreds, and he moved with an expert horseman's physical confidence.

He loved the sport, but he had serious concerns about it. Serious enough to make him take action. When he'd been asked to run for the presidency of the International Thoroughbred Racing Federation, ITRF, he'd taken it as a great honor. But an even greater responsibility.

When he spoke of reforms, he *meant* reforms. Reforms in breeding, equine safety—and the ugly inroads crime had made into the sport. There were people, powerful people, who didn't like his ideas, especially about cleaning out the criminal element.

Mick had kept company with him this week to personally introduce Andrew to the racing set in the Northern Territory. He believed passionately in Andrew's cause and wanted it clear that Andrew had solid connections to Australia—both family and friends.

Both men knew that Andrew faced a grueling fight against Aussie candidate Jackson Bullock. Australia was the deciding contest. There would be other elections the same day in smaller Pacific countries, but Australia was where the presidency would be won or lost. Bullock was the favorite here, a native son with longtime ties to the racing community.

Andrew's dark brows drew together. "Bullock's going all out to beat me?"

Mick's good-natured face clouded. "Right. He didn't expect you'd get so much support in Europe. He thought he'd win easy, and now he's pissed off. Here, he means to dominate you. On his airwaves. In his papers. Through *all* his media connections. He'll fight hard. And if he has to, he'll fight dirty."

A deep voice called from behind them. "Misters—can I speak with you?"

Andrew glanced over his shoulder and saw a dark-skinned man dressed in jeans, a bush shirt and cowboy hat. He was a burly fellow and carried a blacksmith's anvil as if it weighed but a few pounds. Mick stopped, and so did Andrew.

"Raddy." Mick grinned, "I didn't see you."

"I was just inside the stable," the man said with a laugh. "I came to borrow Barney's small anvil." He tucked the anvil under one brawny arm.

"Andrew, this is Conrad Nakumurrah, best blacksmith in the shire. Raddy, this is my Yank friend, Andrew Preston. He's running for prez for the ITRF."

"Pleased to meet," said Raddy. He shook Andrew's hand with a grip appropriately like iron. Andrew feared for his finger bones.

"Same here," he managed to say.

"I heard what you said to Bleak," Raddy told him. "I like what I heard. You have sympathy for horses. That's good. You going to my boss's place?"

"Dead cert," Mick answered. He started walking again, and the other two men fell in step on either side of him.

"My pickup's parked by your Jeep," Raddy said. He looked up at Andrew shrewdly. "I heard the way you talk about the animals. Some people—" he nodded back toward Bleak's stable "—they don't care for the horses. Only the money. Breed 'em for the long legs until the long legs break. And so forth. You are against such things, right?"

"Right," Andrew replied with a sideways smile.

Raddy cocked his head and narrowed his eyes. "You know about the Song Lines? The Dreaming Tracks?"

"Only a little," said Andrew. "I read a book about it."

"Ha! I hear you talk, I suspect you understand. Australia is part of a song the earth sings. Part of the dream the earth dreams."

Andrew smiled and nodded. "Yes. So is Kentucky. Where I come from."

"Ha!" Raddy exclaimed again. He turned to Mick and pointed at Andrew. "This is a good fellow, yes?"

"Yes," Mick agreed. "He is. But tell me, Raddy, how's your family."

"I have a new child. A beautiful boy child. It is odd you ask about my family."

"Why?" asked Mick.

"Because last night, my wife had a feeling that today something special would happen. She made a charm. 'Someone will need this,' she said. 'You'll know him when you see him,' she said. Aha!" Again he pointed at Andrew.

Andrew blinked in surprise. Mick gave Raddy a dubious look. "I can never tell about you. If you believe this stuff or if you're pulling my leg."

"Maybe I'm doing both at once," said Raddy, flashing a smile. But he reached into the back pocket of his jeans and pulled out a wooden charm. It was a beautifully carved bird with a beak painted yellow, its body black and white and red. It hung on a necklace of red string.

"Here," Raddy said, handing Andrew the charm. "Wear this. It will bring you something important. My wife knows these things."

"It's—wonderful," murmured Andrew, touched, yet puzzled. "What is it?"

"Put it on, put it on. It will bring change to your life. Because you know the earth sings songs, it dreams dreams."

Andrew put the string with the charm about his neck, feeling odd. Did he have the right to do this? But Raddy only smiled more broadly. He swung the anvil into the back of the truck, opened the door and got in. "I will see you later?"

Mick nodded. Raddy grinned. "Catch you then!" He backed up, changed gears, and drove off.

Andrew and Mick got into the Jeep. Andrew looked skeptically at the carved charm hanging from his neck. "What's it mean?"

"I don't know." He glanced at Andrew. "Do you believe all that rigmarole? Song lines and charms and stuff?"

Andrew shrugged. "What do you think of it? You understand it better than I do."

"I'm never sure. Sometimes I think the Aborigines see things we don't see. They know things we don't know. I'd treat that charm with respect, if I were you."

Andrew fingered it uneasily, then dropped it inside his blue shirt. Beneath the painted wood, his heart tingled strangely.

At that same moment in the Northern Territory, in the city of Darwin, Marie Lafayette had finished her day's classes at the university and fought the unusually heavy traffic.

She weaved and darted on her secondhand bike, moving with surprising speed for one so small. She was barely five foot two, hardly more than a hundred pounds, and although she was petite, her body was toned and muscular.

Legs pumping, she headed for the Royal Darwin Hospital where her mother lay in the critical care unit. A heart attack had felled Colette Lafayette, her third—and worst—attack in as many years.

Although it was February and still "the Wet," the rainy season, today the sun shone, and the clouds were distant. But Marie knew better than to trust the Northern Territory's fickle weather. She had a secondhand rain poncho in her secondhand backpack.

In the hospital parking lot, she chained her bike to a rack, and headed for the main entrance. The building, one of the tallest in Darwin, was a miracle of engineering, designed to withstand the cyclones that were the curse of the city.

Marie made her way to the elevator, pulling off her helmet and shaking her head. Her hair was thick and golden, and she trimmed it herself into a short, smooth bob. Her eyes were her most arresting feature; they were long-lashed and a pure crystalline light green, unmarked by even a touch of hazel.

Her high cheekbones, straight little nose and full lips gave her a delicate femininity in spite of her boxy unisex clothes. She wore the university uniform for cookery classes, a white shirt and plain black trousers.

She got off at the critical care facility. She no longer had to identify herself at the desk. The entire staff recognized her by now. She headed down the hall and quietly opened Colette's door.

Colette lay with her eyes closed, and Marie's heart tightened in alarm. Her mother looked even frailer than she had yesterday. But her eyes immediately fluttered open, as if she sensed that Marie was there.

"My good girl," she said in a small voice.

Marie caught Colette's hand in her own, as if she could pump some of her own strength and energy into her mother. "Mama," she said softly and bent to kiss her.

Colette smiled and stared up at her. "My good girl," she repeated. "This is a school day. Isn't it? How were classes?"

"Good, Mama. And my job at the Scepter's going well. Last night they told me they wanted to train me for management when I finish this round of certification."

Marie worked evenings waiting tables at the restaurant in the Scepter Hotel and Resort, one of Darwin's finest. The manager considered himself a perfectionist, but he'd said Marie had exceeded even *his* expectations.

Now the older woman sighed and smiled. "Ah. You're so smart, and you work so hard."

"Mama, let me bring you something homemade tomorrow. You're getting too thin. You're not used to hospital food."

Colette grimaced. "I have no appetite. Eating tires me."

Marie squeezed her hand more tightly. "Home cooking will make you feel better."

Colette shook her head. "What makes me feel best is how well you do. You've got an education, opportunity, prospects. That's what's important. You'll have a good future—secure."

Marie swallowed. Education, opportunity, prospects, security.

These were things her mother had never had. But she'd worked unstintingly for Marie, and now it was Marie's turn to care for Colette. And she would—she was prepared to drop out of school for a semester, even take a leave of absence from her job if she had to.

"I'm doing fine, Mama. And you're going to *be* fine."

Colette's mood shifted strangely. "I've been thinking. I have something to tell you. Something I've held back. You know about Reynard and me."

Marie nodded, but was concerned: Colette had been repeating herself lately—was this a bad sign? She kept talking about the past as if she were struggling to make it clearer to Marie, although Marie knew it well.

Reynard was Colette's brother by law, but not by birth. The Lafayettes had first adopted Colette, then four years later, Reynard. But the family had almost been ruined by the 1950 cyclone. The cyclone, unnamed, destroyed the little building where the Lafayettes lived above their pastry shop—everything they had.

Colette's father, overwhelmed by depression, never recovered. The family began a spiral into near poverty. Neither Colette nor Reynard could finish their schooling.

"I told you I never knew who my birth mother was," Colette murmured.

Marie nodded; she knew that part of the story by heart. But then Colette surprised her. "But maybe I *do* know. I didn't know how to tell you. I started writing to people. A nurse in Queensland answered me—two years ago. This is her letter. Remember that little wooden box I asked you to bring? The letter was in it. But don't read it here. Read it at home and think about it. Yes, it's time I put it in your hands. I feel it."

It was time? She felt it. What did Colette mean? Marie fought down a wave of alarm. She forced a smile, as cheery as she could make it. "You're being very mysterious."

With an unsteady hand, Colette picked up an envelope from the bedside stand. "I didn't know what to believe, what to do, so I did nothing. I just have no idea…"

Colette seemed exhausted. "So I'm passing it on to you. To find out or—I'm so tired," she said. "I'm sorry. You've come all this way, but I think I'm going to fall asleep. It's all I do lately."

"Don't apologize. You need rest. Sweet dreams." Marie bent and kissed her mother's cheek again. Already Colette's eyelids were lowering, but she managed a smile.

Marie studied the envelope, feeling an indefinable uneasiness, and then tucked it into her backpack. She stared at Colette's face, once smooth and delicate, but now shadowed by illness.

Making her way to the elevators, Marie punched the down button, her stomach queasy with anxiety. She and Colette were not only mother and daughter, but the closest of friends. Colette had to recover. She *had to*. Life would be empty and loveless without her.

The elevator doors slid open, and Marie blinked in surprise. A cupid, a very tall, chubby cupid, stood inside. At first glance he seemed naked except for a large white diaper and two inadequate wings sprouting from his back. Cupid's blue eyes widened, and he gave Marie a smile and a leer.

She quickly realized he wasn't naked, but dressed in flesh tights and a leotard.

A gilded bow hung from one shoulder. Slung over the other was a little gold quiver of darts with pink heart-shaped tips. His mop of curly blond hair was clearly a wig.

"Hello, Dearie," he said, looking her up and down. "Happy Valentine's Day."

"It's a bit early for Valentine's Day," Marie returned, hardly in a mood for silliness. She noticed he carried two large pink tote bags, each labeled BNC for Bullock News Corporation and showing a jolly, smiling caricature of its founder, Jackson Bullock.

Cupid jiggled one of the bags, which seemed to be empty. "BNC's sending me to children's wards to hand out goodies— candies and crackers and balloons."

"Very admirable," Marie said between clamped teeth.

"I got a lovely Scallywag biscuit left. Want it?"

"No, thank you," she said in the same tone.

"Aww," he said. "Troubled? You look worried. Shame, a

pretty thing like you. You need Dan Cupid in your life. All of him you can get. How about a spot of supper tonight?"

She looked at him as if he were a bug. She rolled her eyes and muttered, "Puh-leese."

"Please pick you up? With pleasure. What time? Where do you live? Do you like the Pizza Shack?"

She flashed him a disgusted glare. "Thanks, but no thanks. I'm not in the mood. Please just leave me alone."

"Oh, ho!" he said in a hostile tone. "Aren't you little Miss Snip? What's the matter? Don't you like men?"

She was saved by the door opening into the lobby. She was smaller than he was, but trimmer and faster. She sprinted toward the hospital's main entrance.

"Hey!" he bellowed. "You shouldn't run off from Dan Cupid. You'll be sorry."

She dashed out the door and toward the bike racks. She glanced over her shoulder in case he was following her, but she could see no trace of him. Thank God, she thought. Could life get any more surreal?

She was sick with forebodings about her mother, and now she'd been harassed by an overweight man in a diaper. Things could *not* get worse.

Seven seconds later, just as she reached her bike, a flash of lightning nearly blinded her, and a thunderclap almost broke her eardrums. The sky was no longer blue but roiling with storm clouds. She felt the first drops of rain.

A strong, wet wind sprang up, almost flattening the hospital's flower garden, and the rain began to cascade in earnest. She slipped out of her backpack, got out her heavy weather rain cape, shook it out and started to put it on.

Another gale of wind made her stagger, and it ripped the cape from her hands and sent it flying off like a strange yellow bat over the storm-tossed shrubs. It flapped as high as the trees and disappeared. The whipping rain half blinded her.

She'd have to walk the bike home, as fast as she could. She swore softly, then gritted her teeth and told herself to buck up. She needed to be at her job within three hours.

* * *

Marie felt like the proverbial drowned rat when she reached the apartment that she and Colette shared. Curious as she was, she knew there wasn't time to read the mysterious letter. She laid it atop her dresser, showered and got ready for work.

She put on a plain black skirt and another white shirt, this one with frills and clip-on black bowtie. She studied herself in the mirror and thought that her life was a series of changing uniforms. Even when not in a work uniform, she had a sort of uniform. Bush pants and shirt—sturdy and sensible wear.

Now she fluffed her hair to make it look softer and gave thanks that she had a ride to the Scepter Hotel. Her coworker, Izzy, would pick her up and bring her home. Marie chipped in for petrol and Izzy's trouble.

When Isabella honked, Marie snatched up her raincoat and dashed for the car. She made small talk with Izzy, but didn't confess her fear that Colette seemed worse. She couldn't bring herself to put her anxiety into spoken words. She feigned her usual natural cheer.

That night, distracted as she was, she performed her job with utter professionalism, perfect courtesy and genuine charm, as if she hadn't a care in the world. She spoke Chinese to the Chinese businessmen, Malaysian to the Malay tourists, and Spanish to a traveler from Argentina. She had a gift for languages and had studied them at college. She had a smile for everyone.

Well, *almost* everyone. Butch Paul, a busboy, had come close to sexually harassing her lately, but if he tried tonight, he'd be extremely sorry.

When other men tried to flirt with her, she acted as if they were only teasing and smiled at them, refusing to get involved. Nobody came to the Scepter to be greeted by a mope. Her business was not hanging her heart on her sleeve, it was hospitality.

Redheaded Mick Makem was a regular customer, and tonight when he joked with her, she made herself banter back as if she were in the best of spirits.

She vaguely noticed that he sat with a dark, lean man who was strikingly handsome, then rebuked herself for paying attention to a good-looking man at a time like this. She'd vowed to keep herself under strict control tonight.

But then it happened. Butch the busboy gave the side of her breast a hard squeeze as she was leaving the kitchen, and she snapped. She spun about and stamped his foot so hard that tears sprang into his eyes. "That's not fair," Butch accused. "You know kung fu or something."

"Yes, I do," Marie returned coolly. "So don't ever touch me again. Ever." She turned and left him glaring after her. She hadn't spilled so much as a drop from the drinks on her tray.

"Somebody ought to take you down a notch," Butch sneered.

Marie saw that Mick and his dark-haired friend had seen it all. Mick made an okay sign and grinned at her as she came to their table. "Way to go, slugger," he said.

The dark man simply stared at her with a strange intensity. He said, "We both saw what he did. Do you want us to report it? He was completely out of line."

He looked genuinely concerned, but she said, "No thanks. I'll be fine."

"You're sure?" he asked, looking into her eyes.

"Positive," she said. And she was positive. She had a green belt in karate, and someday she intended to work her way up to black. Colette had insisted she take classes. Darwin had its rough elements, and Marie was so small that Colette wanted her to know how to protect herself.

But physical toughness wasn't going to get her through this latest crisis. Colette's illness demanded a different kind of strength, and she wasn't sure how much she had left.

And as the work night wore on, she wondered more and more about the contents of Colette's mysterious envelope. *Why'd she give it to me now? What did she mean, it's time?*

Her uneasiness grew.

Andrew and Mick lingered, nursing their drinks until closing time. They had much to talk about, and in the back of Andrew's mind, he worried about that small blond woman who might be too spunky for her own good.

Sure enough, just as he and Mick were back in Mick's Jeep, about to pull away, he saw two women dash through the mist toward an older model car. One of them was the little blonde, her head down. The rangy busboy stepped from the shadows and blocked their way. He looked as if he might have helped himself to a drink or two at the bar. He grabbed the blonde's arm, scowling, hectoring her.

The dark-haired woman looked frightened, the little blonde seemed incensed. Mick started to say something, but Andrew didn't hear it. He was out of the Jeep, and in six strides he was between the busboy and the blonde. "Look," Andrew said from between his teeth, "leave the lady alone. You want to pick on somebody, try somebody your own size. Will I do? Huh? Will I?"

The rangy kid swore, but after casting Andrew a filthy look, he turned and quickly sloshed off into the shadows, kicking angrily at puddles. The dark-haired woman was already in the car.

"Get in, Marie," she called. "Before he comes back."

"I'll stay until you're out of the lot—and watch that nobody follows you," Andrew said, looking down at Marie. "You have a cell phone in case you need one?"

She stared up at him, her face pale in the parking lot lights. Her pale skin gleamed with moisture from the night's haze. *My God,* he thought, *she's lovely.*

"A mobile?" she asked. "Yes. Yes, I do. I'll be fine. Really, I—I can take care of myself. I—I—"

She amazed him by beginning to shake. Not just a slight tremor, but a real shaking, like someone shivering from intolerable cold.

He seized her upper arms in concern. He could feel her muscles jerking beneath her raincoat's thin fabric. Her lower lip worked helplessly, her chin trembled, and he couldn't tell if her eyes were moist from tears or from the fine rain.

"Are you *okay?*" he demanded, leaning nearer.

"Y-y-you've been very kind, b-b-but—" She couldn't seem to get any more words out. He slipped one arm around her, afraid her knees were about to buckle.

"Miss, I'm going to tell your manager about this incident. And if that fool harasses you again, call the police. I mean it."

She tried to disengage herself, but when she took a step backward, she swayed, as if she couldn't quite support herself. Instead, she sagged forward, clutching the lapels of his rain jacket. She buried her face against his chest. Her back heaved as if she were sobbing silently.

But only for the briefest of moments. Then, as if by sheer willpower, she righted herself again, drew back and looked him in the eye. "I'm terribly sorry. It's not *him*." She nodded in the direction the busboy had fled. "I'm absolutely okay. Just some— an illness in the family. I'm terribly embarrassed. I apologize. And thank you again. But I'm fine."

Before he knew it, she'd slipped from his grasp, opened the passenger door, and was sliding into the car beside her friend. She smiled at him, and there was something in that smile that nearly broke his heart.

The car drove off, and he stood in the mist, looking after the disappearing taillights.

Chapter Two

The rain started to drizzle harder as Marie and Izzy left the parking lot. It was just after midnight. Izzy stopped at a light and said, "What was *that* all about?"

"Butch groped me again," Marie said in a flat, no-nonsense voice. "I stomped on his foot. That's why he came after me in the parking lot. Mick and that other man saw it happen. They must have realized Butch wanted to get even."

"So that handsome guy comes to your rescue?" Izzy asked. "God, I wish Butch'd pinch me so *I* could stomp on him."

Marie said nothing, just sat lower in the seat.

Izzy cast her a sideways glance. "That handsome guy? He was watching you tonight."

"I didn't notice," Marie said. And she hadn't.

"Not notice? How could you not notice? He's been in the papers, on the telly."

"I don't have time for the papers or telly," Marie murmured, gazing out at the darkness.

"He's a high muckety-muck in horse racing. American. He's going to run for some horse-thingy president. Against Jacko Bullock."

"Uck." Marie shuddered. Bullock turned up several times a year at the Scepter during the racing season. She thought he looked like and acted like a pig. "Bullock's nasty. He's worse than Butch any day. He propositioned me right at the table one night, in front of three other men. I almost poured his drink on his head. I'd have *loved* to."

"Well, he's powerful," Izzy said. "He'll gobble that poor Yank up and spit out his bones."

"Sad but true. The Yank seemed like a nice fellow." He had, she thought vaguely. An extremely nice fellow.

"I *guess,*" Izzy rejoined with heavy irony. "And that's why you ended up in his arms? I thought he was going to plant a big smoochie on you."

Marie shrugged irritably. "Look, I went wobbly. I had a bad day."

"Oh, chook," Izzy said. "I'm sorry. Is it your mom?"

"Yes," Marie said, her throat tight. "But I don't want to talk about it."

And Izzy, who had a kind and sensitive heart, asked no more.

But at home, Marie had to think about her mother. She could think of nothing else. She took Colette's envelope, sat on the edge of the bed and forced her hands to stay steady as she opened the flap.

She unfolded a sheet of paper, a letter. It was dated just over two years ago and signed "Willadene Gates." It began:

My Dear Miss Colette Lafayette,
Thank you for writing me, for I think I can answer your questions, as years ago when I was not yet 17 yrs. of age I become an attendant at a home for unwed mothers.

A high-priced place, it promised total discretion, if you

get my meaning. I do remember your birth, for your birthday is the very same day as my own, March 9!

"Your mother's name was Louisa Fairchild. She was 16 yrs. old, unwed & pregnant, & come from quite the posh family.

And I remember *you,* even after all these years. I said to myself, how could anyone give up such a darling infant? But that girl refused to even speak of you. Cold as ice, she was.

In a few days, her parents come and took her home. Louisa F. walked out of the ward with never a backward look. She never even spoke to her own parents!

Now she's grown up and grown old. I see her name in the news. She's rich as Midas and lives on a horse station near Hunter Valley—very hoity-toity! She never married and don't get along with any relatives, I hear tell.

Should you find her, and she recognizes you as her own, I hope you will not forget your friend, Willadene, what give you this info, as I am now elderly and living in reduced circumstances (although as you see the memory is still sharp!)
Your friend, the first to ever hold & kiss you,
Willadene Gates

At the bottom, Colette had weakly scribbled a note.

I wrote Willadene Gates two months later. The letter came back marked "deceased." I didn't know what to do next. My feelings are still mixed about whether I should try to find out more or let the matter go.

Marie, I put some of my nail clippings in a little plastic bag. I pricked my finger and let some blood fall on a piece of cloth. I put them in an envelope in my jewelry box. If we're related to Louisa Fairchild, your DNA and mine should match hers, if I understand what they say on the telly.

It would be good to know the truth, at long last, but I

was never brave enough to search further. I should have done it for your sake and apologize that I did not. I leave it in your capable hands.

Your proud and loving mother.

Marie read the letter again, disbelief mingling with suspicion.

How had Colette found this Gates person? Could the woman be trusted? Her words had a slippery coyness that oozed with hunger for reward.

Marie rose and went to her mother's bedroom and opened the shabby velvet jewelry box on the dresser. An envelope lay in the box's bottom drawer.

Almost fearfully, she opened it. Inside was exactly what Colette had said, a little bag of nail parings and a square of white cotton with three drops of blood.

She also found a second, smaller paper envelope. Opening it, she saw a newspaper photograph with a short article. The article, eight months old, reported that charges had been dropped against Louisa Fairchild, 80. She'd been accused of shooting and wounding her neighbor Sam Whittleson, 61.

The short piece left Marie even more stunned. As a very young woman, Louisa Fairchild had apparently abandoned her daughter. As a very old woman, she'd shot her elderly neighbor. Such a relative didn't seem promising.

But the picture of Louisa Fairchild shocked her more. She saw a lean, imperious woman staring straight and almost arrogantly at the camera. Her mouth was a rigid, unsmiling line. Yet her resemblance to Colette made Marie's nerve ends prickle and chilled her stomach.

Louisa Fairchild still had wide eyes, shaped like Colette's. She had Colette's high cheekbones, slender nose and cleft chin. And Marie herself shared these features, too, except for the cleft chin.

She was suddenly overcome with an almost irrational curiosity. The Fairchild woman lived in Hunter Valley. Not long ago, Marie's uncle had gone to work in that very region. Could he know anything about this woman?

She went back to her room, snatched up her phone and dialed her uncle's latest number. It was after midnight, but Reynard was a night owl. He answered after only a few rings. "Marie!" he exclaimed. "How are you, love? And how's my dear Colie?"

Marie heard background noise and supposed he was in a pub. "Rennie, Mama's not well. She's very weak—and she doesn't look good—I'm afraid for her."

Reynard's voice went serious. "She's taken a turn for the worse?"

"I sense it. She's getting weaker. The doctors don't seem able to help her."

Reynard spat out several colorful oaths concerning doctors. Then his tone grew solemn again. "Should I come? Would it help if I was with you?"

"Rennie, you've got a job. You just can't walk away."

"I can if I need to be with her and you, pet. No man owns Rennie Lafayette."

Marie feared she'd sounded too alarmist. "Wait until I know more. But Reynard?"

"What, love?"

"Mama gave me a letter that a woman wrote her. This woman said she'd worked in a home for unwed mothers and remembers when Mama was born. And she named Mama's birth mother. Do you know anything about this?"

"Stone the crows!" he said in surprise. "I never—she never said a word to me. When did she find this out?"

"Over two years ago. And the woman died shortly after. I don't know how to check this out. Or even if I should. Mama's mother might be dead, too, by now. But she lives or lived in Hunter Valley. Have you ever heard of a Louisa Fairchild?"

"Heard of her?" Reynard demanded. "Crikey, I *know* her! *She's* supposed to be Colie's mom? Hold on. I'm going outside for a bit of privacy."

Marie heard him tell someone to deal him out; he had a family emergency. The background noise faded. She pictured him stepping, alone, into the Southern night.

"There," he said. "Now—Louisa Fairchild is supposed to be Colie's mum?"

"So said the Gates woman."

"That's a jolt. Colie's such a *nice* woman. So much for the bloody theory of heredity."

"Louisa Fairchild's not a nice woman?"

"The old girl's a snorter, she is. But now that I think on it, she does bear a certain likeness to Colie. It's truth."

Marie remembered the photo and somehow she managed to feel both numbed and anxious at once. "You really know her?"

"I live at a neighboring horse station, not far from her. I'm the handyman there. I've actually been in the old girl's house. Fixed the lock on her famous gun cabinet. She's an old boiler, she is, a right old hen. But I get some smiles out of her—pruny smiles, but I get 'em."

Marie didn't doubt it. If Reynard put his mind to it, he could make a cat laugh. She said, "Gun cabinet? Mama had a clipping about Louisa Fairchild. Something about her shooting a man— do you know about it?"

"All New South Wales knows about it. She said the bloke stormed into her house, raving about water rights, and attacked her. Conveniently, she was cleaning a gun at the time. Said it went off accidental-like."

"And people believe that?"

"Some do. And some say she got off the hook because she had more money than Whittleson. She could out-lawyer him."

"What do you think?" Marie asked, frowning in uncertainty.

"I think it's odd to be cleaning a loaded gun. It's a point Whittleson's lawyer never brought up. But lawyers? Pah— they're about as useful as a third armpit."

Reynard always resented authority and officials; unlike Colette, he was a born rebel, and it was part of his raffish charm. Marie tried to nudge him further into the subject.

"You've met her. Do you think she could shoot somebody?"

"She's a scrapper. And she *can* shoot. Rumor says she can blast the head off a snake at thirty meters. Still," Reynard said silkily, "she's rich as a queen. No known direct descendants. If she's your gran, she might open her scrawny arms to you in welcome."

"I might not open mine," Marie said. She liked nothing she'd learned about this woman.

"She's a hard one to know," he returned. "Not a happy person. Lonesome, I think."

Reynard's take on Louisa confused Marie. He sounded critical one moment, sympathetic the next. But he was often mercurial; that was his nature.

"I wonder why Mama waited so long to tell me."

"I don't know, pet. But from what you say, I think I'll drive right up there. She may be franker with me than with you about Louisa Fairchild. I am her baby brother, eh?"

Marie protested, but Reynard insisted. "Today's Monday. If I start early tomorrow, I can make it in two days. Don't argue, dear heart. My womenfolk need me!"

My womenfolk need me! He sounded so swashbuckling, she almost smiled.

"You're sure you won't lose your job?" she asked.

"Who'd be fool enough to fire a jack-of-all-trades like me?" he said with the same bravado. "I'm indispensable, if I do say so."

Marie smiled. Although Colette worried about her footloose brother, he always cheered her as no one else could. "Then come to us," she said.

But shortly after 3:00 a.m., Marie's phone rang. It was the hospital, calling to inform her that Colette had died in her sleep.

Chapter Three

Marie was stunned, but didn't cry. What she'd feared most had happened, but it seemed unreal. It was as if she was trapped in a terrible, incomprehensible dream.

She phoned Reynard, who sounded stricken and said he'd be there as soon as he could.

The next morning, zombielike, Marie arranged for her mother's remains to be cremated. She had it done as soon as possible, without ceremony, for that had been Colette's wish.

Then, somehow, she went to her classes, still feeling trapped in the numb, unbelievable nightmare. That night she waited tables at the Scepter, functioning on autopilot. But under her business-as-usual facade, she was in a maelstrom of emotion.

All of Marie's life, it had been the two of them, she and Colette. When the Lafayette family's fortune failed, Colette went to work as soon as she could and had never stopped. Reynard had left Darwin. Some called him a drifter, but he called himself "a free spirit."

He returned to visit two or three times a year, and then he'd be off again to wherever his whim took him. He was clever enough to always find a job, too restless ever to keep it long.

By her early thirties, Colette was working as a cook and housekeeper. Lonely and shy, she tried always to please. Finally, in the household of a professor whose wife had left him, she tried too hard. He easily seduced her.

Colette soon found herself pregnant—and unemployed. She didn't tell Marie who her father was until Marie was ten, and the man had been dead five years.

He'd never acknowledged Marie's existence, and Colette had never asked him for a thing. So from the beginning of Marie's life, she and Colette had been a family of two, and Colette had been not only her mother but her closest companion.

That night, the first night that Colette was gone, the stupid busboy, Butch, made a move to grope Marie again.

"Where's your fancy toff tonight?" he sneered. "Want a real man?" She looked at him in disgust, her expression cold as Antarctica.

"Why are you so uppity?" he demanded. "Think you got the crown jewels between your legs? You're the same as any other woman."

She turned and walked away. She was not the same as any other woman. All she knew for certain about Colette's mother was that the woman had foolishly trusted a man. Result? She'd ended up unmarried and pregnant.

Colette made exactly the same mistake. Result? She'd ended up unmarried and pregnant—but she'd not been one to give up her child.

Two illegitimate generations were enough.

Long ago, Marie vowed she wouldn't repeat the pattern. She intended never to "fall in love" or into any man's bed. Ever. Marriage? Married women could be as lonely as single ones. Sometimes lonelier.

It had been completely unlike her, nearly collapsing into a stranger's arms last night. She wondered if she'd done it because she'd known Colette was dying. Had she known that from the moment Colette put the letter in her hand?

She wanted this empty, unhappy day to be over.

This, too, will pass away, she thought. But it didn't pass soon enough.

She glanced at her watch, wishing it were midnight. But it was only 7:00 p.m.

On the grounds of Mick's stud farm, Makem's Thoroughbreds, Andrew glanced at his watch and wished the night was older and the party over. But it was only 7:00 p.m.

A gorgeous brunette in a tight red sundress leaned against a palm tree watching him, sultry invitation in her gaze. Andrew ignored her. He intended to keep on ignoring her.

A man in the public eye, a man campaigning for an important office, should not fool with women. He knew he shouldn't have impulsively embraced the waitress in the parking lot last night…yet, still, for some reason, the memory of her rain-misted face haunted him.

But he needed to watch his step. Especially when his opponent had large media holdings—including some of the country's most ruthless scandal sheets. And Andrew's family had just emerged from an alleged breeding crime that made headlines around the world.

Jacko Bullock loved to sling mud. Sexy mud sold best, even if it was lies. Jacko would be delighted to find dirt on Andrew, especially sensational dirt.

Andrew didn't intend to supply him with any. Not a rustle of impropriety. Not a whisper, a wisp, a breath.

Mick Makem, who was hosting the barbecue, gave him a sly nudge. "That black-haired beauty over there's giving you the eye." His freckled face split in a grin.

"Not interested," Andrew answered, taking a sip of beer. "People are taking pictures here. And she looks like trouble."

Mick jabbed with a sharper nudge. "Lovely trouble. All work and no play make Jack a dull guy."

"Better a dull guy than a fall guy," Andrew muttered.

"Oh," said Mick, understanding. "Bullock, you mean."

"Right."

Bullock still repeated the accusations about the American Prestons' breeding fraud. Even though the Prestons had been cleared of any wrong doing in the DNA fraud that had ended the career of their star stallion, Leopold's Legacy, Bullock kept resurrecting memories of the old rumors and implying new evidence might soon emerge.

Bullock's point, Andrew knew, was to keep the Preston family firmly linked to the word *scandal.* And what could be more damaging to a candidate than a good old-fashioned sex scandal?

How many American politicians had lost their reputations, even their careers, by not keeping their pants zipped? *Count 'em,* Andrew thought.

So he had grimly vowed to stay celibate for the duration of the election. Here in Australia, he was the tall, dark, single American from a rich family with a famous stable. Beautiful women signaled him they were ready for kissing and a great deal more. He'd been approached by so many lookers, it made him suspicious.

He knew he was considered handsome. But he was also smart enough to know that he hadn't become as sexy as a rock star as soon as he stepped on the Australian shore. And he knew looks weren't particularly an advantage against the homely, hearty and proudly homegrown Bullock. Bullock looked and acted like somebody's plain and stocky loudmouthed uncle, Australia's answer to a Good Ol' Boy.

Andrew didn't come across as a Good Ol' Boy. He was long and lean, with chiseled features, brown-black hair and deep blue eyes, and he had a slew of college degrees. Next to the rotund Bullock, he didn't look homey and jovial; he looked aristocratic and privileged.

Unlike Bullock, he wasn't a glad-hander or a baby-kisser. He didn't slap backs or lavish smarmy compliments on everybody he met. When he talked about issues, he talked about them with passion, but his passion was measured and earnest. He didn't pound the podium like Bullock. He didn't shout or sputter or chortle or wave his arms or tell raunchy jokes.

The result was that, although some people thought Andrew

the serious, committed and perfect candidate, others believed he didn't have a chance in hell. And tonight, he was haunted by a sensation usually foreign to him: he felt isolated.

Mick's barbecue wasn't just for political reasons. This was Andrew's birthday, his thirty-sixth. Turning thirty-six was sobering. He'd unwittingly crossed some psychological line he hadn't known existed.

Most of his friends had settled jobs, wives and children. He had a campaign.

He was now closer to forty than to thirty…and in the hurly-burly of entering the election, he'd begun to feel disconnected from his real self. He had to watch every word, every action, even every facial expression and bit of body language, especially here in Jacko-Land.

Stop obsessing, man, he commanded. *You've got principles, and you committed to run for the presidency. Forget the private stuff. Fight your heart out.*

So he set his jaw and put on his public persona again. He smiled. He rejoined the party. He had indulged himself in something like a midlife crisis for almost two minutes, and that was two damned minutes more than enough.

He amiably cuffed Mick's arm and complimented him on the feast spread before the crowd. Wine from a local vineyard flowed generously and cold beers seemed to number in the hundreds.

"Want to see something really delish?" Mick asked with a wink. "Look who's coming your way."

Andrew saw the beautiful brunette making her way toward him, her eyes now fastened on his. Her red sundress was cut low over a startling pair of breasts, and she sparkled with jewelry. She was almost too stunning to be real.

She looked like a model or a beauty queen or a starlet. She certainly didn't look as though she belonged at a suburban political barbecue. Distrust edged into Andrew's mind. "Mick," he said, "do you even know who she is?"

"No," Mick admitted. "She's a guest of one of the breeders. But it's you she's got her eye on. She's been trying to catch your attention all night."

My God, thought Andrew, *could she be a plant? Somebody the Bullock people had sent to entice him?*

Photographers, press people, some with video cams, milled through the crowd.

The brunette smiled at him and nodded in more than friendly greeting. He smiled back mechanically.

"Hi, there," she purred. "My name's Sylvia. I just want to say I totally agree with everything you say. I heard you're going to stay with your cousin down in Hunter Valley. I get to Hunter Valley now and then."

"I make my base with him in Hunter Valley," Andrew said. "But I won't be there much. Have to travel a lot. Excuse me. I see somebody I have to talk to. Nice to meet you."

He nodded, a curt movement that signaled goodbye. He turned his back on the woman and left her looking piqued.

Maybe he was being paranoid, but that might be good. No involvement with women—especially one like that—until the election was over. That was that, and it should be gospel.

But suddenly he remembered his strange attraction to the blond waitress. He wondered why he couldn't forget her. Biology could toss even the most cautious man a curveball.

He was more cautious than most because he had to be. He pushed the blonde to the back of his highly efficient mind.

Almost.

But there was another woman, only a memory now, a lively voice that sometimes spoke to him that no one heard except him.

He gazed up at the night. Darwin's cloudy sky showed an obscured, gray pearlized moon. Suddenly the voice in his memory, that long-ago woman's voice, said "There's a door in the moon—if you can find it. And if you open it, you find out the future."

For an instant, he saw the past instead, and another young woman, small and spirited like the waitress. Kellie Maguire.

He'd met her his first year at the University of Kentucky. When she'd told him about the door in the moon, at first he thought she was nuts or trying to grab attention. No. She meant it. He finally asked if she'd ever found the door into the moon.

She'd laughed and said she'd never looked for the future; she was too busy with the present. And she was.

She wasn't like anybody he'd ever known before. She had a sassy air about her and long red hair, always tied back in an unruly ponytail. She was sweet and cheery and as independent as hell.

Unlike him, she didn't come from a family with money. She was a scholarship student, majoring in art and literature. He thought that was stupid. How could anybody make money that way?

She laughed good-naturedly at his business major. How was he ever going to have fun if he didn't learn anything except money? "Hey, Preston," she teased. "Live, why don't you?"

She didn't give a damn for fashion, and she was so original and self-disciplined he was in awe of her. He'd only seen her cry once, when she'd learned her grandmother was dying. She broke down in tears for almost a full minute, and he'd held her. Then she'd pulled herself together and tried to act as if nothing had happened. She'd never spoken again of that moment.

He was secretly shy and, though he hated to admit it, hidebound. She challenged him, she fascinated him, she could get him talking half the night about things he'd never even thought of before.

She enticed him to movies he never would have seen on his own, challenged him to read books he normally never would have opened. She'd changed him, and by the end of his freshman year, he was falling in love with her, unconventional as she was.

And then she was gone. Forever. A swimming accident over the summer. A drunken motorboater didn't see her, and ran into her, killing her almost instantly. And Andrew hadn't come close to loving anyone again since.

Now, for that strange instant, the door in the moon opened, and he saw her standing there, with a smile and her untidy red hair dancing in the cloudy breeze.

"Christ, Preston," she said in his mind. "Now you want to be president of ITRF?"

That question raised a dozen more in his heart.

"Yeah," he said to her silently. "Very funny, huh? I want to be president…"

"Then go for it," she answered with her sidelong grin. "But is that *all* you want? Are you sure? Isn't there something missing?"

And then her image disappeared, and he was staring up at a clouded, doorless moon.

At midnight that night, Jacko Bullock reached across the sleeping body of his mistress and picked up the receiver. "What?" he demanded. He was in a rotten mood because he'd just dozed off, but he hadn't quite managed to make love to Tarita, who now slept beside him, all silken and exquisite and useless. He needed a new woman again.

He heard raspy breathing, and that meant Feeney. Feeney was his contact, his liaison in Jacko's covert war on Andrew Preston. Feeney was a general in this war, one whose face he'd never seen, but who'd been supplied by very dependable allies.

Jacko had a public campaign for president of the ICRF. And he also had an extremely well-hidden private one, as complex as a huge spiderweb. Feeney wasn't at its center, but he was close enough, close enough.

"Preston steered clear of her," said a man's rasping voice. "The dark one. She said he smiled, he nodded. But he didn't let her get near him."

Jacko swore. "What is he, a pansy? Sylvia's gorgeous."

Hell, he thought, she'd kept *him* satisfied for almost three months—that's how good she was. He'd sent orders for her to wear something red and low-cut. And plenty of diamonds. He'd given her diamonds. Cheap ones, but they'd kept her happy.

"He's not a pansy," Feeney said. "He likes women, all right. I think he just was leery of her. Maybe she's not his type."

Jacko swore again. "Not his type? She's the type for any man with a set of working goolies. For a while, at least."

"Well," Feeney said hesitantly, "she's not subtle, y' know? From what we know, he doesn't go for the glam thing. No super-models. His tastes are hard to predict."

If Sylvia'd got Preston in bed, I'd've given her good diamonds, Jacko thought.

He stared down at Tarita's lovely, sleeping form and wondered if *she'd* suit the Yank. If she could turn the trick, he'd give her up in a minute.

"Preston's human," said Feeney in his scratchy voice. "This country's full of beautiful women, and he's a long time here. And he isn't made of iron."

Jacko snorted. "Then watch him. When he finds a piece, she's dead meat, by God. And he'll be done. Ruined."

"He's being watched," said Feeney. "He's being—"

Jacko, disgusted that the bejeweled Sylvia had failed, hung up. He stared down at Tarita, shadowy on the wine-red satin sheet. Should he shake her out of sleep and try again?

No. He was too tired, too disgusted. God, he wished this election were over and he could get on with his life. So much more lay ahead: more power, more prestige—and far more money.

He hoped Feeney was right, and Preston would hurry up and find himself a tasty tart. And then? God help the scumbag. And the unlucky dirty little girl he settled on.

Feeney would help him take care of that, too.

The next morning in Darwin, Marie still moved like an automaton. And like an automaton, she did not feel. She was numb and vaguely wondered if she was in shock.

She managed to get through the day because Colette would have wanted her to.

Reynard arrived late that evening, before Marie got home from Scepter. He'd parked his battered blue truck in front of her apartment and waited in the driver's seat. As soon as he saw Marie, he leaped out of the truck to hug her tightly.

She clung to him with real affection. He'd always been kind to her and Colette, and Colette had adored him. Even though she fretted over him, he could always make her laugh with a funny story or a cheeky song.

"My little love," he said against Marie's ear. "Our Colie's gone where there's no more pain. Had she been born my blood sister, I couldn't have loved her more."

Marie drew back and studied his face, shadowy in the apartment's outdoor lights. He was in his early sixties, but still surprisingly handsome. The only apparent flaw in his health was that he wore two hearing aids. He'd suffered for years from ringing in his ears, and had begun to go deaf in his late thirties.

He was tall, and his body was straight and strong. He had dark blond hair, wavy and going gray. His brows were darker, his lashes bronze-colored and surprisingly long.

In spite of the lashes, his face was strong-boned and years of sunburn had lined his skin, especially with laugh lines. His eyes were medium blue and looked lazy, heavy-lidded. They made him seem as if he was ready to nod off, but she knew his gaze missed little.

She looked up at him. "I'm glad you're here. Nobody else would understand."

He rumpled her short hair. "I know. We're an odd lot, aren't we? Tell me, duck, when's the service? I'll have to go to the Salvos and get me a suit."

Marie looked him in the eye. "There's no service. She was cremated yesterday. That's how she wanted it. We can get the ashes tomorrow. She wanted them scattered in the ocean."

Reynard's body stiffened, and he stared down at her with displeasure. "Cremated? Burned like rubbish?"

"She never told you. She knew you wouldn't like it."

"You did it without me?"

"She didn't want you to have to be there. She thought it…would hurt."

"And what about you, miss? You were there all by yourself?"

She swallowed hard, not wanting to remember. "Yes. I didn't want her to be alone."

He shook his head in what seemed a mixture of dismay and grudging admiration. "But *you* were alone. Didn't you feel wretched?"

"I didn't feel much of anything," she said honestly. "Rennie, it's like an invisible suit of armor fell from the sky and clamped itself on me. It won't *let* me feel yet."

"Ah. I know the sensation." He looped his arm around her

shoulders. "Maybe now that I'm here, you can come back to yourself. Let's go inside."

As she unlocked the door, he said, jokingly, "I hope you've got a drop of something for you old uncle. The long drive made me thirsty."

She nodded sadly. "I bought a bottle of port."

"Then let's have a glass. It'll loosen you up. Your body feels tight as a knot, my girl. You should come back to Hunter Valley with me. Get away from this place for a while."

He was steering her into the living room, but she stopped and stared at him in alarm. "I can't leave here," she protested. "I have classes. I have a job. I have this apartment."

"Details," he said with a careless air. "*I* have a proposition for you."

"What?" she asked suspiciously.

He gave her his most winning smile. "We'll talk about it tomorrow. After...you know. Now let us drink a toast to our Colie. And that old bat Louisa. Who might be your granny."

She could no longer think clearly. She didn't want to think at all about Louisa Fairchild, only Colette. "Yes," she said. "A toast. She deserves that."

Marie had reserved a small hire boat. Reynard, of course, could pilot it, for he truly was a jack-of-all-trades. After her classes the next day, they took the boat out into the harbor to a pretty and private spot that Colette had always loved.

They said their own silent goodbyes and released the ashes into the waves. Then they returned to shore. And nothing, to Marie, would ever be the same.

Afterward, she and Reynard sat in a pub near the harbor. Reynard had a whiskey, but Marie barely touched her wine.

"Oh, knock it back," Reynard urged her. "You've been through bloody hell, my girl. Drink a bit more. It'll help you to sleep."

"Sleep?" she asked dubiously.

"I'll drive us back, and you should take a nap," he said. "You look all fagged out. You're not Superwoman, y'know."

She saw the logic, but still she didn't want the wine.

"You remember what I said last night?" Reynard asked. "About you coming back to Hunter Valley with me?"

"Remember what I said? I have commitments here."

"Perhaps you have commitments *there,*" he argued. "To your mother, for instance."

"Mama?" she asked, puzzled.

"Yes," he said, leaning closer, staring intently at her. "She gave you the letter from Willadene Gates, didn't she? She expected you to deal with it. Knew she didn't have the strength to do it herself, poor thing. Wanted to know the truth. Knew the end was near, I'll warrant. Thought it was time to put things in your hands. Trusted you, she did."

"She didn't know if anything *should* be done," Marie objected.

"She kept the letter, didn't she?" he challenged. "She gave it to you, didn't she? Read her note. She practically begs you. She thought she failed you by not following through. But that you could handle it. And so handle it you must."

Marie felt a bit dizzied by his reasoning. "What difference does it make if Mama was Louisa Fairchild's daughter? I mean, it can't mean anything now that Mama's—"

She found it hard to say the word *dead.*

Reynard looked both saddened and angry. "If the Fairchild woman had been kinder, Colie might not be dead. Years of poverty ground her down. But Fairchild just cast out Colie and let the fates take her. God, I'd show a dog more kindness."

"Rennie, she probably thought that Mama was going to a good, safe home. Mama *loved* the Lafayettes. Didn't you?"

"I was a mere toddler when they lost everything. I don't remember the good times. No, I've no happy childhood memories. They couldn't even afford to get my ears fixed. My life might've run a different course if that had happened."

Colette would agree to this, Marie knew. Reynard said that he did poorly in school because of his tinnitus, the constant ringing in his ears. He was bright, but he knew he'd never get through college, so never tried.

Instead he'd drifted across Australia, back and forth, up and down. He'd lived that way for decades, and Colette had always feared he'd die that way, aimless, rambling and poor.

Marie looked at him in concern. He raised his chin and said, "I think you owe it to her to find out about the old Fairchild girl. And who knows? Maybe you could put things to right."

"To right?" she repeated, frowning slightly.

"Maybe Louisa was forced to give away her baby and that's why she's so sour. You could bring her happiness. And find some yourself. Colette would want that for you. You know she would.

"Besides," he added, "the old girl might settle a bit of money on you. God knows you and Colie never had help from any corner."

"I don't want that woman's money," Marie said firmly. "I can take care of myself."

Reynard shrugged. "I wish I could say the same. If she was my gran, I'd feel her out. She might at least give me enough for better hearing aids. Why, there's even doctors in England and America that say they can cure tinnitus." He smiled philosophically. "But I've borne it this long, haven't I? I can bear it for the few more years I've got."

The few more years I've got. The words struck Marie hard. When she was young, she thought Colette would live forever. And Rennie, vital, mischievous, clever Rennie—why, if he could live by his wits, he'd never have to die. But he was aging. And mortal.

"It seems to me," he said, "if she's your gran, you might close a long, sad chapter in your family history. Bring about a sort of healing. A sort of—fairness. And forgiveness."

Marie could say nothing.

"What do you say? Come back with me," he urged. "It would do you good to get away for a while. You've worked yourself half to death with your school and your job and caring for Colie. Will you think about it at least? For me?"

Her head swam, and she felt emotionally exhausted. "I'll think about it," she said without conviction.

"Good girl," he said with a disarming smile. He patted her hand. "Good girl."

* * *

The next morning Reynard kept after her. He had an answer for her every argument. Perhaps Louisa would have helped Colette and her family—if only she'd known what had become of her daughter.

What was wrong with going to Fairchild Acres, just to see if Marie might like the old girl? "You could work there, you know. Observe her. She lost an assistant cook right before I left for here. You'd be the perfect replacement."

"Go in as a *spy?*" Marie demanded, appalled. "And if I like her, pop up and say, 'And by the way, I'm your long-lost grand-daughter?' No! It's awful. It'd never work."

Reynard then explained for a full hour why it would work. "Again, if you don't like her, she never needs to know. You can leave and never look back."

"I have to take my finals."

"Take them early. You've got fine grades. Tell 'em your mother's died and you've got family business to tend."

"I have a job."

"Colette said they think the world of you. They'd give you a leave of absence. Your apartment? Sublet it. It's an excellent location, the uni so close."

"I can't."

"You can't not do it. It may be the chance of your lifetime."

"I don't want to talk about it. I've got to get ready for work."

"Work, that's all you ever do. You'll end up like your mother. And she'd *hate* that."

He made her head spin. She was glad to escape to the Scepter.

When she came home again, Reynard was watching television. He switched it off with the remote control. "Sit down with me," he said. "I got news."

Now what? she thought. But she sat. "Yes?"

"I phoned Mrs. Lipton," he said with his most benevolent smile.

"And who, pray tell, is Mrs. Lipton?"

"Louisa Fairchild's housekeeper. Lovely woman. I see her almost every day."

"Why do you see her so often?" asked Marie. "And why'd you phone her?"

"I bring her eggs. The old girl—Miss Fairchild—likes her eggs fresh, but she won't keep chickens. Afraid of birds. Was chased by a goose as a child."

This was the first humanizing detail Marie had heard about the woman.

"I called Mrs. Lipton to ask if she was still in search of an assistant cook. She is."

"Reynard..." Marie said in a warning tone.

"She'd found nobody suitable yet. So I told her about you, that you have your certificate in cookery and hospitality from the uni, that you work at the Scepter, that your mum was a cook, too, and she taught you to make wonderful desserts and pastries. She said you sounded perfect."

"Reynard," she exclaimed in shock. "How *could* you?"

"I told her you need a change of place with your mum just dead and all. So tomorrow just e-mail her some references or whatever. I didn't tell her you were workin' on a second certificate. Didn't want you to sound overqualified. I told her it'd take you about two weeks to make arrangements to leave here. She said fine."

She stood, torn between laughing or exploding in anger. "*No.* And that's an end to it."

That was not an end to it. He argued, he cajoled, he flattered, insisted, urged, coaxed, wheedled, pleaded and finally goaded. It was when he called her a coward that she snapped.

"You're afraid," he taunted. "You've never had an adventure in your life. I defy you to name a single one. You're a lovely young woman, but you're becoming a drudge. Now adventure comes knocking, and you pretend you're not at home."

Marie, sad, exhausted, worn down, finally agreed. She went to bed, wondering if she'd gone insane.

Reynard had to go back to Hunter Valley, and Marie, still filled with doubt, scurried to put her affairs in order. Always efficient, she'd finished her arrangements in just over a week.

Two days after he got back to Lochlain, Reynard phoned to say there'd been a spot of trouble at his employer's, a stable fire, but not to be alarmed by anything she heard on the news; the fire had been contained. Nobody had been seriously hurt. All was well.

Marie, who had no time to follow current news, took him at his word and told him she'd see him soon. "I can't believe I'm doing this, but I'm buying my bus ticket today."

"No you're not," Reynard told her. "I got you a plane ticket to Newcastle. It's only a skip and jump from there to Fairchild Acres. I'll meet you at the airport."

His generosity stunned her. He couldn't afford such a gesture. "Reynard, you *can't*. That's too much money. I can't allow it."

"The ticket's in the mail, duck. And like a duck, my duck, you *will* fly. Think of it not as a gift for you, but for Colie. It'd make her happy."

She bit her lip so that she wouldn't cry. "Thank you, Rennie. I'll pay you back some day."

"You'll pay me back by coming here. And that's *your* gift for Colie. To find out the truth about her and Louisa Fairchild."

PART TWO

Hunter Valley, New South Wales
March

Chapter Four

On a morning in early March, Marie found herself in a cramped economy seat on the cheapest airline out of Darwin. It was small and a bit shabby, but she was thrilled, for she'd never before been on a plane.

The inside of it looked no more glamorous than an elderly bus, but it was a magical thing, for it quickly whisked her up into the clouds and in an unbelievably short time, she was hundreds of kilometers away, in the Newcastle, New South Wales, airport, hugging Reynard.

He flinched at her tight embrace, and when she kissed his cheek, her lips touched a long cut just starting to heal. "Oof." He drew back from her slightly, and she realized that under his work shirt she could feel something suspiciously like bandages.

"Rennie, what's wrong?" she demanded.

"Oh, the bloody fire," he said dismissively. "Cracked a few ribs, that's all. Don't worry, love. I'm a tough old bird, I am."

Instantly she suspected his injury—and the fire—had been more serious than he'd let on. "Reynard, tell me more about this whole thing. Were you in the hospital?"

"Only overnight. Come on. Let's go find your luggage. Ah, it's lovely you look. Flying agrees with you?"

"It was wonderful," she answered. "But I want to know more about what happened to you. And about the fire."

As he steered her toward the baggage claim area, she saw that he carried himself gingerly and walked with a slight limp. "Rennie," she prodded, "what *happened?*"

"A horse panicked, rammed me against a wall," he told her. "That's all. The scratch? The wall had a nail in it. And for a few seconds, so did I. A bit of a bashing, nothing life-threatening, I assure you."

"And the fire? How bad was it?"

Gruffly he explained that in terms of money, the fire was a disaster for Lochlain Racing, where he worked for Tyler Preston. Several horses had died, and many more had been permanently damaged by smoke inhalation. There was one human fatality, a body that had finally been identified as old Sam Whittleson.

"Sam Whittleson?" Marie echoed in disbelief. "That man Louisa *shot?*"

"The very one. Somebody killed him this time. They found a gun half-melted in a burned fertilizer barrel, and a lab's trying to identify it. The cops say the fire was arson, and—"

"Wait," Marie interrupted. "Arson? Murder? You told me nobody was seriously hurt."

"When we talked, I didn't think anybody was," Reynard said defensively.

"Who killed him? Why?"

"Nobody knows," Reynard said with an impatient shrug. "Anyway, the authorities said the fire was set, and some yobs whisper Tyler Preston himself set it. To hide that he was drugging his horses.

"But," Reynard said flatly, "he didn't drug horses, and he set no fire. That's the trouble living in the sticks. Too much gossip, too many rumors. Now, take Louisa Fairchild. Some even say *she* done Sam in—ridiculous. An eighty-year-old woman steals out in the wee hours. She lures a man who wouldn't trust her for a second into a neighbor's barn? And she guns him down? Not bloody likely."

The luggage carousel buzzed, and suitcases began to cascade onto the moving belt. Her bicycle appeared with a clatter. "God's holy trousers," Reynard exclaimed. "You brought that bloody old wreck of a bike?"

"I have to get around. I don't have a car."

"You'll frighten horses," he grumbled. "Nobody rides a bike up there. You ride something with four wheels or four legs, and that's *it*."

"I'm not afraid to be different," she countered, lifting her chin.

He shook his head. "You never were. And I don't know if that's your blessing or your curse. Indeed I don't."

Reynard refused her help in loading his old blue pickup, even though the job was clearly a strain on his taped ribs. Soon he and she were in the truck, and she gawked at the quaintness of Newcastle and then at the beauty of the Hunter Valley countryside.

Woods and peaceful fields and hills and vineyards stretched on until they met the shadowy lavender of mountains in the distance. Rain poured daily in Darwin, but in the Hunter Valley, the sky was cloudless and blue.

"It's more beautiful than I imagined," she murmured. "So tranquil."

"Appearances deceive," Reynard said. "Too dry. There's spot fires near the Koongarra range. There's wildfire warnings all over the valley. It's not tranquil, and neither are the people. The stable burning, the killing, it spooked everybody. And the locals were still squabbling about Louisa's shooting Sam Whittleson last year."

"Tell me more about that," Marie said. "They were feuding about water rights or something?"

Reynard nodded. "And there were factions from the start. Some say it was Sam's own fault. Some say it was Louisa's. Now at Lochlain, where I work, Sam's son's the head trainer. So the Prestons sided with Sam. That irks the old girl. But then she never really took to the Prestons in the first place."

"Why not?" Marie asked, the familiar uneasiness stirring again.

"The Fairchilds've been in Hunter Valley for a century and a half. The old girl sees the Prestons as upstarts and Yanks to boot. Still, they say she was usually civil to them—until they sided so strong with Sam. Now she's offended about racing politics, too. Really offended. You see, my boss, Tyler Preston, he's got this cousin. Well, the cousin—"

They rounded a curve and the view was suddenly dominated by a huge set of gates, framed by stone pillars ornamented with bronze and red crests. "Ta-da!" said Reynard with a chuckle. "Behold—Fairchild Acres."

The security guard let them in, and Marie looked at the great lawn and the seeming endless pastures and paddocks beyond. Did Louisa own *all* this land?

They bounced down a broad drive between jacaranda trees, plots of bright flowers and the flash of water from a myriad of sprinklers. The rest of Hunter Valley might be browning and dry, but not Louisa's lawn.

They rounded another curve. "And there is the humble abode of Louisa."

At the end of the drive stood an enormous house. Gray stone and stucco, it rose three stories, with a gabled roof and rows of mullioned windows. The jacarandas gave way to a wider sweep of manicured lawn, decorated with large formal gardens. There was even an ornamental marble pool with a three-tiered fountain at its center.

She gaped at the house, the grounds. Reynard took a fork in the drive that led to the back of the house. "You'll meet Mrs. Lipton first."

Marie's heart beat hard. Too hard. But Reynard had kept reassuring her that she wouldn't need to lie. Her identity was true, her experience real, her credentials excellent. She should simply be closemouthed about her family.

"Just remember the nursery rhyme, love." With a sidelong smile, he recited the poem:

"A wise old owl sat in his oak.
The more he heard, the less he spoke;
The less he spoke, the more he heard;
Why aren't we all like that wise old bird?"

She eyed him thoughtfully. "Is that how you know so much about what goes on here? And you've only been here—what?—two months?"

He winked. "That's it, love. Eyes open. Ears open. Mouth shut. *That's* how you learn."

He parked, got out stiffly, and opened Marie's door as smoothly as if he were a trained chauffeur. Perhaps he'd once been one, for she didn't know all of his past. Not by half.

He escorted her to a back door and gave the bellpull a smart ring, and then two more.

A girl of about eighteen opened the door. She had curling red hair and freckles all over her ruddy face. She wore navy-blue shorts, a white short-sleeved blouse and a white apron.

"Oh, Rennie," she said with a grin. "Come in. And this must be your niece. Marie, is it?

"I'm Belinda, but everybody calls me Bindy. I'll get Mrs. Lipton."

Bindy talked fast, and she dashed off into a hallway just as fast. Marie stood, dazzled by the huge modern kitchen, gleaming with whiteness and chrome.

"Hello, Rennie," said a man's deep voice. The accent was American.

Marie turned to see a tall figure standing near a table. She looked up into his face, and her heart, already pounding, almost leaped out of her chest.

He was the man who'd defended her in the parking lot of the Scepter that night, the stranger she'd clung to so foolishly, so desperately. Suddenly the room seemed to swim round her, dizzying her.

Did he recognize her? Would he remember her? She prayed not.

"Mr. Preston," said Reynard, heartily shaking hands with him. He grinned.

"What are you doing here? Miss Fairchild must be gone."

"She is, and somebody had to do your work. So I brought the eggs today."

Rennie grinned more widely. "Thanks kindly, mate. And meet my niece, Marie Lafayette from Darwin. She's the new assistant cook. Marie, Andrew Preston from the U.S.A. He's running for the presidency of the ITRF. Staying with his cousin over at Lochlain."

Marie was still struck dumb and immobile. Andrew Preston stepped over to her and offered her his hand. Somehow she raised her own and placed it in his. It was like having tiny flames shoot up her fingers, through her arm, and into her heart.

She remembered he'd been handsome, but not as handsome as this. He might be the most beautiful man she'd ever seen, but it was a purely masculine beauty. He wore a white T-shirt that emphasized his shoulders and chest and revealed tanned, muscular arms. Around his neck was a peculiar necklace, a carved bird on a red string.

Low-riding blue jeans hugged his narrow hips and long legs. His riding boots were tall, black and dusty. "Pleased to make your acquaintance," he said.

His eyes were such a dark blue they seemed nearly black. His wavy hair was a dark and gleaming brown, and he seemed fully a foot taller than she.

Assume a virtue if you have it not, she thought. She raised her chin and gave a perky smile. "Pleased to meet you."

He smiled back and released her hand. Again, strange sensations tripped through her body, making her giddy.

"I heard about your mother," Andrew said. "I'm sorry for your loss." He sounded as if he actually meant it.

"Thank you," she said, her smile dying.

Andrew turned to Reynard. "I was just starting back to Lochlain," he said. "See you there later. And I hope we meet again, Miss Lafayette."

Marie nodded. She'd let down her guard, so she gave him a mildly friendly, totally professional and completely manufactured smile.

Andrew smiled again, almost hesitantly, and left by the back door.

"Well, you seemed a bit gobsmacked at the sight of him," Reynard said, eyes narrowing.

"I didn't know anyone was there. H-he surprised me," she said defensively.

"I'll bet he did, I'll bet he did. And you surprised *me.*"

Before Marie could reply, an interior door opened and a tall woman entered. She had perfectly sculpted gray hair, a strong jaw, a kind face and a firm, stout figure. She wore a navy-blue skirt and blouse, and a ruffled white apron with a bib. "Rennie, you rascal," she said, obviously pleased.

"Ah," he replied, his tone silky. "And what mischief are you up to, entertaining gentlemen in your kitchen? Miss Louisa doesn't know he was here, does she? You're a bold one, you are."

She made a shooing gesture at him. "She's in Sydney getting her annual checkup. She won't be back until this evening. Ah. And this is your niece, Marie?"

"The very one. Marie, Mrs. Lipton, the housekeeper. A marvel of organization, she is."

Mrs. Lipton almost smiled, but her face grew serious. "Marie, I'm very sorry about your loss. It's good you've come to join your uncle. It's a very empty feeling, losing one's mother. I remember all too well."

"Thank you, ma'am," Marie almost whispered.

Reynard said, "My sister was a darling woman and a lovely cook." He pinched Marie's cheek affectionately. "And this one's every bit her mother's child. She'll do you proud."

Mrs. Lipton moved to a small cabinet built into the wall. She opened it and pulled out a set of keys. "Rennie, will you be a dear and take Marie to her quarters? I suppose she has things you'll have to help her move in. Then bring her back here, and I'll explain her duties to her. Marie, did you bring a uniform?"

Marie said, "Yes, ma'am." Mrs. Lipton had e-mailed the uniform requirements.

"You needn't wear it until this evening. We'll also provide

you with one of our staff T-shirts with the Fairchild logo. Now, help her settle in, Rennie."

He gave her an appreciative look from beneath half-lowered lids. "Right away. By the way, Mrs. Lipton, you've changed your hair somewhat, haven't you?"

"Oh. Just a bit," she said, toying with a gray curl. "Now run along. I know Tyler will want you back at Lochlain."

"He's a good enough cove, Andrew Preston," Reynard said, as they parked in front of the staff bungalow. "I see him around Lochlain all the time. Not our sort, of course, but a good cove. The old girl doesn't like him, of course. She's got her back up because he's a Preston and a Yank and dared come here to campaign against her candidate—Jacko Bullock."

"I see." But Marie didn't really understand; she was still in shock at seeing the man again. Andrew Preston. She hadn't even known his name. Andrew Preston.

Reynard parked and unloaded the truck, talking the whole time.

Numbly she listened as he explained that Bullock had used all his media clout to defend Louisa in the shooting case the year before. He'd been her loyal supporter, and she intended to be his. She therefore hoped that Andrew Preston would not be merely beaten, but crushed like a bug.

"When it gets to racing politics, she can be hell on wheels," Reynard said as he unlocked the door to her room. The cottage was sparklingly clean, not fancy, but comfortable, with a shared living room and kitchen.

"It's nice." Marie nodded in approval. "And Mrs. Lipton is a nice woman."

"She is indeed."

"She seems to like you," Marie said with a hint of mischief. "And *you* flirt with her."

"She needs a bit of fun in her life. So does old Louisa, if she'd admit it. I do my bit, is all. I'll bring your things. There's a place to chain your bike near the main entrance. "

Reynard put her bike in place and carried her secondhand suitcases inside. "You need help unpacking?" he asked.

She shook her head.

"Then let me take you back to the kitchen and I'll be off to Lochlain."

"Your boss has been generous, letting you off this long."

"Tyler? Very decent fellow, a good mate. Andrew Preston's cousin, did I say?"

"You did." Her pulse speeded up at the mention of Andrew. It was ridiculous, she scolded herself. *Seeing him again wasn't exciting. It was just a surprise. And—awkward.*

"I thought he eyed you like you were something special," Reynard said.

"Don't be silly. I'm a kitchen worker."

Reynard frowned as if in puzzlement. "Bad as my old ears are, I thought I heard something when you saw him."

She threw him a puzzled look. "Heard something?"

He scratched his chin. "A clickety-clackety. Like maybe someone finally shook those hormones of yours into action."

She smacked him lightly on the arm, but her eyes flashed in irritation. "You're impossible."

"Unfamiliar sensation, wasn't it?" he asked. "Hormones romping around?"

She smacked him again. He threw his head back and laughed. But then he sobered. "He's a handsome devil. But out of your league, love. Be careful of men like him. Would to God that Colie had been."

Andrew, who'd borrowed Tyler's Jeep for the trip, drove back to Lochlain in a pensive mood. It had been odd, when he'd delivered the eggs, to be welcomed so warmly by the kitchen staff. It meant not everyone at Fairchild Acres hated his guts. Just Louisa.

But that wasn't what most interested him. Images of Reynard's niece, startlingly vivid, kept flashing into his mind. Marie. She'd stood so demurely in the kitchen—yet with confidence.

He'd recognized her almost instantly, but he never would have taken her for Reynard's niece. While Reynard exuded a raffish air of good fellowship, Marie seemed carefully controlled, sure of herself, yet at the same time a bit shy. It was a paradoxical combination, and it intrigued him.

He remembered holding her in his arms so briefly. Too briefly. He rubbed his chest, which sweated in the rising heat. Then he realized Raddy's charm was gone. He stopped the car, searched the seat and looked on the floor.

Where in hell was it?

Reynard insisted on driving Marie back to the kitchen, although the distance was short. She kissed him in thanks, said she'd phone, then hopped out of the truck.

"Oh, wait," Reynard said. "There's something I forgot to tell you."

She came to his opened window and looked at him in puzzlement. "What?"

"Louisa's great-niece and nephew are here, staying with her. Megan and Patrick Stafford."

"What?" she demanded, swept by both surprise and anger. "You said she wasn't close to *any* of her family."

"I never did. Willadene Gates wrote that. And Louisa *wasn't* on speaking terms with them. I think this is kind of a test. To see if they're worthy of inheriting her money bin. Maybe they are, maybe they're not. Either way, there's enough to go around."

Marie, appalled, stared at him. "Reynard! If she's reconciling with them, I shouldn't even be here. It makes me feel— underhanded. Why didn't you tell me, for God's sake?"

"I didn't know until they arrived. There were just rumors."

She put her hands on her hips. "Why didn't you tell me when they got here? Why'd you wait until now to spring the news?"

He shrugged. "You wouldn't have come. Now you can't go. You're moved in. You might like them, love. They're probably your cousins. I've heard the woman's nice, but the bloke's a bit of a layabout."

"This is unforgivable," Marie accused.

"I'm doing it for your own good. It's what Colette wanted and I did it for her, as well. Don't go all high and mighty on me. Just do your job like the trouper you are. It's not just me that drew you here. It's destiny. Bye, love. Talk to you soon."

With that, he blew her a kiss, drove off and left her standing there.

She stared after him, bewildered, fighting back tears. But for now she had no choice but to brazen it out until she could make her escape. She squared her shoulders and forced herself to march to the kitchen door.

A red-and-yellow object lying in the grass caught her eye, and she bent to pick it up. She stared at it curiously: it was a carved wooden bird with a large yellow beak. The rest was patterned in black and white and red, and it hung from a broken red string.

It was the charm Andrew Preston had worn. He must have lost it, she thought numbly. She slipped it into the pocket of her slacks as she entered the kitchen, her mind dazed, her body working on automatic pilot.

"Welcome back," said Mrs. Lipton. "I'll be with you in a little while, but must catch up on my paperwork. I'll be in my office if anyone wants me. Tonight's staff menu is on the bulletin board. You could start the potato salad if you like. We need to feed about eighteen."

"I'll be glad to," Marie said. The baked potatoes were already cooling on a large metal sheet on the counter.

"And could you make a meringue for tonight? Miss Louisa loves her meringues and Pavlovas."

"Certainly," Marie said, still stunned, but hiding it with all her might.

Mrs. Lipton bustled off.

Alone, Marie again felt almost overwhelmed by the modernity of the shiny white-and-chrome kitchen. *What would Mama have done in a kitchen like this?* she wondered with a pang. *What couldn't she have done?*

Yearning for Colette stabbed through her. *I'll find out who this Fairchild woman is,* she promised her mother's spirit. *And if she's not worthy of you, I'll walk away and never look back. And she'll never know what a fine daughter she had—and lost.*

But she couldn't yet think about Colette or Louisa or Megan

and Patrick Stafford who might be cousins—and she couldn't yet deal with what Reynard had done. She simply couldn't sort it out yet. It was all too sudden.

Get control of yourself, she thought sternly. *Get control and keep control, no matter what. There's work to be done. Do it.*

She began to peel potatoes.

Andrew pulled up again at the Fairchild mansion's kitchen door. He knew he'd been wearing the charm this morning when he'd left Lochlain Stables. A hand from Whittleson's, Sandy Sanford, had been helping build a sleep-out addition onto the main house. Sanford had given him a condescending look. "Hey, mate, goin' native?" he'd asked with an unpleasant grin. Andrew'd ignored him and gotten into the Jeep.

The charm must have dropped off on his walk from the Jeep to Mrs. Lipton's kitchen—or the walk back. If it had hit the kitchen's tiled floor, he would have heard it, wouldn't he?

He had no rational reason for attaching any importance to the thing, except it had been given as a friendly gesture. And the Aborigine culture fascinated him; it seemed rich and mysterious. He'd spent a lot of time in Kentucky reading about more exotic cultures than his own. And now, at last, he was seeing them first hand.

He got out of the Jeep and retraced his path to the back door. He looked three times, but saw no sign of the necklace. He pulled the bell, and an instant later Marie Lafayette appeared, wiping her hands on a dish towel she'd pinned round her waist for an apron.

She didn't seem taken aback to see him, and smiled her cheery smile. She looked like a woman almost totally sure of herself. "Oh, Mr. Preston. Can I help you? Mrs. Lipton's not here, but she should be back in a minute. Would you like to step inside where it's cool?"

She swung open the door and he entered, glad to escape the heat. He said, "Sorry to bother you. I was driving back and I missed a—a kind of charm someone gave me. I thought maybe I'd lost it here."

For a moment she looked strangely blank. But then her face lit up, and he realized for the first time that she was not merely pretty, she was exquisite. Her thick cap of hair shone like spun gold in the artificial light. She wore no makeup except pink lip gloss, but she didn't need makeup. She was stunning without it. And those dimples. Good Lord.

She reached into the pocket of her slacks and drew out the charm. "Is this it?"

She must have seen by his expression that it was and held it out on her palm. "I thought it was yours. I meant to tell Mrs. Lipton, but she was involved in something else."

Her smile flickered away as he took it from her, his fingertips brushing the smoothness of her palm.

But that too-brief smile made his heart quicken with pleasure. It had been a smile that hinted at mystery and complexities. And her eyes, he suddenly realized, were the most startling and pure green he'd ever seen. Men must fall at her feet like flies. What was such a woman doing, working in a kitchen?

"Thank you," he managed to say, wondering why he seemed to have something stuck in his throat. "I—I don't really know much about it, but a blacksmith gave it to me, and…"

She looked up, listening, and he realized he didn't have an end for the sentence.

"And?" she questioned.

"I hated to lose it," he finished lamely. "In this age of plastic and—"

"Mass manufacturing?" she supplied.

"Exactly," he said, trying not to get lost in those depthless green eyes. "That's it."

Maybe she wasn't as poised as she seemed. Almost subliminally he sensed emotions coursing through her, emotions she guarded carefully.

"The string wore through." She pointed at the frayed edges. "Odd. It looks good and stout." Her voice was low and soft, her accent delightful.

He forced some words out. "I hope I didn't interrupt you."

"No," she said, with a nonchalant shrug. "I'm just making potato salad."

"Potato salad," he repeated.

"I was looking for the mayonnaise," she said. His gaze must have been too intent because she glanced away.

"Mayonnaise," he echoed. *Good Lord. I'm talking like a parrot, and I was the captain of the college debating team. What's wrong with me?*

But her bearing was almost carefree. Almost. "Yes. None in the fridge. I thought there must be some in the cabinet. I couldn't find a kitchen stool to see on the top shelf."

She was petite, almost tiny, beside him. He cleared his throat and said, "I'm tall. I'll like if you look," he offered. "I mean, I'll look if you like."

"That's very kind of you."

He peered at the row of top cupboards. He went to the nearest, opened the door, looked on the top shelf, and behind eight jars of mustard found four quarts of mayonnaise. He pulled one down. "Do you need more?"

"Oh, no. Thank you. That's plenty."

He handed it to her, careful not to touch her this time. He realized he still had the charm in his hand.

She licked her lips, and the tip of her tongue was daintily pointed and daintily pink. He felt carnal stirrings. She set aside the jar and murmured, "Maybe you should buy a thong."

"A thong?" he asked, picturing her in a thong, her arms crossed modestly across her breasts. It was a most arousing image and not the sort that often popped into his head. He was usually a man of stern self-control.

"Leather," she corrected. "A strip of leather for the bird."

"Yeah," he nodded. "Leather. The very thing. Thank you."

"Thank *you*," she replied.

"I'd better be going," he said. "Um. See you later."

"Yes. Perhaps." She gave him an unreadable smile.

He made his way out the door and into the Jeep. He got onto the road again and felt the blood roaring in his ears.

What the hell had gone wrong with him back there? When he'd seen her earlier this morning, he'd thought she was singularly pretty, but this time—she'd affected him as few women ever had. Why?

Because you got a closer look at her, he told himself. *You looked into those green, green eyes for the first time. And she had such a unique air about her. You touched her. You were alone with her.*

He'd slipped the charm into the front pocket of his jeans, and it seemed to spread the heat of desire through his groin. He smacked himself in the forehead with the heel of his palm. Why did she make him react this way?

But he knew why, and had known, perhaps unconsciously, from the moment he'd seen her again.

She somehow reminded him of Kellie Maguire, whom he'd loved all those years ago. The girl who'd been so strong of purpose, but turned out to be so vulnerable.

Marie was small, like Kellie, and beautiful, but in a completely different way. He remembered her at the Scepter, speaking foreign languages fluently, working so gracefully and with such sparkle—and defending herself like a champion. And yet there was vulnerability there, he could feel it, and it brought out an almost fiercely protective urge in him.

Again he seemed to hear Kellie's voice. "I don't know how you did it, Preston. It's broad daylight. But maybe you just found the door into the moon. Glimpse of the future, Mr. Serioso?"

Chapter Five

That afternoon, the Fairchild household bustled, readying itself for Louisa's return. Helena, the kitchen assistant, made sure all spices and condiments and baking goods were in perfect alphabetical order; Bindy and Marie polished the counters and appliances to an even higher sheen.

"How long has Miss Fairchild been gone?" Marie asked, puzzled by cleaning things that already seemed spotless.

"Only since last night," Bindy said. "But she gets irked if there's any sign of people slacking off when she's not here. And *nobody* wants her irked."

Marie wondered if the very ground would shake when Louisa Fairchild drew near and if small animals would run for cover. "Is she as fearsome as everybody seems to think?"

Bindy rolled her pale blue eyes. "That girl who was here before you? Annabel? Fired for kissing one of the Lochlain stable boys. He was always hangin' about. Miss came and found them snogging and groping outside, while inside eight apple pies was burning. She made Annabel weep like a waterfall and told her to get off the property by sunset. She watches her single girls, Miss does. She's *strict.*"

"But what if you want to go out?" Marie asked.

"We go on our time off and we have to be back here by midnight—alone. The guard lets us in."

"Do you go out?" Marie asked curiously. Bindy wasn't traditionally pretty, but she had a lot of bubble and bounce to her.

"Me? Oh, yes. I mean, there's nothing to do around *here* at night except watch detective shows on the telly. I've got a boyfriend, but I'm careful. Still, lately I've found my eye roving. That Andrew Preston's major sexy."

Marie hoped her cheeks didn't flush. "Is he?" she asked with false innocence.

"Can't you *see?*" Bindy demanded. "My word! Every woman here's noticed, even the laundress, Mrs. Fife, and she's at least a hundred and fifty!"

"He's too tall," Marie said, improvising. "Looking at him's like staring up at a giraffe."

Bindy laughed, then suddenly looked alarmed. She went pale. "Oh, dear! I see Miss Fairchild's car! She's home early. I need to change my apron. And hide my book. She hates it if she catches me sitting about reading."

She snatched her mystery novel off the counter and rushed to the restroom off the kitchen, just as Mrs. Lipton ran in from the dining room. "She's here, she's here. I must make coffee," she cried. "She's at least an hour early."

"She's driven all this way alone?" Marie asked.

"No, no. The deputy housekeeper drives, Agnes. Have you started those desserts yet? Oh, my God, she'll be expecting her coffee and a lovely snack."

"I've done a banana meringue with raspberry-brandy sauce," Marie said. "I can have it ready in a few moments."

"Bless you, my girl," Mrs. Lipton panted, flying about the kitchen. "Oh, Lord, I hear them at the front door. Can you do the espresso? I must go greet her."

"Certainly," Marie assured her, but her heart hammered. How long before she faced this dragon that sent everyone into such a frenzy?

It was not long. Mrs. Lipton came back to the kitchen, puffing from rushing about. "Millie took the tray up," she said, fanning herself with her hand. "Miss Fairchild is having it on the terrace. She tasted your meringue and pronounced it adequate."

Marie's heart sank, but her pride made her feel bristly. *"Adequate?"* she repeated.

Mrs. Lipton patted her arm. "From her, that's a high compliment. She'd like to meet you. She asked that you bring her more meringue."

Now nervousness stole through Marie. "Am I supposed to curtsy or anything like that?"

"No, simply call her 'Miss' and be on your best behavior. Don't act intimidated. She doesn't like people she can easily intimidate. But don't be overbold, either."

Marie headed for the terrace with another serving of banana meringue. Mrs. Lipton had given her a short tour of the house, and Marie thought that to live there must be like dwelling in a museum. Everything was rich, elaborate and perfectly placed.

She went through the French doors to the terrace, and saw Louisa Fairchild, sitting at a small table, her back to Marie. Her spine was extremely straight, and her hair pulled back into a meticulous bun.

"Excuse me, Miss," Marie said, going to face her. "Mrs. Lipton said you'd like for me to bring you more meringue. I'm Marie Lafayette, the new assistant cook."

Louisa gazed over her teacup, unsmiling. She had an aristocratic nose and a humorless mouth. Age had hollowed her cheeks and wrinkled her skin, but she wore pink lipstick, perfectly applied, and gray eyebrow pencil. Marie could not help feeling nervous meeting those critical eyes.

"Marie Lafayette," the older woman said, slowly. "The niece of Reynard Lafayette, who works at Lochlain?"

Marie nodded. "I am."

"He's a rascal and a scamp. I'm not sure I trust him," Louisa said in clipped tones. "But he amuses me. Will you *amuse* me?"

Marie couldn't help herself. "I hadn't planned on it, Miss. I thought my job was to cook, not entertain."

Louisa lifted an eyebrow. "Ah. You're saucy. And there's something in your bearing that reminds me of someone I didn't like."

Marie could only gaze at her as calmly as she could, but her pulse galloped.

Louise gave her a wry look. "I mean to say myself. I was saucy at your age. I thought I knew everything. Do you think *you* know everything, Lafayette?"

"Not at all," Marie replied as pleasantly as she could.

Louisa gazed at her so intently it made Marie's nerves prickle, but she met the old woman's eyes unflinchingly. At last Louisa said, "I'm not on good terms with the Prestons, especially lately. I know they think I killed that bugger Sam—the dolts. Your uncle works for them. And you work for me. Don't you find that strange?"

"No," Marie said calmly. "People such as us work where we can."

"Mrs. Lipton showed me your credentials. They're surprisingly good. That raises questions in my mind. I'm not the easiest woman in the world to work for. I know it, and so does your uncle. So why did he bring you *here?* Do the Prestons want you in my house?"

Marie took a deep breath and tried to say something that wasn't precisely a lie. "The job was open. I wanted to be near my uncle. He's my only remaining relative."

"In my experience, relatives are vastly overrated," Louisa said. "I have only a great-niece and nephew that I hardly know, and they're more than enough family for me, thank you."

She paused and added, "I'm leaving for England in a few days. I intend to tell Mrs. Lipton that if you're caught in my rooms or going through my private things in any way, she's immediately to sack you. I cannot abide a snoop. *Comprenez-vous,* Lafayette? Do I make myself clear?"

"Perfectly clear," Marie answered with a polite smile. But with distaste she thought, *What a cold woman. Why should I want her to claim me as her granddaughter? I'm glad my mother never met her, never knew what she's like. I'll talk to Rennie. I want no part of this.*

Louisa tapped her fork against the dessert plate. "How much of this is left?" she asked.

"Two servings," Marie said.

"I want you to take them over to Lochlain. Tyler Preston always lords it over everyone about his cook's 'perfect' meringues. Give them to him and tell him they're a neighborly gift after his troubles. Ha!"

She laughed with seeming satisfaction. "But if that upstart cousin of his is there, that Andrew, tell Tyler *that* man may not taste my gift. I don't like his gall. Coming to *my* country, to *my* shire, to run against *my* candidate."

Marie's stomach did a slight loop-the-loop. Louisa wanted her to deliver an insult meant for Andrew? She stood straighter still. "I'd take it, Miss, but I have no car, only a bicycle."

"Then ask Mrs. Lipton for the keys to the truck. And come straight back. No dallying."

She paused and looked Marie up and down as if she were livestock on the sale block. "And leave word for your uncle to bring more eggs. By the way, my sympathies, etcetera, to both you and him about your mother. You may go now."

"Thank you, Miss," said Marie, wanting to add *And get stuffed, you imperious old bat.*

Marie took the blue pickup truck that was treated like common property by the staff of Fairchild Acres. Its bed was littered with hay and straw, and oil and paint stained it.

She followed Mrs. Lipton's directions and easily found Lochlain Racing. She flinched when she saw the burned barn, leveled now, heavy equipment parked near it, men sifting through the ashes.

She pulled up at the back door of the house, and chagrin flooded through her. Andrew stood a mere twenty feet away, and beside him another man, his arm in a sling. He resembled Andrew enough to be his brother. Tyler Preston? It had to be.

Andrew wore jeans, a white T-shirt and his riding boots. He looked at her as if in disbelief, and he didn't smile. Her heart pummeled her breastbone. But she carefully picked up the box holding the meringues and reached for the door handle.

Then Andrew was beside the truck, opening the door for her. He clasped her elbow to help her step down, and his touch tingled through her like an electrical shock. She found herself staring at the carved bird that rested against his chest.

"What brings you here, Miss Lafayette?" he asked in his low voice.

She looked up, met his dark blue gaze, and did her best imitation of a perfectly composed woman. "Miss Fairchild sent me over with something for Mr. Tyler Preston."

"That's me," said the other man. He gave her a lopsided grin. "Who are you? And what did you bring?"

Andrew dropped his hand from her arm and hooked his thumbs into the front pockets of his jeans. She sensed too much self-consciousness between them, too much mutual awareness. She tossed her head, smiled cheerfully and mentally commanded her nerves to behave.

Tyler took the box and glared at its contents. He gave her a quizzical look. "Is this a joke? She *covets* my cook's meringues. She's green with envy and has been for years. What's she up to?"

Marie had been pondering what to say about that. "I think it's her whim, sir."

"She must have sent some barbed remark," Tyler said. "What'd she say to tell me?"

Marie tried to be honest but softened the message as much as she could. "She said these were a neighborly offering. After your recent troubles." She did not repeat Louisa's "Ha!"

"Really?" Tyler commented with an amused expression. "And there must be more—I know Louisa. What else did she say?"

Marie kept her composure and gave him a sympathetic smile. "That you shouldn't share them with your cousin." She gave a nod in Andrew's direction and tingled because his eyes were on her.

Tyler laughed outright. "Because he's a foreigner and he advocates change?"

"She implied something to that effect, sir."

"So I'm left out?" asked Andrew, with mock disappointment.

"That's Miss Fairchild's wish, but it's Mr. Tyler's decision," Marie responded. "A gift belongs to the recipient, not the giver."

"Do you always choose your words so carefully?" Andrew commented.

"I am an employee," she answered, with just enough pertness to make him cock his head in surprise.

"And who, Miss Lafayette," Tyler asked, "made these meringues? Was it you?"

"Yes," she said. "Desserts were my mother's specialty. I'm afraid mine aren't nearly as good as hers. She had a genius for all things sweet."

"So it would seem," Andrew said with an unexpectedly roguish glint in his eye.

She backed toward the Fairchild truck. "Now I need to get back. Oh—and Miss Fairchild said she'd like more eggs sent over."

Tyler bowed slightly. "Tell her that Reynard will bring them. And thank her for her gift. Tell her I won't let Andrew have even a taste. No matter how much he begs and whines."

"I don't beg or whine," Andrew said, with a lazy smile. "I'll just steal."

She managed to stay poised when Andrew took her arm again to help her back into the truck. "So you've met the old girl," he said to her. "What did you think?"

"She's quite the grande dame."

He leaned his arms on the rolled-down window. She tried not to notice the muscles that played beneath his tanned skin. "I hear she's the *grandest* of grandes dames," he said. "She makes hard demands on her staff. Don't let her wear you down."

Marie, inside the truck again, felt safer. She lifted her chin. "I'm not easily worn down."

He smiled, almost diffidently. "Yes. I get that feeling."

"Good day, gentlemen," she said, and putting the truck in

Reverse, she backed up. Then she changed gears and sped away as fast as was polite.

A glance in the rearview mirror showed that both men stood watching her, Tyler smiling, Andrew looking more contemplative, almost puzzled.

She thought of his expression all the way back to Fairchild Acres.

By the time Louisa and her niece and nephew were served that evening, and the workers fed in the staff dining room, Marie was exhausted. But everyone on the staff seemed pleased by her contributions to the menu.

Afterward, Marie helped Bindy with the dishes, even though it wasn't part of her job.

"That was a delicious spread," Bindy said, scrubbing the casserole dish. "We always have the same thing every week. Cook doesn't have much imagination when it comes to us."

"Thanks. Does Cook have a name? Or is Miss Fairchild so old-fashioned she just prefers to call the woman 'Cook'?"

Bindy grimaced. "From what I hear, there's been so many cooks, it's easier to call them all 'Cook' than keep learning new names."

Marie stared at her, a horrible suspicion creeping into her mind. "And Cook left because she had to have a knee operation? In Sydney? Why'd she go clear to Sydney?"

"That's where she's from. She likes the hospital better. And she's got family there to help her convalesce." Bindy squinted skeptically. "Or so she says. I think she also has an old boyfriend there who just got divorced. She's been in touch with him, too."

"But she *will* be back?"

"So she says," Bindy repeated. "If she doesn't have complications. Or get a proposal."

Marie's suspicion grew larger. What if Cook was making her escape from Fairchild Acres? Would Marie be responsible for *all* the cooking? It would be the equivalent of doing two people's work.

As soon as she got to the privacy of her room, she took out her cell phone and rang her uncle. "Rennie, I need to talk to you.

Could we go somewhere? I could meet you at the gate if you can pick me up and get me home by midnight."

"Of course, my girl," he said cheerily. "I'll take you to a pub in Pepper Flats. It's got a ladies' lounge. It's all as proper as a prioress."

A pub wouldn't be Marie's first choice, but she knew Reynard liked his drop. "Fine. How soon can you be here?"

He told her, and he arrived at the gate exactly when he said he would. He drove her to the nearby township of Pepper Flats, where there were two pubs with brightly lit signs. One was garish, one rather demure with pale pink neon letters spelling out The Secret Heiress.

The name made her clench her teeth. "A bit too appropriate, perhaps?" Reynard teased. "Don't mind. The woman who runs it named it after a racehorse. One of Louisa's first champions, in fact, very famous filly hereabouts. The proprietress is a Mrs. Tidwell. A widow woman, but she can still bat her eyelashes like Bambi."

Once the two of them were seated in the decorous ladies' lounge, Marie found that Mrs. Tidwell could indeed bat her eyelashes, especially at Reynard. She looked suspiciously at Marie until Reynard explained she was his niece.

"Oh, lucky you to have such a jolly uncle," Mrs. Tidwell gushed. "Such a joker!"

Marie assured her that Reynard was simply heaps of fun and ordered a white wine spritzer, while Reynard asked for a schooner of ale. Mrs. Tidwell fluttered off happily.

"Another of your conquests?" Marie asked.

"She's lonely. I try to give her a smile when I can," Reynard returned. "Now tell me, duck, what's on your mind?"

Marie leaned closer, moving a pink, scented candle out of the way. "Louisa's already suspicious of me, I can tell. And she said she didn't trust you."

"Poor old dear. Her mind must be going. That would explain a lot, wouldn't it?"

"She also made it clear that her great-niece and -nephew were more than enough family for her."

"Ah, the niece and nephew. Seen 'em yet? Nothing extraordinary about him. But the first time you see *her,* you may get a jolt."

"I haven't had so much as a glimpse of them. My point is why would she say such a thing to nearly a total stranger?" Marie asked with feeling.

"Don't be so sensitive. What she said's not so bad. I'll tell anybody I've got only one niece, and she fills up my world. What more family could I want?"

"I'm serious, Reynard. She thinks it's odd that I work for her, and you work for Tyler. Especially with Andrew Preston there. As if he's some evil puppeteer or something."

"Piffle. More paranoia. And Andrew's no evil boll weevil. Truth is, he's trying to be Mr. Goody Two-shoes. Doesn't want Bullock getting any ammo stockpiled against him. Won't even look at a woman—not so's people'd notice—until after the election. Heard him say so myself. Said it to his cousin."

For some reason Marie's heart sank. "So he's Mr. Clean?"

"Mostly. I've only seen him look with lust at one Sheila."

"And she was—?"

Reynard leaned closer. He smiled his most beguiling smile. "Why, you, love. And you know it as well as I. For you gave him that look right back. But don't fall for him. He sees you as a little nobody who might be fun on the side once or twice. Keep your distance, duck."

His words shocked her, and she stared at him with a challenging spark in her eye.

"Rennie, I'm not interested in being anybody's 'fun on the side.' And stick to the subject. I don't like Louisa Fairchild. She has a mean streak in her. I don't want to go through with this—this impersonation. It's not worth it."

"Really, love," he purred, "you've known her half a day. Give her a decent chance. Mrs. Lipton's a good sort, and she's stayed with her for years. Her best trainers and stable men have stood by her. She can't be all bad if she inspires such loyalty."

He smiled wisely and sipped his beer.

"She may have good in her somewhere," Marie argued. "But she was beastly to me. And I feel like I'm just here after her money or favors. It makes me feel dirty. We've seen that one highly questionable letter from Willadene Gates—that's all."

"Ah, but there's talk," Reynard observed. "Small community like this? Oh, the gossip's everlasting. And I've heard the same rumor a dozen times."

Marie shot him a dubious glance. "What rumor?"

Reynard smiled, and gave her his heavy-lidded look. "Louisa left home for six months when she was sixteen. Her family said she was going to New Zealand to study. *But* others say she had a bastard child. She came home changed. Cold and bitter."

Marie's spine straightened in surprise. "But you say it's only a rumor."

"It's also a question of math. I was told that she left here in the last part of 1945. Colette was born in March of 1946. It fits. Look at old pictures of Louisa. You'll see the resemblance between her and Colette. Can't miss it."

"How'd you see pictures?" Marie challenged.

"Mrs. Lipton showed me. At the end of the hall on the second floor. Look for yourself."

"Why didn't you tell me this sooner? About the rumors? And her going away?"

"I thought I'd save it until you started going wobbly. Didn't expect it would be this soon. Don't you want to learn more? You owe it to Colette to find out. You know you do."

Marie was struck speechless.

"Stay a bit longer?" he asked in his most beguiling voice.

"Only a bit," she said, once again feeling cornered. "Only a bit."

Chapter Six

The next morning Marie helped make a simple breakfast for the staff and a complicated one for Louisa and her great-niece and -nephew.

Reynard showed up with the eggs just in time to eat breakfast. "Luscious, love," he told Marie as he took another cup of tea. "You're truly your mother's daughter."

She smiled, but wondered if her mother was truly Louisa's daughter. No two women could be so different in spirit, the gentle Colette, and the crotchety Louisa.

"And by the by," Reynard said, "the cook over at Lochlain wants to know if you've got any stoneware onion soup bowls she could borrow. Andrew Preston's campaign manager, the fabulous Miss Darci Parnell, comes for lunch day after tomorrow. Loves onion soup. Nobody in the history of Lochlain's ever wanted onion soup before. A loan would be appreciated."

Marie was taken aback by the words "the fabulous Miss Darci

Parnell." Of course, Andrew Preston would know fabulous women. And she was his campaign manager? They must be *very* close.

She stiffened her back and said, "You'll have to ask Mrs. Lipton. I don't know yet what this kitchen does or doesn't have."

He got up, leaned over the table and kissed her on the cheek. "Then I'll ask Mrs. Lipton—and take a few of her brandy snaps with me. And thanks, love, for a bonzer brekkie."

A moment later, Reynard practically had his lips buried in Mrs. Lipton's ear, and she couldn't have looked happier. He blew Marie a kiss and was out the door, whistling.

Mrs. Lipton came to Marie. "Onion soup bowls? Yes, we have extras. I know you're already worked to bits, but if I find them, could you run them over to Lochlain later in the day? Perhaps you'd welcome a little break—you haven't had a chance to see much of our valley."

Marie nodded, but was curious. "Miss Fairchild has a grudge against Lochlain. Why would she want to loan them anything?"

"Miss may bear a grudge against whomever she likes, whenever she likes. But people on the two staffs have been friends, neighbors—and some of them relatives—for years. She may go on the warpath, but we keep our separate peace. And by the way," Mrs. Lipton added, "Miss would like to see you at nine sharp. You'll be able to oblige?"

Marie nodded again. And wondered what the old woman wanted this time.

At five to nine, Marie climbed the stairs to Louisa's second-story suite. Just as Reynard had said, there were many gold-framed photographs arranged on the wall at the end of the hallway. All were of Louisa, from babyhood to the present.

As a young teenager, Louisa was lovely. In one photo she stood by a horse, giving it an adoring look. The sight shook Marie, who saw a clear resemblance not only to Colette, but to herself at that age. *My God,* she thought, *this can't just be coincidence.*

She studied the pictures with growing perplexity, until her watch said nine. Then she rapped at Louisa's door.

The suite included a sitting room, a private dining room, bathroom and an office that was being remodeled. When Marie entered, she saw Louisa sitting on a couch in riding clothes. She was amazed that the old woman still rode.

Louisa seemed to read her thoughts. "Once I could sit a horse like nobody's business. Now? The groom has to help me into the saddle. Such, such are the joys of aging. You see your lovely pleasures slipping away, one by one."

Marie thought, *My mother didn't live to be truly old and had few pleasures. Would her life have been better if you hadn't turned your back and left her life to chance?*

She said nothing, simply stood with her head held high.

"On occasion," said Louisa, "one of my pleasures is complaining. You've deprived me, for my breakfast was disappointingly without flaw. Still, I went out on the balcony and sniffed the aroma of the staff's breakfast. It smelled *better.* How could that be?"

"I'm just trying to make their meals more flavorful. Mrs. Lipton said that your breakfast was what you'd requested."

"In making meals more *flavorful,* won't you also make them more expensive? I don't intend to spend money on truffles for men who scoop manure."

"It'll cost only a bit more and be worth it. Well-fed people will work harder for you and want to keep you happy."

"And what are you feeding these people for lunch?" Louisa demanded. "Oysters on the half shell?"

"I believe that's your lunch, Miss," Marie said with just a touch of tartness. "They'll have German tuna salad, rye bread and a medley of vegetables, also a German recipe."

"Then bring me the same. I haven't had simple food in years. Perhaps you can make it tolerable. That's all I have to say. Except tell your uncle I wish to speak to him tomorrow when he brings the eggs. And tonight I want a strawberry Pavlova."

"Certainly," Marie said and managed an imitation of an obedient smile.

"Now I have bloodlines to study for my breeding program," Louisa said with an irritable flutter of her fingers. "Blood will tell, you know. I can spot an excellent Thoroughbred the instant I see one. I have an unerring instinct. Blood will tell, it's true."

Marie nodded. "If you say so, Miss."

She left, her heart beating hard and high in her chest. Louisa's words kept echoing in her mind: "Blood will tell."

Early that afternoon, Andrew was restless. Ever since he'd met Marie Lafayette, he couldn't get her out of his head. Or out of his dreams, which were disturbingly erotic until some inner censor switched them off and hurled him into semiconsciousness.

He had too much pent-up energy, he told himself. He was a physical man, not used to an endless agenda of giving speeches, taking meetings, doing interviews and touring the countryside talking to an endless series of owners, trainers and breeders.

He wanted to go for a gallop over the hills or hike ten miles or chop wood. Then he'd be back to normal and not become tongue-tied in the presence of a cute cook. Because that's all she was. A really cute cook.

Tyler was busy with a vanload of tourists from Sydney, led by a guide who'd cooked them a barbecue in a shady grove next to a pasture of grazing Thoroughbreds. Afterward, some visitors would go horseback riding, some would take a trip in a horse-drawn carriage, and the rest would stay in the shade sipping Hunter Valley wine.

Tyler made some sorely needed spare cash from this, but Andrew would as soon stay off the riding trails while the tourists were there. He opted to chop wood, which in Australia was not just a chore, but a national sport. One of the stable men, Winkler, had taught him to underhand block chop and said Andrew showed a talent for it.

A woodsman had to stand atop a log, chop halfway through one side, turn it over and chop through the other side as fast as possible. There was a danger of chopping a foot, but only a sissy wore steel-toed boots.

So Andrew chopped in a special area beside the yearling barn until he'd worked up a fine sweat and all he could think of was his aching muscles. He'd pulled his T-shirt off after a few minutes and thrown it onto the grass. The charm Raddy had given him nestled against the hairs of his chest.

A few tourists drifted by, wineglasses in hand, and paused to watch him.

"Why's he doing that?" a woman in a big hat asked. "That's a funny way to chop a log."

"Probably a little sideshow for you ladies," a potbellied man said snidely. "Let's go look where the fire was and they found the body."

Andrew thought he heard the click of cameras and immediately stopped chopping. He snatched up his shirt and strode off to put the ax away. He gleamed with perspiration.

Winkler, a large man with a shaved head, had been lounging by the barn, watching him. "We'll have to enter you in competition, mate," he said.

Andrew was disgruntled by the tourists, but managed a smile. "I'd be no competition against you guys," he said, and headed for the house to take a shower. He'd spoken at a breakfast gathering in a nearby township, had a cocktail party to attend late this afternoon in the next shire, then yet another banquet and another speech.

He wasn't satisfied with his performance lately. He felt stiff, self-conscious, unnatural. It was probably from knowing that he was so different from the professionally beaming and effusive Jacko that he held himself far more in check than usual.

Then he saw a blue truck, familiar to him now, the Fairchild Acres all-purpose vehicle.

He noticed it with only passing interest until he realized who was behind the wheel—Marie Lafayette. He stopped as if paralyzed, then moved to open her door.

"Oh," she said, looking at him in surprise.

Suddenly he realized he was half-naked and dirty to boot. "Miss Lafayette," he said with all the chivalry he could muster. "What brings you here?"

She stared up at him with those hypnotic green eyes, her full lips slightly parted. The sun gleamed on her thick golden hair, and he had an almost irresistible urge to stroke its smoothness.

She dressed in the Fairchild standard uniform, dark blue shorts and white blouse, but the no-nonsense cut of her clothes couldn't hide her neat little figure, the intriguing thrust of her breasts, the smallness of her waist, the curve of her hips. He took in all these details instantly and greedily.

My God, you're bewitching, he thought. *What goes on inside your head? Are you as sure of yourself as you seem? As sunny-natured?*

She took a deep breath. "Rennie—my uncle—said that the cook here needed to borrow some soup bowls. Could you point which way to the kitchen?"

"I'll walk you there," he offered. "And carry the bowls."

"Oh, you don't have to do that," she said, her eyes still on his.

"I want to." There. That was easy. And honest.

She reached into the cab of the truck and picked up a cardboard box. He took it from her and tucked it under his bare arm. "This way," he said, cocking his head toward the office, but still not looking away from her.

He heard a clicking noise, but it barely registered on his consciousness. "So Louisa let you escape for a while?"

She laughed, a delightful sound. He was sure that sound would be in his dreams tonight.

"Just a while."

"Can you stay for a cup of coffee, er, tea?"

"Thanks, but I have to get right back."

"Your uncle says you put in long hours over there. That it's a killer workload."

She shrugged philosophically. "I'm still learning my way around the kitchen. And we're short a person, the chief cook. But I'll get my schedule under control before long."

"You're an organized type?" he asked. He wished he had his shirt back on. It seemed she was trying not to look at his chest.

"I have to be. Don't you? With all your campaigning?"

"I try. Ah. Here's the kitchen."

He called out the cook's name, but no one answered. "Come on in," he invited. "I'll set these on the counter. And tell her you brought them."

"Thanks," she said, all chipper pertness. "Well, I suppose I may see you around now and then, after all."

"Oh, yeah, I suppose," he said casually. In truth, he wanted to see her far more than "now and then."

"Thanks again. I'll find my way back."

She gave him a lovely smile of goodbye, but he was immediately at her side. "I'm going out. I'll walk you to your car."

Her smile faded, as if such treatment wasn't wanted. She said nothing, only nodded. He strolled beside her toward the truck. "Do you ever get a day off over there?" he asked, again trying to sound casual.

"Tomorrow I do. The staff each gets one day off, but we have different days."

"What will you do?" he asked, looking out over the lawn so he wouldn't seem too interested.

"I may catch a bus to Scone or Aberdeen and buy another set of uniforms. I have to keep washing my everyday one and ironing it in the morning."

He wrestled over whether he should volunteer to drive her. Louisa Fairchild would probably snort fire over such a thing, and he didn't want to get Marie in—

Suddenly he had her in his arms, hoisting her up so her feet were off the ground, holding her tight, so that she was pressed against his hot, naked chest. He stepped carefully backward.

She stared at him, her mouth a luscious pink O of surprise. "What—" she started to say.

"Snake," he replied in a low voice. "I'm just backing out of his range."

She followed his gaze and saw a large brown snake, well camouflaged in the dry grass. It was over a meter long and sluggish with the afternoon heat. It seemed to be heading for shade under a nearby bush.

"I'll set you on the porch," Andrew said, still moving backward slowly. "Then get the ax and kill it."

"Oh, no," she protested. "It's quite harmless. A very nice snake, actually."

He stopped moving. "Nice? It's nearly four feet long. And

you've got some of the most poisonous snakes in the world here."

She laughed. "It's only a rock python. It's not venomous, and it's so docile that it's called the 'children's python.' People who fancy snakes keep them as pets. Now will you put me down?"

"You're sure it's harmless?"

"Certain." Yet she looked at him with amused admiration. "But you did exactly the right thing. You didn't know what it was, so you walked off slowly."

He didn't want to put her down. He liked having her in his arms, and it felt *right* that her body was so close to his; it felt wonderfully right. But reluctantly he set her down again. The front of her blouse had damp spots from his sweat, and some wood chips clung to it.

"I got you—uh—kind of grungy," he said. "I'm sorry."

Winkler, the barn cleaner, still leaning against the wall, guffawed. "Cuddle-wuddle snake," he snorted. But Marie didn't seem to hear him, thank God.

"Don't apologize," she told Andrew. "You were very gallant."

He almost blushed. *Gallant?*

He found they were looking in each other's eyes again. For a moment, the rest of the world seemed to drop away. He wondered if she felt the same. He said, "I could drive you to Scone tomorrow morning, if you'd like. I have to go over that way."

She edged away from him a bit. "That's kind," she said, smiling, but she looked almost nervous. "But I can go alone. So, no, thank you."

He wondered if she didn't want to be with him, or if she feared Louisa Fairchild's wrath. "If it's Louisa," he said, "can she control you on your day off? She doesn't own you."

She shook her head, the gold hair swinging slightly. "Right now I'm just trying to keep life simple."

He didn't understand what she meant by keeping life simple; he hadn't proposed anything complex. He sensed a sadness hiding under her chipper facade, and he didn't understand that, either. Was she thinking of her mother? He wanted to put his hands on her shoulders, look into her eyes again and ask her to tell him her feelings.

But he couldn't do that, and the scene around them was getting more hectic as the guide started trying to herd the tourists back into the van and on to their next destination, the petting zoo, where they'd coo at the koalas, chuck cockatoos under their chins and hand feed the young kangaroos.

"I really need to go," Marie said. "And thanks again for your concern about my safety. You were very quick-witted." She smiled and showed her dimples, then turned and moved toward the truck.

"Cuddle-wuddle snake," repeated Winkler, running his hand over his shaven head. Andrew wanted to drag him into the barn and shove that shiny head up to its neck in horse manure.

Marie left quickly, the dust puffing out behind her, then settling back to the scorched and thirsty earth. But her body still tingled from where it had pressed against his.

Her heart banged as if a small, crazed snare drummer had hijacked her chest. She felt dazed, yet excited. Being swept up by Andrew so swiftly, so powerfully, had left her breathless with surprise.

She'd had to grab his bare shoulder to keep her balance, and she remembered the hardness of his muscle, the damp smoothness of his hot skin. He'd held her so tightly that her breasts had flattened against his wide chest, so she could feel the heat and strength of his body.

She'd inhaled his scent, clean sweat and the smell of freshly hewn pine. She was close enough to see just how darkly blue his eyes were, the fine bone structure of his face, and the sweaty, waving tumble of his hair.

She could see every detail of the carved bird that rested on his breastbone. In those moments, physical awareness of him had shot through her so intensely she'd almost gasped.

Now, alone in the truck's cab, she could still feel the faint moisture of his perspiration on her blouse, smell the piney tang of wood. So this was what Reynard meant when he'd said he'd heard her hormones rattling free at last.

It was a wonderful feeling. And terrifying. Reynard had warned her, and he'd meant it. She didn't want to have these emotions about any man, especially one as wealthy and influential as Andrew Preston. It was insane to take a fancy to a man whose social status was so much higher than hers. Look at what had happened to Colette—and to thousands of other young women.

Then the rest of the world came crashing back into her consciousness. She'd had another assignment at Lochlain—not just delivering bowls. Louisa Fairchild had ordered her to have Reynard come talk to her tomorrow morning. Marie had forgotten even to look for him.

She pulled over to the side of the road to call him on her cell phone.

"Hello, love," he said, clearly in a merry mood. "Nice to hear from my girl. What can I do for you?"

"I have a message for you from Miss Fairchild. She wants to talk to you tomorrow morning when you bring the eggs."

"Oh?" he replied, sounding even more pleased. "And what would she like to talk *about?*"

"I have no idea. I hope it's not more silliness about us being— in league with Andrew Preston or something."

He laughed. "I'll just chat her up and see what's on her mind, that's all."

They said their goodbyes and Marie drove on.

Mrs. Lipton met her at the kitchen door, saying that Louisa wanted to see her in the library. Marie hastily tied on her bibbed apron to cover her rumpled shirt and ran up the stairs.

Louisa sat at her massive desk, surrounded by sheaves of paper with large print. Several obviously expensive books on Thoroughbred breeding were stacked beside her elbow.

She looked at Marie over the tops of her spectacles. "Hello. I wanted to tell you that I liked your luncheon for the staff better than I liked my usual. How can that be? It's not right, young woman."

Marie clasped her hands in front of her. "I've noticed from the menus that you don't vary your diet much. Every Monday you have the same thing, every Tuesday, and so on. Perhaps you were unconsciously growing tired of the repetition."

Louisa gave a snort of disdain. "I never unconsciously do anything. I am probably the most conscious person you'll ever meet."

"I apologize, Miss. I gave you the only reason I could think of."

"Well, it tasted good. Like the food of my youth. I think for a while, I'd like to try the staff meals. And see what my niece and nephew think of them."

Shocked, Marie was silent.

Louisa gave her a stare that was almost pitying. "Don't look so gobsmacked. Did you tell your uncle I wish to speak with him?"

"Yes. When he comes with the eggs, as you asked."

"And do you wonder why I want to talk to him?"

"That's between you and my uncle, I'd think."

Louisa slitted her eyes and patted the sheaf of papers with one gnarled hand. "Do you know what these are?"

Marie shook her head. "No, I'm afraid not."

"They're the records of my horses. I pore over them every day. The horse business is complex. It takes a great deal of rigorous study and hard work to succeed. Do you know anything of it?"

"No, miss. I'm quite ignorant on the subject."

"If you're to stay around here, you'll need to learn," Louisa said crisply. She pushed a book toward Marie. "Take that. Study it. I may quiz you when I get back from the U.K."

Reluctantly Marie took the book and gazed at its cover. It was a thick book, and a heavy one; its title was *The History of Australian Horse Breeding.* It looked daunting, but Marie told herself she would tackle it with all the determination she had.

But Louisa's move puzzled her. Did it mean that the old woman wasn't as hostile as she seemed? Did Louisa want her to stay?

At Lochlain, Reynard bent over the kitchen counter, repairing one of the microwaves. Andrew sat at the kitchen table, nursing a cup of coffee that he'd made himself. It tasted terrible, but he was tired of tea.

"So my girl brought over the soup bowls, eh?" Reynard asked, "and you saved her from a kiddy snake."

Andrew wanted to bury his face in his hands. "How was I supposed to know it was harmless? Australia's full of snakes. It might have been a viper."

"In Oz here, we got about 140 different snakes, but only ten percent are poisonous. 'Course we do have nine of the most deadly in the world. But some are lovely to look at. The sea krait. The desert death adder. True beauts, those two."

"How do you know so much about snakes?" Andrew asked grumpily.

"Used to work at a reptile farm farther south. I handled the snakes. Grew rather fond of some of them. But they're not much at making conversation. So I moved on—and here I am."

Andrew eyed him dubiously. Reynard always had stories, but were they all true?

He could repair anything, build anything, he could even invent things. But with all his imagination and talent, he seemed more in love with drifting than security. Could he really be related to Marie?

Sometimes it didn't seem possible.

"You look a bit glum," Reynard remarked. "Don't let the kiddy snake embarrass you. Most Yanks would have run like hell. Your reaction was spot-on. You even tried to rescue the damsel. Many a man would've worried only about his own skin."

"The damsel must think I'm an idiot."

"Naw. She's not like that. She's good, sensible, and kind—she truly is. She'd never think ill of a chap trying to do the right thing."

"You've known her all her life?"

"Indeed. I'm even her godfather."

Andrew finished the last of his coffee. "So you know everything about her?"

"I reckon. But she hasn't had much of a life. Work and college. College and work. And taking care of her poor mum. Her mum hadn't been well for years."

Andrew suspected he should be cautious about what he said to Reynard, but he couldn't help himself. "She's really pretty. I mean, I'm surprised she's still single."

"Her parents' union was brief and unhappy," Reynard replied smoothly. "That affects a girl's outlook, y' know. Plus, she keeps busy. Hardest little worker you'll ever meet. Love her as if she was my own. And I appreciate your protecting her. I'd protect her with my life, I swear it. Any man ever trifle with her, hurt her, I'd break his skull with pleasure and bite his brain in two. I'm like an old lion with one cub, I am."

Tyler's housekeeper opened the kitchen door. "Reynard, the cuckoo got stuck outside the clock again. Can you make him go back in? I'm always afraid I'll break him."

Reynard smiled engagingly. "With pleasure, love. I'll put the budgie back in his bunk."

He turned and winked at Andrew. Then, a slightly lascivious gleam in his eye, he followed the broad-hipped housekeeper.

Andrew stood up and rinsed his cup in the sink. Again he was perplexed. Had Reynard just warned him away from Marie? It sure as hell had sounded like it.

Was Reynard smart enough to sense his attraction to his niece? For an amiable man, he'd spoken with remarkably grim conviction about skull breaking.

And why did the warning make Andrew even more curious about Marie? Didn't Reynard think Andrew was good enough for her?

Shaking his head, he stood, knowing he had to get ready for the cocktail party.

But he wondered if, in his free time tomorrow morning, he might just see where the bus took Marie. And perhaps run into her....

After he talked to her for half an hour or so, he'd wager that he'd find they had nothing in common, and that his attraction was simple lust, easily controlled. He and she might not even be able to get through a half hour of bland chitchat.

And after that, he'd forget her. The enchantment would be

broken, the mystery would vanish. He'd be a free man again, with nothing to distract him from his true work: beating Jacko Bullock.

That night Marie again felt exhausted. She'd stayed late in the kitchen, preparing ahead for Louisa's meals and the staff's so she could take her day off with a clear conscience.

Now she lay down and tried reading *The History of Australian Horse Breeding.* Weary, she began to nod off.

Her thoughts drifted from horses and Louisa to being in Andrew Preston's arms. She remembered the way he'd held her, tightly, almost possessively. She found herself wanting to press her mouth against his bare chest, just above where the wooden charm rested over his breastbone.

She wanted to raise her lips to meet his, to run her hands over the smooth skin of his torso, the tautness of his muscles and the crispness of his chest hair. She wanted to guide his strong hand to her breast. His kiss would be like a soft key that unlocked her timid lips and unleashed feelings in her that were strange and wonderful, but that were also new and frightening.

She'd put her arms around his neck, and the sensation of their touching would make her feel as if she were swaying, losing control of her body and her will and—

Her eyes snapped open with an embarrassed start, her body throbbing.

She never had thoughts like this. *Ever.* She didn't have sexual fantasies. She didn't *allow* herself to have them.

In fact, she'd come to suppose that she was frigid, but so what? It would keep her safe from the fate of Colette and Colette's mother.

Marie was shaken by that thought and by the sensual hunger she'd discovered in herself. Why, after all the years she'd repressed such feelings, had quiet, gentlemanly Andrew Preston awakened them? A man with whom she had no chance. No. None at all.

Chapter Seven

The next morning Marie dressed in one of her short-sleeved blouses with a ruffled front and her best nonuniform shorts, blue-and-white seersucker, with a blue belt.

She walked a mile to the bus stop, and once aboard, she stared out at the rolling countryside. The irrigated vineyards were green, but much of the land was browned and yellowed by drought, and she could see a smudge of smoke along the Koongarra Tops.

In Scone, the morning heat was already burning, and the sultry breezes whirled dust through the air. She walked to the library, got herself a card and checked out four books, a cookbook of gourmet desserts, two collections of poetry and a volume on dealing with grief. They would fill the empty nights when she didn't see Reynard.

She tried not to think of her uncle. He'd have his private conversation with Louisa Fairchild. Heaven only knew what Louisa wanted from him and what the outcome might be. Reynard was good company, but Marie had long suspected that he picked up spare money wherever and however he could. Did he get involved with shady dealings? She fiercely blocked the notion; it was too painful—and too possible.

She made her way to the town's shopping district and looked in a thrift shop. She was amazed to find a half a rack of Fairchild Acre-type uniforms for both men and women. She found two informal sets that were her size, and put them into her shopping cart.

She browsed awhile more. Although she had little money, she decided to buy another secondhand outfit, a three-piece set in her size; a simple top, shorts and a nicely cut skirt. It looked nearly new, simple to care for, and was a silky apple green.

She paid and walked outside, carrying her purchases and cradling her library books in the crook of her arm. She paused on the steps of the store and set down her books, then took off her backpack, and put her new clothes inside.

A man's voice, from behind her, startled her. "Shopping? Find what you wanted?"

She whirled and saw Andrew standing with one hip cocked. He wore freshly pressed khakis, bush shoes and a T-shirt of such dark blue it almost matched his eyes. The day was breezy, and the wind ruffled his hair so that a dark forelock danced over his brow.

"Oh," she said, stunned. She remembered last night's drowsy sexual fantasy and felt her cheeks turning hot. "What are you doing here?"

"Took some stuff to the cleaner's," he replied, tilting his head at a shop farther down the street. "I go to a lot of lunches and banquets. I keep spilling gravy on my power ties. It negates their power. I have to get their potency restored."

I doubt if you have any trouble with potency, Marie thought, then blushed harder.

"That's all?" she asked, not believing he was really there.

"Nope," he answered with a one-sided smile. "I've got to buy some stuff to take back to Lochlain. Are you through shopping?"

She forced herself to give a lighthearted shrug. "Almost. I have to go to the grocery store. Check it out and buy a few things."

"That's where I'm headed," he said, squinting into the distance. "It's a long way. Why don't you let me drive you?"

Oh, yes, yes, yes! shouted her emotional side.

No, no, and no again! warned her rational side. *He asked yesterday if he could bring me here. Did he follow me? Somehow figure out how to meet me?*

Her cynical side scolded, *You're daft. Why would he bother? He said he was coming this way this morning. We met by accident, not design.*

"Well," she said half-reluctantly, "if you really have to go…"

"I do. But it's hot. Want to get a cold tea or lemonade? There's a tea shop over there. Isn't it time for morning tea or, what do they call it—smacko or something?"

"Smoke-oh," she corrected, smiling. "Yes, that's what workers call the morning break. "They have tea or coffee—or a smoke."

"Okay," he said with a serious nod. "You've taught me something. So let's have a smoke-oh across the street. And then get on with business."

No, her mind told her. *Yes. Shouldn't do it. Not at all. But maybe…*

"Certainly," she said in her most business-like tone. "But I'll need to be quick about it."

"I'll carry your books," he said, scooping them up from the steps.

Andrew thought, *Am I ruthless? A stalker? Has political work paid off—I now talk out of both sides of my mouth?*

But they were in the tearoom, a quaint place with dozens of framed etchings of Thoroughbreds on the walls and horse brasses decorating the side beams. She ordered lemonade and he had iced tea.

Once again he had to search for something to say. She had a way of befuddling his usually quick and careful powers of speech. At last he said, "I hear Louisa's leaving for London soon."

"So she said," Marie replied amiably enough. "But I haven't the foggiest why."

"A foal, my cousin says," Andrew told her. "A descendent of one of her great mares, Secret Heiress. If she likes what she sees, she'll buy it."

"I wonder when she'll be back."

"This is Louisa we're talking about. She'll come back when she chooses. Who knows?"

Marie made no answer, so he gazed at the spines of her books, which he'd set on the table top. He looked at a title and frowned. "Gourmet desserts? I thought you already knew all about cooking."

"Do you know all about horses?" she asked with a mischievous smile.

"No," he admitted. "I'm still learning."

"So am I," she said. "Miss Fairchild has a sweet tooth. I need to learn more about her favorite types of desserts, give her some variety."

"You're very solicitous," he said, not knowing what to think of her. She seemed too sincere and unaffected to be trying to cozy up to Louisa for her own advantage.

He looked at the last book. Dealing with the Death of a Loved One. He paused. "You got this one out because of your mother?"

She stared at the tablecloth. "Yes."

"You and she were…close?"

"Extremely." She still didn't look at him. "Listen. I need to say this." She took a deep breath. "That night in the parking lot when I cried? It wasn't because of that idiot busboy. My mother was…very ill. That's why I broke down. I'm so sorry about that—it must have been very embarrassing for you. But I—" She struggled to keep from faltering and almost succeeded. "She died only a few hours later."

His heart twisted for her. She'd been so brisk and efficient and poised inside the restaurant. How had she hidden her fears so well? She must have been sick with worry the whole night.

"*I'm* sorry. Do you have brothers and sisters to help you through this?"

"No. I just have Reynard."

He examined her. This lovely, valiant little creature had only one living relative? He said, "That must be hard. I can't imagine life without a big family. I miss mine all the time. My brothers, my sister, my folks, my granddad." He paused, then asked, "Your father's gone, too?"

She looked him straight in the eyes and said, "He never married my mother. He didn't want a child, and I never knew him. He died when I was five."

He gazed at her, astonished by her frankness, her matter-of-fact air. "I'm sorry," he repeated.

She gave him a philosophical smile. "Thanks, but you don't have to be. We did fine without him. Let's talk about something else. What made you want to run for Federation president? It sounds like a hard job to get and then even harder once you've got it. You'll have to keep most people happy, and they're *all* going to want a piece of you. No matter what you do, someone will be mad."

He stole another look at her. She was astute, all right. And she'd deftly changed the subject from herself. Still, she looked truly interested in what he had to say. He took a swig of his tea, wishing it were a whiskey and soda.

"There are causes I believe in strongly," he began. "One's equine health. There's too much irresponsible breeding. Treating horses like commodities, not living creatures like us that can feel pain, catch diseases, have needless accidents... There's a serious problem with overbreeding—and too much chasing after money."

The more he talked, the more closely she seemed to listen, until he realized he'd been speaking almost ten minutes, and he'd been serious as a judge and earnest as a preacher. "I—I'm sorry," he stammered. "I sound like I'm stumping for votes. But I really believe in what I say."

"I can tell," she said, gazing at him with something like approval. "Mrs. Lipton says you're taking a strong stand on gambling reform."

He let a harsh sigh escape from between his teeth. "Where there's gambling, there's crime. And crime, like wolves, tends to travel in packs. You have bookies and offshore betting and expensive horses. You get money-laundering. I read a report— shady business may account for as much as twenty per cent of today's economy."

He paused. "So, yeah, we've got some pretty dirty people and some pretty dirty business trying to muscle in on ours. It's time to clean up."

She looked at him as if seeing him for the first time. "Aren't you afraid?"

"Not for me," he said, and meant it. He knew danger, lots of it, could come with a run for the presidency. "For my family. That's another matter. The arson? Tyler was threatened before I ever got there."

"Isn't *he* scared?"

"Somebody began threatening his best horse months ago. He won a race nobody expected him to win. Made him some enemies of his own. It's a high-stakes world. And sometimes the stakes are more than money. I hope my staying with him doesn't make him a target again."

She cocked her head and stared at him in disbelief. "And you just calmly sit there and talk about it, like it's the weather."

Good God, was that *admiration* in her look? Or did she just think he was crazy? His heart did a wild, dangerous cartwheel. "I've talked too much. Let's go hit the grocery store."

Soon they were doing the most ordinary of tasks, each rolling a cart through the Coles store in the mall. Andrew had a short list from the cook, and Marie bought only a few items, fresh raspberries, sliced almonds, grapes, a large turkey and sausage spices. But Andrew saw that she was expertly casing the joint. She looked over almost every category of food, making notes in a small spiral notebook.

"What are you—a spy?" he joked.

She gave him a startled look.

He said, "I mean some kind of professional comparison shopper? All those notes?"

"I—I just have to know what's available and how fresh the produce is," she stammered. "I'll eventually have to do some of the shopping."

He smiled and shook his head. She was a thorough pro, as observant and businesslike and efficient as a rising young executive.

"Miss Fairchild's difficult to please?" he asked, wondering how honestly she'd answer.

"She is. She compliments me in backhanded ways, but she doesn't seem to like me. I'm not sure why."

"That makes two of us. She doesn't even want to see me."

"Well, she's very moody of late, Mrs. Lipton told me." She paused and nipped at her full underlip in a way that made him want to taste her mouth, explore its softness. She shook her head and murmured, as if to herself, "I shouldn't talk about her. She's my employer."

"I shouldn't have asked," he replied. "I didn't mean to pick your brain about her. By the way, do you want to check out any of the other markets? I'll be glad to take you."

"No, thanks. I can't let you do that. I'll come another time. You must have things to do."

"Not until the afternoon," he said. "There's a tea in Maitland I've got to go to. Besides, you've got a lot of bags to wrestle. Ride back with me. It'll be a lot easier than the bus."

She hesitated. He leaned closer, looked into those flawlessly green eyes. "Come on," he coaxed.

She gave him a sardonic smile. "Miss Fairchild might think that I'm consorting with the enemy. I'm sorry to say that, but I have to face facts. You're very kind, though."

"Let me drive you to the bus stop, at least. There's no harm in that."

She agreed, although she had her reservations. "I suppose you have a full schedule with the election coming up," she said, fastening her seat belt. "A lot of engagements."

"Enough," he said without enthusiasm. "I have to go to Sydney for the next few days—if we can get there. There's a lot of trouble there. Riots. Sabotage. All over APEC, and it looks like it's getting worse. After that, it's back to Tyler's. And then I *really* hit the road. I see Oz from coast to coast."

"Sounds grueling," she said.

"Absolutely," he agreed. "I'm no raconteur and entertainer like Jacko. And lately I feel off my game. Like the fire in the belly doesn't burn hot enough. I think I'm coming across as too stiff, too dull compared to him." He paused and cast her a curious glance. "You ever see me on television?"

She looked almost guilty. "Well—yes. I've seen you a few times."

He cocked his head. "Well, what did you think? Don't be afraid to give it to me straight."

She drew a deep breath, deciding if he wanted honesty, she'd give it to him. "You don't come across the way you do in person. It's hard to know who or what you are on television."

He frowned slightly, looking puzzled. "What do you mean?"

"A lot of times you come across as so measured, so studied. Mr. McPerfect."

"I'm not perfect," he said with a wry smile. "I assure you."

"Nobody is," she replied. "But on the telly, you *seem* perfect. Or like you're trying to be. So completely controlled. Maybe *too* controlled. You don't talk the way you talked in the tea shop. So if I only knew you from that, the face you show the public, I'd wonder who's the real Andrew Preston."

Darci had hinted at the same thing. He came across as serious and deliberate, sometimes too much so. He'd been the eldest son, the one who was supposed to set the example, carry on the Preston tradition and his father's high standards.

What Marie said brought the simple truth home to him. "I don't want to make any mistakes," he said, almost to himself.

"Maybe it's a mistake to be afraid of mistakes," she offered. "Holding yourself in for the sake of—of decorum or something."

She smiled. "You were plenty eloquent in the tearoom. If you speak half that well every place else, you'll be great. Maybe you should pretend you're talking to just one person. Forget about crowds and cameras."

Damn! he thought. It was old advice, but good advice that he'd forgotten, and she reminded him of it when he needed to hear it the most. Her words were like a pleasant wave of cool, blue water washing over him. And he knew he wanted to see her again.

"I'd like to take you to tea again," he said, his heart jarring his rib cage. "Maybe on your next day off."

"That might not be wise. Miss Fairchild has mixed emotions

about me. And quite strong ones about *you*. It makes me feel as if you and I come from warring houses."

Like Romeo and Juliette, he thought. And he remembered what had happened to those two.

"I understand," he said.

But he didn't accept it. He couldn't. And wouldn't.

Hot and dusty, tired by her walk from the bus stop, Marie was glad to reach Fairchild Acres. She put away the groceries she'd bought and gave Mrs. Lipton the bill.

"My dear," said Mrs. Lipton putting her hand to her breast, "you didn't have to spend your morning shopping. You should take time from your workday to do that. I'm sure you can use the truck to carry back supplies. You mustn't take the bus."

"I just wanted to look over what's available," Marie said. She didn't mention Andrew Preston and wondered what would have happened if she'd driven up to Louisa's gates with him.

She excused herself and went to her room to put her books and clothes away. Suddenly, in the little room that was still strange to her, a pang of loneliness pierced her, and for the first time since she'd been at Fairchild Acres, she let herself get misty over Colette. The way Andrew spoke about his family made her lonely for her mother and homesick for a home that would never again be complete.

The phone rang, and she was pleased to hear Reynard's voice. He asked her if he could pick her up and take her to The Secret Heiress again that night—they ought to get together and have a good chin-wag, he said.

She agreed. Then, keeping on her white shirt and seersucker shorts, she went to the house to eat. She'd made the lunch the night before: a country chicken and veggie casserole with coleslaw.

Upstairs Louisa and her guests would dine on this, as well. So far Marie had heard no negative reviews from Louisa about the humbler fare—could she actually be happier with the simpler food? Or was this just another of her whims?

Marie was roundly welcomed back by Bindy, Helena, another kitchen worker and Mrs. Lipton. Two grooms, Mike and Walt, stood up and made mock bows to her. Mike pretended to tip his hat. "Welcome back, Miss Lafayette. You've fed us well even on your day off."

Walt put his hand over his heart. "You've made our lives worth livin' again. Maybe the Old Girl isn't as hard as she seems. You must never leave this place."

"Here, here!" cried someone.

Mrs. Lipton put an arm around Marie's shoulder. "She's working very hard for you. And I'm glad you appreciate it."

Marie smiled because it was lovely to be appreciated. Someday even Louisa might show her gratitude. And then again, maybe not.

Would Marie really care?

She had yet to meet the niece and nephew, though she had seen Megan Stafford lounging by the swimming pool. The woman had worn a large sun hat, large sunglasses and a tiny bikini.

Marie wondered why Reynard said the niece's appearance might give her a jolt. To Marie, who'd never worn a bikini in her life, the only surprising thing about the woman was the skimpiness of her swimwear.

That night Reynard again took Marie to The Secret Heiress. She didn't want her uncle prodding her to hurry up and win Louisa's trust so she took the initiative and started by quizzing him.

"All right," she said, "how was your conversation this morning with Miss Fairchild?"

Reynard sipped at his schooner of beer. "Interesting," he said with an innocent expression. "How was yours this morning with Andrew Preston?"

She gasped in angry disbelief. "How do you know about *that*?"

He shrugged and gave her a resigned smile. "In a small community like this? I told you, love, the main recreation's gossip. One of the hands from Whittleson's, Sandy Sanford, spent his day off in Scone and saw you go into a tearoom together. Then leave and drive off with him in his car. Oh, you'll keep few secrets *here*."

She glowered at him. "I see. I now live in a goldfish bowl."

"Indeed. And be careful of this Preston. All he wants is a quick roll in the hay."

Marie narrowed her eyes. "You told me he wasn't getting involved with any women."

Reynard lit a cigarette, and stared at her through the spiraling smoke. "That's what he said. And he won't. Get involved with anybody the public might recognize, that is. But a girl such as yourself? Out of the limelight? Susceptible to his charms? Perhaps if he thought he could discreetly dally with you. He fancies you, it's clear."

"I don't dally, discreetly or otherwise," Marie shot back. "And I asked *you* what you and Louisa talked about."

"She wants me to keep an eye on Andrew Preston and the fabulous Miss Darci Parnell, that's all. She wonders what they're up to."

"And you *agreed?*" Marie demanded.

"I told her I wasn't an insider at Lochlain. But I'd keep my eyes open and my ears as sharp as I could."

Marie gave a sigh of disgust. "Your eyes are always sharp."

He tapped one of his hearing aids. "Well, the hearing isn't, duck. And it's getting worse."

"I think you've learned to compensate. You seldom seem to miss what people say."

"Under the right circumstances. Not in a crowd, not with background noise, not when people talk low."

"So—will you tell her that he met me in Scone?"

"She probably already knows. And what's your version, love? Did the two of you plan it after he swept you up in his arms to protect you from the kiddy snake?"

"I planned *nothing,*" Marie said emphatically. "Good grief, does everybody know my business? I walked out of a thrift shop, and there he was. He offered to take me to tea, and I accepted. I was going to the grocery store, and so was he. He gave me a lift, then drove me back to the bus stop."

"Do you think he followed you to Scone?" Reynard asked mildly.

"Why would he? He's an important man. I'm nobody."

"A very lovely little nobody." Reynard tapped his fingers against his cheek contemplatively. He took another drag, then exhaled slowly. "Did he volunteer to drive you back to Fairchild Acres?"

"Yes, he did," she retorted. "And I told him no. That I didn't think Louisa would like it, and that he and I shouldn't mingle."

Reynard smiled. "Wise. You know, Andrew seems a decent chap, but he's only human. And not just any human. He's one with powerful enemies. Extremely powerful."

Marie sat straighter in her chair and stared at him. This was the second conversation of the day about enemies. Andrew had mentioned Tyler had enemies, too. "Exactly what do you mean by that?"

Reynard raised his brows speculatively. "There are people who may try to hurt him. Him and those around him. I'm only saying it's a possibility. I mean, there *has* been arson and murder at Lochlain. *And* there are rumors about Jacko Bullock and his associates. That for all his bright smiles and quick jokes, he's got a dark side."

"How so?"

"Ties to organized crime," Reynard said offhandedly. "Don't know if it's true. But there are some very tough people out there who want the racing world here to stay just the way it is. They'd much rather see Jacko as president. Andrew would be their worst nightmare."

She looked at him skeptically. "That's rather a cloak-and-dagger statement, Rennie."

"Ah," he said, "in the racing world, these are cloak-and-dagger times. Do you know how the Internet affects betting? Do you know about offshore betting and money transfer by wire? The opportunities to launder money? Irresistible, my dear. *Irresistible.*"

"And that's a reform Andrew Preston wants to make?" she murmured. "To stop the money laundering?"

"Exactly. He'd do his damnedest. Which would make certain people unhappy. Even violently unhappy, if you get my drift."

He patted his side with the bandaged ribs. "Everybody knows the fire was arson. Most likely set to get at the Prestons. Tyler was getting death threats about his best horse, y'know. Anonymous."

Marie straightened in her chair, her body tensing. She remembered, too, that Tyler had gotten threats before the fire.

"Somebody may very well have it in for the Prestons. Andrew's going to be a magnet for trouble. Keep your distance."

"Rennie," Marie challenged, "aren't you being a tad melodramatic?"

"No. Realistic. During this election, keep away from him. Will he be interested in you when it's over? That *might* be a different matter. Another glass of wine, love?"

"Thanks, but no," she murmured. "It's been a long day. I think I'd just like to go back."

"Righto," he said. "Don't want you all tired out. I'm sure the old girl intends to keep you on your toes. But you won't have to worry about Preston for a while. His campaign schedule's tight. His campaign manager's doing her job. Fabulously, of course."

"It's no concern of mine," Marie said, trying to sound airy about it.

But inside, she felt a sickening turmoil. This afternoon she'd seen a newspaper photo of Darci Parnell. She *was* fabulous, beautiful, perfectly coiffed and made up, and exquisitely dressed.

Marie couldn't believe there wasn't chemistry between such a woman and Andrew. They looked like a perfect match. They were Thoroughbreds themselves. She said, "I suppose she'll be spending all her time with Andrew. That's her job, isn't it?"

Reynard gave her a sly smile and arched one brow. "Curious, are you? Well, she's definitely interested in Mr. Preston. Mr. Tyler Preston, not Andrew."

"You're certain of that?" she demanded.

"I have two good eyes in my head and a knack for using them. I could see it from the minute she got here. My mum used to say I had the gift of foresight." He yawned and tapped out his cigarette. He drained his beer. "And now my foresight foresees me in bed."

He gave her a knowing smile. "And do remember, m'dear. It's safer to have a rich old granny who's fond of you than a rich lover. Lovers are far more fickle than grannies."

Maybe not more fickle than my granny, Marie thought bleakly—*if that's who she is.*

* * *

Reynard dropped her off at the gate shortly after 10:00 p.m. When she reached her bungalow she changed into her sleeping uniform, which was how she thought of her pajamas, read a chapter in the horse breeding book and turned out the light. But she couldn't stop thinking.

There was Rennie's startling news that beautiful Darci Parnell was interested in Tyler Preston, not Andrew. That had somehow comforted her. And yet Reynard had warned her emphatically against Andrew.

There was too much intrigue in Hunter Valley. Once again she was ready to tell Rennie she wished she'd never set out on this Quixotic journey, that she wanted to go home and be herself. Louisa's great-niece and great-nephew seemed settled in, and from the little Marie had heard, their visit was going well. If Louisa liked them, she would write them into her will as her heirs.

Marie thought it wrong to meddle with their relationship. She'd made no claim on Louisa's affections or her fortune. Even if she had the right to do so, she'd feel compromised if she did. She'd insinuated herself into Louisa's household, and she didn't like herself for it.

As for Andrew, Reynard was right. If he felt anything at all for her, it was only physical, a passing lust, a testosterone hiccup.

She'd made the mistake of going out with a few well-to-do men when she first worked at the Scepter. They'd thought she'd be easy because she was only a waitress. And Andrew, although he seemed sincere, would be the same. She must face the fact.

The next morning at Fairchild Acres began badly.

"I have unfortunate news," Mrs. Lipton announced to Bindy, Helena and Marie. "Cook has phoned from Sydney. She won't be returning. She says her doctor insists she take on a less demanding job."

Marie's heart plummeted.

Mrs. Lipton looked at her sympathetically. "I'm sorry, my dear. You've being doing your work and Cook's, too, and I'm afraid you'll have to keep it up until I can find a replacement for her.

You'll have to keep on doing extra duty. I know it's hard. But can you?"

Marie swallowed hard. She hated to make a commitment. But Mrs. Lipton looked both apologetic and desperate. Marie swallowed again. "I—I'm not sure. But I can try, ma'am."

"You're a treasure," Mrs. Lipton said, looking infinitely relieved. "I can't believe how that woman played out her sick leave and insurance benefits. I think she planned it this way all along, the conniving thing."

"She always was a sly one," Bindy put in. "She used to nip at the cooking wine, too. I seen her. I'll bet it was her liver, not her knee, that ailed her."

Mrs. Lipton gave her a look that bespoke of long suffering. Bindy was inclined to inject as much drama as she could into life.

The older woman sighed, "And suddenly, with no notice at all, Millie announced late last night that she was leaving. She may already be gone."

"Millie? The upstairs maid?" asked Marie. Millie had been a curvy, doe-eyed girl who'd seemed a bit too elegant to be a housemaid. Her makeup was always flawless, her hair perfectly done, and she seldom talked, only listened.

"Yes," Mrs. Lipton said with a trace of disgust. "Just up and announced she'd be going. That leaves me with two positions to fill. At least Miss will be going to the U.K., and the guests will be going back to Sydney as soon as they can. Otherwise, how could we cope?"

"Millie told me once she'd been a skimpy," Bindy offered, "a barmaid who didn't wear hardly anything at all. She said it was much more peaceful here, but boring, and it didn't pay nearly the same. I bet she'll be back in a bar before you know it."

"Bindy, *please* be quiet," pleaded Mrs. Lipton. "I have a headache."

Later in the morning, Marie finally got her first clear look at Megan and Patrick Stafford when she went out to pick fresh parsley. She saw Louisa inspecting the flower gardens arm in arm with her great-niece and great-nephew. They looked like a friendly trio, but not quite a cozy one. The nephew was tall and square-jawed with perfectly barbered hair and conservative sports clothes—a stockbroker, said Mrs. Lipton.

The niece, too, was tall, and dressed in what must be designer clothing, flowing silken black slacks and an exotically patterned tunic. But as Marie passed them, she glanced from Megan's clothes to her face. She got the jolt Reynard had predicted.

Megan Stafford had hair the same sunny blond as Marie's—and remarkably similar features. Her eyes were almost the same unusual green, perhaps only a shade darker with the irises ringed by a hint of hazel.

She looked at Marie, and Marie looked at her and realized that they were both startled, though neither spoke. Patrick, who was talking, didn't seem to notice, and Louisa, who gazed up at him with judgmental interest, acted as if Marie wasn't even there.

Marie passed on, her stomach tightening.

Another coincidence? The young woman who might be related to her had almost identical coloring. She, too, looked remarkably like the young Louisa in the photographs.

Marie marched on to the kitchen to start her breakfast shift. Megan Stafford, she'd been told, had a law degree and worked for a collective of art galleries. No wonder she wore such eye-catching clothes.

What, Marie wondered, if they *were* part of her family? What would she ever talk about with a lawyer and a stockbroker? Nothing: she was from a different world, the common world, and she didn't belong in theirs. Of course, Louisa had ignored Marie. Her attention had focused solely on her sophisticated guests. On her kind of people.

It's time to leave. It's a terrible thing to do to Mrs. Lipton, but Louisa's going to England, and the Staffords are leaving as soon as possible. That will give her some breathing space. I should go while the getting is good. It's time. I'll tell Rennie that I have to go by week's end. I'll make an excuse that there are complications about Mama's estate.

* * *

But that night at The Secret Heiress, Reynard counseled her not to be impulsive. He leaned closer, lowering his eyelids as if imparting a secret. "Why should you leave? You have as much right to claim kinship as those two. *More* right—you're her direct descendent. So you saw the Stafford woman up close? You saw the resemblance between the two of you? And both of you to the Louisa of yore?"

"I don't care," Marie retorted. "I don't like this, and I don't much like Louisa, and she doesn't much like me. If I claim I'm her granddaughter, she'll despise me. She'll think I'm a sneak and a fraud, and I couldn't deny it. So why should I stay?"

"Because she hasn't fired you," he said with a crooked smile. "Why hasn't she? Maybe she doesn't *want* you to go. Why? Maybe she's watching you, just as you're watching her. Oh, she's a mysterious one, all right."

"Why would she pay any attention to me?"

"Maybe she's noticed the resemblance, too. Who knows? And besides, love, what'll you do if you quit? Your job's filled for the next couple months. Classes have started without you. And your place is rented to somebody else. You've got to stay long enough to set aside some money, at least."

He had her there. He certainly did.

For the next day Louisa had planned a special parting feast for her young relatives. They would stay a day or two longer— Sydney was still blockaded. But Louisa, who would take tonight's flight to London from Melbourne, had told them to stay as long as they needed.

The day of her departure, cooking was a full-time job in the Fairchild kitchen. Louisa had requested a feast for supper, and Helena and Marie would work all day to make it.

As evening approached, Marie was dashing into the dining room with the crystal decanter of wine, when she saw a police car gliding up the front drive. She heard someone knock loudly at the front door. She slipped into the dining room and set the decanter on the buffet.

A man was saying something to Mrs. Lipton. Marie peered furtively from the doorway and saw the housekeeper, her expression reluctant, lead two policemen into the library.

Then Louisa came stalking in the front door to the kitchen from the direction of the stables, wearing her riding costume. Mrs. Lipton met her.

"Miss," called Mrs. Lipton in a low voice, "Officer Hastings wishes to speak to you. He and another officer are in the library." Louisa thrust her riding helmet into Mrs. Lipton's hands and strode into the library, Mrs. Lipton scurrying behind her protectively.

"What in hell do you want now?" Louisa demanded, and then the doors crashed shut again.

Marie nearly cringed in nervousness. Mrs. Lipton had told her that the police had already come to question Louisa once. Why were they back again? She waited, listening hard, but she only heard her own pulses pounding in her ears.

Then, moments later, she heard a cry of outrage and distress, and sounds suspiciously like a scuffle, then Louisa's tearful voice crying out for help. In alarm, Marie ran farther into the hall, stopping near the library's entrance.

The door burst open and Mrs. Lipton ran out, looking frantic, and the door slammed shut behind her. She hurried to one of the doors that led to the swimming pool and pulled it open.

"Megan! Megan!" she cried. "Come quick! It's Miss Fairchild!"

Megan's voice was faint, but clear. "What is it?"

"They're arresting her!"

"Arresting Louisa? What for?"

"Murder!"

Arresting Louisa Fairchild? For murder? Marie's heart raced in disbelief.

But it was true. A few moments later, the two men in uniform hustled an angry, sputtering Louisa out the front door. She was pale, her footsteps tottering. Handcuffs glinted on her thin and fragile wrists.

Chapter Eight

Tears glistened in Mrs. Lipton's eyes. "That gun they found? That killed Sam Whittleson? They think it's Louisa's—the same one she used to shoot at him last year. And it wasn't in the cabinet. It's gone. So th-they arrested her."

Marie gaped at Mrs. Lipton in astonishment. "They *think* it's hers? Have they *proved* it?"

"I'm not sure. All I know is they accused Louisa of murder."

Marie's mind spun. Murder? How could a woman over eighty commit the crimes at Lochlain? It was impossible.

"Didn't they find the gun days ago?" asked Marie. "Why'd it take them so long to decide it's hers?"

"Fire damage, I suspect," said Mrs. Lipton. "And that gun was given to Louisa by her cousin James when he came home from the war in the Pacific. She loved it and had it refitted many times. That might also make it harder to ID."

Marie frowned. "But why would she leave it at Lochlain? Why not dispose of it where it couldn't be found? And why would she use the same gun that she'd used to shoot him before? That makes it awfully tidy to link her to the murder. Too tidy."

Mrs. Lipton's eyes narrowed. "I think you should say *exactly* what you've just said to Miss's lawyer when he manages to get back from Sydney. Perhaps you should be the detective—and not that hothead, Dylan Hastings."

Marie shook her head in puzzlement. The evidence all seemed circumstantial. And she couldn't imagine Louisa setting a fire that would destroy horses. No. She'd never do that—ever.

Someone, for some reason, was framing Louisa Fairchild.

But who? And why?

Megan was gone, and Patrick had lost his appetite. The lavish supper went uneaten.

Marie and Helena put everything in the refrigerator, saying little, too lost in their own thoughts.

Bindy, rinsing pots and pans, looked wanly over her shoulder at them. "If they find her guilty," she said in a tremulous voice, "I suppose we'll all be sacked, won't we? Who'll own this place, anyway? The new people that just came?"

Helena said nothing and shook her head as if she had no idea.

Marie said, "They *can't* find her guilty. How could she have done it? She might have her problems with humans, but she'd never hurt a horse. *All* those horses could've died."

Bindy frowned. "But what if—"

The door swung open and Mrs. Lipton stood staring at them, her expression distraught. "The great-niece—Megan Stafford—just phoned. Miss Fairchild's had a heart attack. She's been taken to the hospital."

"What?" Marie cried.

Helena gasped, and Bindy stood openmouthed.

Mrs. Lipton sank to a chair. "The gun's been positively identified as hers. They were fingerprinting her. And she had an attack. They'll do an emergency angioplasty on her."

"An attack? How serious?" Marie asked, shaken.

"Serious," Mrs. Lipton said. "Oh, how could they take her off like that? Why didn't they even *consider* her health? This is a crime against her. The police are the criminals, not her!"

"If she dies we'll be sacked for sure," wailed Bindy. "Unless those Stafford people inherit everything! And even then—"

"Hush!" Marie commanded. Her mind was in turmoil, and she felt swept by a strange sense of impending loss. Louisa shouldn't die; she was old but vividly, powerfully full of spirit.

Marie went to Mrs. Lipton and put her hand on her shoulder. "I was going out with Rennie tonight, but I'll stay here. If the hospital calls, I want to know right away."

Mrs. Lipton covered Marie's hand with her own. "My dear, go with your uncle. I'll phone you as soon as I hear anything, I promise. Go—it'll do you good."

Marie tried to insist that she stay, but Mrs. Lipton was firm. "No. It'll help you, being with family. And you need a break from this sad house. You put in such a long day."

At last, reluctantly, Marie agreed.

That night, however, Reynard was not the best of companions. "You've been there for weeks," he grumbled, "making yourself indispensable. And now the old girl might cark? Die on us?"

"Reynard!" Marie snapped. "How can you say such a thing?"

"What?" he demanded. "Speak up. My ears are bad tonight. Sound like a bloody carillon tower."

The two of them sat in The Secret Heiress. Marie hadn't touched her wine, but Reynard was already signaling for a second schooner of beer.

"How can you talk about Louisa like that?" she asked.

He gave her a sideways look. "How? Because I'm concerned about your welfare, that's why. You've got just as much right to Fairchild Acres as those two toffee-noses from Sydney. More right. You're her direct descendent, you are."

"Rennie, they seem like perfectly nice people. And she *invited* them here. I wasn't invited. I came under false colors. It gave me a bad feeling from the start. I'm the interloper here, not them."

Reynard shook a finger at her. "Wait, wait, wait."

"No. You wait," she countered. "If something happens to Louisa, God forbid, I'm not going to start yelling that I deserve part of her estate."

"But you do deserve it," Reynard shot back. "There's a law on the books for people like you. I've got a copy and—"

"No. It's low, it's moneygrubbing, and I won't do it. Not after I've lived here and never once talked to her about it. I'd feel like a sneak and an opportunist."

"I've heard she's got a will," Reynard said. "In her lawyer's safe. That D'Angelo fellow."

"How do you know that?"

"I pick up information the way a dog does fleas," he said with a self-satisfied smile. "Now think of that—a will. But what if she hasn't put these Sydney upstarts in it yet? Who *is* in it, do you suppose?"

"I haven't the faintest idea," she said with disgust.

"She might be leaving it to her dogs," Reynard said sarcastically. "Or her horses. It's been done, you know. Who's written into that will? I find that a *very* interesting question."

She sighed. "Rennie, I want to go back to Fairchild Acres. I'm too upset to have this conversation—now or ever."

"I am only a poor, concerned old uncle," he said righteously. "But you know what? I think the old girl's got under your skin. I think you like her."

Marie refused to answer, but she knew he was close to right. Somehow, in spite of everything, she'd come to have a peculiar respect for Louisa Fairchild, an intense, if complicated, relationship with her.

"Let's go back," she said again.

"Eh?" He cupped his hand to his ear. "Oh, bloody hell, I'm getting worse. Then where'll I be? A bludger, I s'pose. Living on the dole."

"I want to go back," she said as loudly and clearly as she could. *"Now."*

Marie and Reynard were in the truck, bumping their way back to Fairchild Acres, when Marie's phone rang. Heart pounding fast, she picked it up. It was Mrs. Lipton. Megan had called from the hospital. The angioplasty seemed successful and with luck Louisa could come home in less than a week.

Marie shut the phone and told Reynard.

"Well, there," he replied genially. "That should ease your mind. Everything's back to normal again. Almost."

I don't think anything's going to be normal for me until I leave this valley, she thought.

She was back in her bungalow, showered and ready for bed. She was about to slip between the sheets, when her phone rang again.

More news of Louisa? She snatched her cell. "Hello?" she said breathlessly.

"Hello, Marie. It's Andrew. I just got back from Canberra and ran into your uncle. He told me the news about Louisa. I got your number off the cook's list in the kitchen and I hoped you'd still be up."

She took a desperately deep breath, not knowing what to say to him.

But he didn't wait for a reply. "Reynard said Louisa was arrested and suffered a heart attack. She had an operation and it went well. Is that right?"

"Yes," she managed to say, her throat tightening. She'd never realized how low his voice was, how dependable it sounded.

"There are rumors the police were rough with her."

Marie swallowed. "Th-they handcuffed her. They shouldn't have done that. And their evidence seems thin. Ridiculously thin. They said they found the gun that killed Sam Whittleson, and claim it's the same gun she used to shoot him before. But *that* shooting could have been an accident. Nobody's proved otherwise."

"That's all they've got on her?" He sounded appalled. "Hell, somebody could have stolen the gun and planted it. Where's that hotshot lawyer of hers?"

"He's trapped in Sydney. That's what Miss Fairchild's great-niece said. And all the state police are down there, too. So it's just the Pepper Flats police on the case."

"But I thought the New South Wales State Police were supposed to handle homicides," Andrew said.

"They are." Her voice broke in frustration. "It—it's the same in the Northern Territory, where I c-come from."

"Marie," Andrew said, "are you crying?"

No, she thought, *although she was long overdue for a good cry. It's you who's shaken me up. And there's no sane reason for it.*

He said, "Tyler says the Pepper Flats cop, that Dylan Hastings, doesn't like Louisa. He's got a grudge against her."

Marie's heart still beat unsteadily, but she felt another emotion, anger, flicker up strongly.

"You mean they've got an amateur heading this investigation, and he *dislikes* her? That's not fair! That's not just!"

"Ah," he said with a smile in his voice, "that sounds more like you. A woman who stands up to trouble."

She held back a bitter laugh. She didn't think she was standing up so well. But she tried to sound tougher than she felt. "I don't care what the police say—she's innocent," Marie insisted. "She has to be. Someone's set her up. Why?"

There was a pause, and then he said, "I've got a few ideas. And I want to hear more of what Tyler's got to say. This is getting complicated—and damned ugly. It'd be easier for you and me to talk about if we could see each other face-to-face. On your next day off? We could just go have lunch. Or tea. I swear to God, that's all."

She felt a strange, warm fluttering in her stomach. "It wouldn't work," she said. "It wouldn't be wise for me to be seen with you. Megan managed to reach the lawyer, D'Angelo. He said it wouldn't be smart for us to mingle with anybody connected to the case in any way."

"You mean like Tyler or anyone connected to him? Because it happened on his property?"

"Exactly. And anybody connected to Sam Whittleson, too."

"But I want—I need to talk to you in person. I know a place where we wouldn't be seen. Trust me."

Trust him? Dear God, she wanted to. "What good would it do? We come from opposing camps. You know it, I know it, and D'Angelo doesn't want us communicating."

"Damn D'Angelo," he said in frustration. "Listen, Marie. When Tyler heard about Louisa being arrested, his first reaction was that it was ridiculous. That it'd be funny if it weren't so outrageous."

His voice grew lower, more intense. "God knows he's got no reason to love her, but he does not—I repeat does *not*—think she'd do such a thing. If both our sides unite, Sergeant Dylan Hastings is going to have a much tougher time making an arrest stick."

"You…and Tyler would help her?"

"And others here at Lochlain. I know Louisa's got a good PR woman. But so do I. There are people at Lochlain who've known Louisa for years. She may be eccentric, she may be cranky, but she's no killer. If we stand together to protect her, we're stronger than if we stand alone."

"Why would you want to help Louisa?" she asked, more uneasy than before.

"Because it's the right thing to do. Is that so hard to believe? My family's been in her position, Marie. We were accused of breeding fraud. I know how it feels."

She'd heard the staff talk about the so-called Preston breeding scandal. She knew that Andrew was running for president partly to fight the kind of fraud that had threatened his family. But she could think of nothing to say.

"So," he said, "tomorrow's your day off, right? Meet me, will you? I have to leave again tomorrow night, but first I want to hear what you think. And tell you what I think. Just talk with me for Louisa's sake, all right?"

She closed her eyes, feeling dizzy. She should say no. But she said, "Yes. I will. But I need to help around here a bit first. And then get back. We're shorthanded."

"Fine," he replied. "How about around ten-thirty? Could you meet me on the road at that little grove by Lake Dingo? Where Louisa's land abuts Sam Whittleson's? There's a secluded spot close by."

"All right," she said, knowing she sounded tentative, unsure about agreeing.

"Then good night, Marie. And sweet dreams. Very sweet ones."

"The same to you," she said automatically, then instantly wished she hadn't. She closed the phone, thinking that he seemed almost to be pursuing her. But why? She was a nobody compared to him. And Rennie had told her to be on her guard.

Full of conflict, she went to bed, knowing that sleep would be long in coming. She took up one of her poetry books and stretched out on her bed. Opening to a random page, she read:

Sweet Peril
Alas, how easily things go wrong!
A sigh too much, or a kiss too long,
And there follows a mist and a weeping rain,
And life is never the same again.

She could read no more. It was too much like some warning from beyond.

Next morning Megan Stafford was in the kitchen when Marie arrived. Marie was amazed that she'd be up this early. She'd made herself tea and toast.

"Can I get you anything else?" Marie asked.

"I'm fine, thanks," Megan said, tossing her long hair back. "What I really need is information from you and the other staff. May I ask you a few things?"

"If you don't mind my working while I answer."

"Not at all. The doctor asked some questions I can't answer. He knows Louisa has blood pressure medications. He wants to know if she takes any other medicines or pills. Do you know?"

"Yes," Marie said, "some herbal things. And some brand-name ones. Do you want samples to show him?"

"That would be incredibly helpful," Megan said.

Then Helena appeared, and then Bindy, who looked unhappy and a bit hungover. Marie wondered if she was having boyfriend problems.

Helena volunteered to take over watching the bubble and squeak, and Marie dashed upstairs to Louisa's suite and to the medicine cabinet. She opened the door. Pills, vials, inhalers and boxes of cough drops crowded the shelves, and she took a sample of each, stuffing them into her apron pockets.

She left the suite as fast as she could, for one of the first warnings Louisa had given her was not to snoop among her things. If she knew Marie had rifled through her medications, she'd fire her immediately.

And suddenly, perversely, Marie didn't want to go. Not yet. Not until she knew Louisa would be home and well and cleared of any accusations—until she was *safe*.

Marie hurried back to the kitchen, where Helena was just sliding the bubble and squeak cakes into the oven. Bindy boiled water for tea and spooned coffee into the coffeemaker.

But Megan was gone.

"Where is she?" Marie asked, puzzled.

"The hospital called," said Mrs. Lipton. "Miss Fairchild's awake, so Miss Megan's gone to see her. Miss Fairchild also wanted Agnes to pack a case for her."

"As for you," Mrs. Lipton said wearily, "Miss Stafford wants you to make Miss Fairchild some decent snacks and a thermos of strong coffee. She hates hospital food."

"Shouldn't I make sure that any food I take is healthy?"

"Yes. She won't like that, so I don't envy you," Mrs. Lipton said. "Also, the niece and nephew were going to leave as soon as they could. But now that Miss Fairchild's unwell, I sense that Megan, at least, will want to stay on. She seems genuinely concerned about Miss."

"Or her money," Bindy put in, starting the coffeemaker.

"Hush!" ordered Mrs. Lipton, glowering at Bindy.

"I watch detective shows on the telly," countered Bindy. "I read mystery books. I've been thinking. Who stands to profit from this happening to Miss? The niece and nephew, that's who. She's a lawyer. Lawyers think shifty, they do. She could have set all this up and—"

"Hush!" Mrs. Lipton repeated, clearly furious. "I *don't* appreciate that sort of talk. For shame!"

She turned back to Marie. "Will you have any trouble coming up with menus for Miss Fairchild?"

"Not at all," Marie said. "My mother had heart trouble. I know the food issues."

She sat down at the counter and scribbled a list of heart-friendly recipes. Her own heart beat uncomfortably fast. Why did Louisa have so many pills? Had they affected her health? And what about her addiction to espresso, her insistence on strong tea?

Marie also worried about Andrew. Soon she'd meet him.

Seeing him again suddenly seemed like pushing her luck. Pushing it to the point of folly.

Andrew leaned against the white pipeline fence at Lochlain, his elbows resting on the top rail. Tyler stood beside him, and together they stared out at the north paddock. The two-year-olds grazed there in the morning sunlight, and most looked good; coats shining, legs elegantly long.

But every one had suffered from smoke inhalation. Outwardly, they were beautiful. Inwardly, they were compromised, their lungs damaged. Not fatally damaged, but injured enough to impair their running. They would never recover the wind to race.

Tyler shook his head. "I still can't believe it. I don't want to believe it."

Andrew said, "At least you've got Darci's Pride." The horse had won the Outback Classic and was now Tyler's biggest equine asset.

"Thanks to Darci," Tyler said, almost smiling. "God love her."

Darci had sold a half interest in Darci's Pride to Tyler. Along with the horse, it seemed, Tyler had acquired a fiancée, as well, Darci herself.

Andrew studied his cousin's profile. "Can I ask you something?"

"Have at it."

"The first time you saw Darci, did you know that—well, did you suspect that she'd end up—you know…"

Tyler cast him a sideways glance. "The woman I wanted to marry?"

"Yeah," Andrew said, gazing out at the paddock again. "That."

"I guess so," Tyler said with a shrug. "Didn't want to admit it, but I pretty much knew. A few minutes with her and wham! That was it. Got a little complicated but it worked out...."

"Um," murmured Andrew.

"Why're you asking?" Tyler said innocently. "That blonde over at Fairchild Acres?"

Andrew felt as if he'd been hit across both knees with a ball bat, except it didn't hurt. He just seemed to lose his sense of balance, his breath, and he gripped the top rail very hard. He could think of nothing to say.

"Gotcha," Tyler commented with satisfaction. "I'm not blind. The way you swept her up that day, when the vicious kiddy snake wiggy-wiggled up to give you his friendly grin."

Andrew swore. "Would you please never mention that again, you sadist?"

Tyler said, "Hey, she's a very attractive woman. Makes a hell of a meringue. Looks great in shorts. Handles herself well. Seems smart as hell. What's the problem?"

"The problem is that we don't have anything in common. I don't really know her. But I'm kind of—obsessed with her. Like there's something in her nature or her character or—forget it. I don't need to get involved with anybody right now."

Tyler laughed for the first time in a week. "Andrew, you've made my day. You, the intellectual one. The imperturbable one. Mr. Self-control. The one with the world at his feet. At last— brought to your knees, like an ordinary mortal. Ah, my life lies in ruins about me, but you've brought a ray of brightness into my life. Thanks, mate."

Andrew had had enough. "Yuck it up. Now change the subject. Tell me again why you don't think Louisa's guilty."

"Because she's Louisa. She shot Sam once—right? But that was spontaneous. He came storming into her house, ranting at her; she had a gun and she reacted. I mean, of course she shouldn't have shot him. But it wasn't premeditated, it was a stupid reflex.

"Louisa's not the type to secretly lure him over to my place and kill him. If she really wanted to shoot somebody, she'd do it in the middle of Main Street in Pepper Flats. Louisa's forth-right, not sneaky.

"And," he said emphatically, "she wouldn't set fire to the stables. She used to come over here and help me doctor sick horses. All night long, if need be. Many a time. All right, that was before the blowup with Sam. But even if she's in a snit at me, she wouldn't hurt my horses."

"Then who would?"

Tyler's eyes moved back to the gleaming horses, so illusory in their seeming perfection. "That's the big question, isn't it? And like I told you, I have a feeling we've got no idea what we're really up against. But I've got my suspicions."

Marie found Megan standing outside Louisa's hospital room, talking on her mobile. "D'Angelo," she mouthed. "The lawyer."

Marie nodded and handed her a small plastic bag of medications she'd taken from Louisa's suite, and then slipped into the room.

Louisa looked Marie up and down rather ferociously. "Where have you been? I was starving at breakfast time. They brought me some ghastly drink that smelled like a dead wombat. And on top of that, I'm now a *felon.*"

"Megan said you're not officially charged yet," Marie said, setting her backpack on the bedside table.

"I'm in bloody limbo," Louisa muttered. "I'm arrested, but not charged. They're going to put a guard at my door. A guard! As if I might leap into the hall and start rending people asunder. Pah!"

Marie stared at her in a mixture of disbelief and admiration. It was going to take more than a mere arrest and heart attack to quell Louisa's rebellious spirit.

"So," Louisa demanded, "what did you bring? Eggnog with rum would be nice."

"You have to have healthy food," Marie said firmly. "I've brought you homemade energy bars, low sodium, low fat, nice fruits and grains. This red thermos has bean soup. It's got no cholesterol, lots of vitamins, fiber and decent protein."

"My God," Louisa said in disgust. "You're a food Nazi."

"You're in no position to indulge yourself. I know about these things. My mother had heart disease. It killed her."

She didn't add *And I think she was your daughter, Louisa. She didn't inherit the hardness of your heart, but she inherited its weakness.*

"Oh, be quiet. Give me one of those wretched 'energy bars.'"

Marie said, "I'll send Bindy with lunch and supper. And the food's going to be healthy. You need to watch what you eat. And drink. I brought you herbal tea. No caffeine."

"I could fire you, you know," Louisa threatened.

"Go ahead," Marie shot back. "Eat hospital food instead."

Louisa slid her a sideways, measuring look. "You're getting to be no fun at all. I used to be able to make you nervous. Quite jumpy, in fact."

"Eat and get your strength back," Marie informed her sweetly. "Maybe you'll be able to make me jumpy again."

She started to turn to go, but Louisa said, "You've given me unwanted advice. May I give you some in return?"

"Certainly."

"I've heard you've made goo-goo eyes at Andrew Preston. Don't. Men like him toy with girls like you. Beware. He'll use you like a paper tissue. As a receptacle for some troublesome bodily fluids. And then he will toss you away. You may count on it. Cheerio."

Marie felt as if she'd been struck across the face. But she didn't allow her expression to change or her body to flinch. "I know my place, Miss. Good day."

"G'day," muttered Louisa. "And I didn't mean to offend you. I try to look out for my girls, that's all."

"Yes, Miss. I understand."

But she didn't. She left the hospital, her mind awhirl. Louisa's mood this morning was peculiar. She'd seemed almost glad to see Marie and to *enjoy* sparring with her. She'd even apologized—almost. Unbelievable.

Maybe Reynard was right; Louisa intimidated people too easily and she wanted someone to stand up to her. Yet she had meant the warning about Andrew; Marie could tell.

Chapter Nine

Andrew parked the truck off the road, in the grove of eucalyptus near the bend in the road. In a hamper in the back of the truck, he'd brought some food and drink he'd bought in Pepper Flats. He thought this particular occasion might demand an icebreaker.

Marie arrived on her bike, the sun shining on her golden hair. She wore her seersucker shorts again and one of her white blouses. She seemed so fresh, so natural, that she almost glowed. He couldn't imagine her looking any better.

He got out of the truck. "Hi," he said.

She dismounted her bike. "Hello." She gazed at the truck in surprise. "Whose is that?"

Andrew felt a tension radiating from her, a distrust. "The cook let me borrow it. I thought—well, it might throw people off our trail. I usually drive Tyler's Jeep."

She looked at him with greater suspicion. "People are on our trail?"

"Not that I know of. But you're not comfortable about us being seen together."

"But we're right here in plain sight," she said. "What are we supposed to do? Crawl under the truck and chat?"

Lord, she was a spunky little thing. And she said what she thought. Was that what heightened his attraction to her? Because he was attracted, damnably so.

She looked about. The grove was one of many dotting the hillside. He said, "I was out riding one day. I found an odd place down the hill. I asked Tyler about it. Come see for yourself. I brought some stuff just for a sort of—uh—snack."

He tucked the cooler under his left arm and took up the hamper with his left hand.

She hoisted her backpack more firmly into place. "I brought something, too. I figure it's my place in life."

He almost winced. Did she think that he looked down on her?

But all he said was, "Chain up your bike and come with me."

She chained her bike to a tree behind some large shrubs, hiding it almost completely. He said, "Down this way. Be careful. There's no path, and it's steep in spots."

He fought back the desire to offer her his hand. He set off in front of her. The hillside dropped off, growing steeper once past the grove. He wondered if he, with his long legs, was walking too fast for her. But she'd kept pace perfectly and didn't even seem out of breath.

He took a hard turn right, following a ridge of limestone, like a rocky spine thrusting through the crust of the earth. Then there was an almost stairlike set of limestone slabs, leading down precipitously beneath the spine. He negotiated the stones easily, but turned to help her. She had beautiful legs, and strong, but they weren't long enough to make such long steps.

She seemed reluctant to take his hand, but she did, and when he touched hers, it was like touching a painless flame that jolted down his arm and flooded his body. He noticed the smooth muscles in her legs, the sureness of her movements. And then he said, "Here we are. A cave. Sort of."

He saw her look up suddenly and almost smile. Above, the limestone formed an overhang that arched over an opening about fifteen feet across and ten feet deep. The floor was almost flat. There was a black spot where long-ago fires had been repeatedly built. In the farthest back corner sat an ancient blue enameled teakettle.

He set down the hamper and cooler. "A private dining room," he said, straightening up and gesturing around them. "Does it pass muster?"

"Indeed," she said. "What is this? Why the teakettle?"

"A hermit lived here once," Andrew answered. "The kettle was his."

"A hermit?" she asked, this time really smiling. And Lord, what a smile.

"Yes. Tyler told me. Said he had a long scraggly beard and hair. He'd go from house to house selling herbs and game. Otherwise he left people alone, and they left him alone. He was an old Scotsman. He'd lived here since he was a young Scotsman. They say his spirit still keeps guard here."

She blinked. "He doesn't want people to come here?"

He couldn't believe how green her eyes were, how sparkling and alert. "No," he said softly. "They say he's a kindly spirit. That he watches over the place."

He opened the hamper and took out a checkered oilcloth and laid it on the ground. "That's why nobody's ever taken the teakettle. There are some metal cups hidden up in the chinks, but their bottoms are rusted out. Still no one takes anything. Out of respect."

He lowered himself to the oilcloth. "Sit," he invited. She took off her backpack and sat, too, placing it between them.

"So why was he a hermit?" she asked.

"Legend says some girl broke his heart, so he left the world of people and became a solitary. It makes a nice story. I don't know if it's true."

She looked skeptical. He said, "Don't you believe in broken hearts?"

Her expression went wary. "I'm more concerned about unhealthy ones, like Louisa's."

Touché, he thought. "Right," he said. "Have you seen her today?"

"I took her breakfast. She already hates the hospital. And she's furious about being arrested."

Marie actually looked worried about the old woman. She caught his gaze and held it. "You said you had information. You said maybe you could help her. Tell me, please."

"Fine," he said. "You want a glass of tea? Fruit? Cheese? Crackers? I've got wine, too, if you wa—"

"I don't drink at this hour," she said, rather sharply. "I'll take tea. I brought lemonade and some cheese Danishes. You want any?"

"Sure," he said, sounding as laid-back as he could. "Some of both." Why had he offered her wine at this time of day? What had he been thinking, for God's sake?

He poured her tea, she poured him lemonade. They exchanged glasses, and she handed him a Danish pastry on a paper napkin. "Now," she said, "what do you have to tell me?"

That you're lovely and brave and you fascinate me, he thought. He said, "Tyler pointed out that the fire victimized mainly three people, Sam Whittleson, Tyler himself, and me. Me as a candidate. By casting suspicion on Tyler—guilt by association. But he points out there's a fourth victim—Louisa."

She regarded him coolly. "That's obvious. She's been arrested, had a heart attack and they're putting a guard at her door."

"All right," he told her. "When I want to be paranoid, I think some syndicate, say one that has to do with racing, would strike out against Tyler, and consequently me. Somebody, say, who wants Jacko Bullock to win."

She cocked a dubious eyebrow. She took a sip of tea and waited. Hadn't Reynard said almost the same thing?

"It's a nice conspiracy theory," he said. "But why kill Sam? And why frame Louisa? Because Tyler and I both think she's been framed. And she's a good friend of Jacko. One of his strongest supporters. Why would he turn on her? If he's behind all this, why would he let his people implicate her?"

She frowned, reached into the open hamper and took an apple. "I don't know. Why?"

She bit the apple and waited again.

"Imagine a map of this region," Andrew said. "Can you see it in your mind?"

"I think so," she said.

"Sam Whittleson's land abuts Louisa's. They fought about rights to the lake, which touched both their properties. Whose property is kitty-corner from Louisa's?"

"Tyler's," she said without hesitation. "What are you getting at?"

"Add the three together and you get thousands of acres of the best Thoroughbred territory in the country. What do you think will happen to Sam's place?"

She made an uncertain gesture. "Well, Daniel, Sam's son, will inherit it, won't he?"

"The place is falling down. Sam's neglected it, and his horses didn't do well last season."

"There's rumor he was badly in debt. You think Daniel can turn that around on a trainer's salary?"

"I don't know. It depends if Sam left Daniel any money."

"And if the rumors are true? He had no money?"

"I suppose Daniel would have to sell it," she said. She took another bite of apple, and he wished it didn't make him think of Eden. It was too easy to imagine her as Eve.

"Tyler swears he's going to rebuild Lochlain Racing. But he's short on barns, and he's got only one horse he can race. If he can't make it, what do you think will happen?"

She looked thoughtful. "I suppose he'd have to sell, too."

"Now here's a big question for you," Andrew said. "What if Louisa gets charged, convicted and sent to prison?"

Marie's face went taut. "She'd never survive it."

"She might not even survive this heart attack," said Andrew. "And if she dies, what becomes of Fairchild Acres?"

Suddenly her expression changed, and she seemed shaken by the question. "I—I really don't know."

"Does somebody inherit it? Like her great-niece and -nephew? Who's in her will? I don't know. But she was estranged from the niece and nephew. Now she might write them into it, but what would *they* do with it? They're not really horse people."

Marie shook her head, as if truly confused. "I don't know. I mean, they do have careers of their own. They're not into racing. Not the way people around here are."

"So *they* might sell it?" Andrew asked.

"I—I suppose they might." She pushed her hand through her bangs as if in agitation.

Andrew leaned nearer. "So it's possible that in one short period, three prime properties could go up for sale. And if someone could afford to buy them all, he'd be king of Hunter Valley. And Hunter Valley is second only to Kentucky in horse racing importance."

She shook her head. "But how does that help Louisa? I mean *really* help her?"

"Ask D'Angelo," he suggested. "Because looking at it that way, Louisa can be cast as another victim. Not the perpetrator, but a victim. Dylan Hastings has a very thin case against her, Marie. Hammer it hard enough, I think it'll shatter into bits."

She stared off into the distance, as if torn by what he said. He made the mistake of biting into the Danish. It was so delicious that it made him dizzy. *My God,* he thought. *It's a love potion.* He took another bite and watched her. She seemed caught up in a private conflict.

At last she said. "It's not enough to clear her. It's a theory."

"It's one that makes sense," he told her. "Do you know what organized crime is like? How complex it is? It's like a great spiderweb. No. It's more like an unimaginably huge maze of interlocking spiderwebs, with strands connecting in all sorts of directions."

"Maybe it is," she said warily. "So who's the spider?"

"That's the point," he said earnestly. "There isn't just one spider. It's like a network of spider kings. Some big, some little. There's probably no great, all-powerful one. The webs are constantly shifting and changing all around us. But they're there."

"Excuse me," she said, her expression dubious. "But this is starting to sound like science fiction. The invisible spider kings of Australia?"

He laid his hand on her bare arm. It made his fingers tingle, but he forced himself to concentrate on his message.

"The invisible spider kings of the *world,*" he corrected. "Do you know how many kinds of syndicates, cartels, narcotics rings, smuggling rings, mobs, money launderers and crime families exist? Organized crime comes from everywhere, Europe, Asia, the Americas. And Australia." He gave her a penetrating look. "Remember what I told you about horse racing and gambling?"

He felt her muscles stiffen under his touch. "Where there's gambling, there's crime."

"Now," he said, bringing his face nearer to hers, "for years there've been rumors that Jacko Bullock has ties to organized crime."

"Rumors again," she said, her expression tense. "Is Jacko supposed to be a big spider? Or a little spider?"

"Nobody seems to know," he said, gripping her arm more firmly. "Maybe he's a very small spider who's well connected. If he's president of the ITRF, he's in a position to help many, many spiders. Who would help him in return."

"All right," she said, tilting her jaw. "Help him what?"

"First, help him get what he wants. First, the presidency. That's obvious—if he has those connections. Right?"

"I suppose. But, Andrew, this is still just speculation."

"It may be. I don't know how much the government knows or how hard it's looking. But what if another thing he wants is the Hunter Valley? The combination would make him one of the most powerful men in the racing world."

For the first time she looked almost as if she might believe him. "And he could make things happen to people here?"

"Perhaps. Or his friends could. Look at it again, Marie. Sam's gone. Louisa's in serious trouble, and Tyler's hanging on by the skin of his teeth. Hunter Valley could be changing hands."

"And what about you?" she asked. "As president?"

He smiled a humorless smile. "I could lose. Fairly or unfairly. But I've got to try to win."

"If you believe in all these webs and all these spiders—some are poisonous, I take it?"

He nodded. "Deadly."

"Aren't you afraid?" she challenged.

"Yes," he admitted. "And for my family. Look at what's happened to Tyler."

He saw fear dull her eyes, as if a cloud passed over them. "What if they—hurt you?"

"That's not what worries me most," he said.

She searched his face. "Then what does?"

"You," he said. "Losing you."

He heard the sharp intake of her breath. "I don't understand."

"If any of this is right—and I think it may be—I don't want you drawn into it. That's why I had to see you face-to-face. To tell you that. You may be right, for now. About keeping our distance. But I don't want to lose you."

Her mouth trembled and she looked at him in bewilderment. "Why? Why say such a thing?"

"Because I feel that I need you. I need something in…your spirit. Remember how in Scone you told me to loosen up when I spoke. You said, 'Maybe you should pretend you're talking to just one person.'"

She nodded, smiling faintly at the memory.

"It works," he said. "I'm doing much better. And the one person I pretend I'm talking to is you."

Her smiled turned to disbelief. "Me? But why?"

"Like I said. Your spirit. Your character. Your courage."

He moved his glass aside, as well as the love-spell Danish. He took her glass and placed it beside his own. He drew her to him and kissed her. He kissed her the way he'd never kissed any other woman.

She'd known this was going to happen. They both had known. It had shivered in the air like electricity building itself into a blaze of lightning. She could have stopped it from happening. But she hadn't wanted to stop it.

For the first time in her life, she felt almost helpless with desire, filled with the need to have his mouth upon hers, to be close to his body, as close as possible. This was the forbidden delight that she'd never wanted to experience, never wanted to admit was real.

His mouth moved expertly against hers. Too expertly? His hands cradled her face firmly yet tenderly. But was that touch too practiced? Part of her wanted to analyze what he was doing and how he was doing it and why.

Another, newly discovered part of her wanted not to think at all, only to feel and desire and to desire more still. His body was strong and hard against hers. He smelled of spicy aftershave.

His lips were warm, strong and supple. They opened slightly, inviting her to follow suit. She did. He tasted like lemonade and richness.

His hands moved from her face to her shoulders, drawing her nearer, so that her breasts grazed the solidity of his chest. Her hands rose shyly and rested on his shoulders, and she felt the subtle movement of his muscles beneath her fingertips.

His arms folded around her, pulling her so close that her upper body pressed against his, and his kiss grew deeper, and she raised her face and strained to make it deeper still.

The tip of his tongue traced her upper lip, then her lower, then thrust gently into her mouth, and she found hers ready to greet him. She felt herself wanting to open like a flower to him, open slowly but completely.

When his hand settled over one tingling breast, it felt wonderful, but *too* wonderful.

Alas, how easily things go wrong!

A sigh too much, or a kiss too long…

She jolted back to reality, struggling to find her usual self-control. She tried to jerk away from him, although his arms still held her fast.

"No," she said breathlessly . "No. This is going no farther. It shouldn't have gone *this* far."

She put her hands against his chest and pushed until he reluctantly let her go. She didn't want to meet his eyes.

But he challenged her. "Look at me. Marie? Come on. Look at me."

Around them, the dry leaves rattled like a whisper of percussion, a light but irresistible rhythm. Defiantly she lifted her head and met his dark gaze. A brown-black lock of hair had fallen over his forehead, and his expression was intense.

He caressed her face. "You're complicated."

"I don't know what you want from me," she said. "And I can't let myself get tangled up in something like this. I—I don't want to be like my mother. She had an illegitimate baby—*me*—and she was born to an unwed mother herself. I promised myself long ago I'd never join that club. Women who—who—"

He felt a wrenching, gut-deep sympathy for her. "I never asked you for that. For sex. I moved too fast. I'm sorry. But I'll prove I mean what I say about you."

Tears welled in her eyes, but she blinked them back down and squared her jaw. Her back was rigid with tension. "How?"

"I'll do everything in my power to clear Louisa."

She shook her head, as if he spoke only nonsense. "All you've got is a theory, and a fancy comparison about spiders. But with no proof to back it up."

He edged nearer again. "You need proof?" he said in a low voice. "I'll get it. Tyler and Dan Whittleson hired a private detective. I'm not from here, so maybe that's why I wasn't asked to chip in. But I can hire a detective myself. I can hire the best."

She turned to face him. "Why? To buy Louisa's favor for you in the election?"

"No. To help her. Because, like I said, I saw my own family go through the same thing. But not just for her. For you."

"But *why?*" she asked again. She tossed her head so that her golden bangs stirred and glinted in the dappled light. "I don't understand."

"Because you're not like most of the women I meet. You're not like any of them. And I think I figured it out. You need to be courted. The old-fashioned way. I don't mean roses and chocolates, I mean getting to know each other.

"I want to know you better. Much better. And I'm going to have to prove I care for you. So—though I'd like to see you at least once in a while—we'll keep this platonic for a while. Because I think you're a woman worth waiting for. So, will you let me get to know you?"

She went pale and wide-eyed. "And—and for that you'll try to save Louisa."

"For that," he nodded. "And for the principle at stake. My father raised me to stand up for principles."

She seemed to diminish a little, like a flower starting to fold in on itself. "I'm afraid," she said. "Afraid of getting tangled up in something like this with you."

He gave her a perplexed smile. "Something like this is only human. I was drawn to you the first time I saw you in Darwin. And then you turned up here, and I felt it again. And you felt something, too. Can you deny it?"

"No," she whispered. "No."

He put his hands on either side of her face and kissed her again until his groin tightened and his forehead seemed to be spinning out of place.

She drew back more quickly this time. "I should get back to Fairchild Acres."

"Keeping my distance from you is going to be hard. Ungodly hard."

Unable to think of a reply, she began to load her backpack up again. "Keep the Danishes," she murmured self-consciously. "Feed them to the birds or something."

Quickly, she rose, and he, too, stood. He put his hands on her shoulders and looked into her eyes.

"Thank you," she said.

Then she spun away and fled, fleet as a little deer, leaving him alone in the Hermit's Cave, clenching and unclenching his fists. He put his hand to his chest and fingered the painted charm inside his shirt.

At The Secret Heiress that evening, Reynard bought Marie supper. "You spend your life cooking for other people. Let somebody else cook for you for a change. Mrs. Tidwell's no Colette, but she makes decent tucker. Try the lamb chops."

Marie smiled her gratitude, but then looked at him quizzically. "You never told me where you were last night. I tried to call you."

"I was at the Crook Scale," he said, jerking his thumb in the direction of the other pub. "Met an old mate who just moved up this way. Got into a card game, and then went partying, I guess you'd say. All work and no play, that sort of thing, y'know."

She didn't know, and Reynard was being maddeningly vague.

She'd come to realize that he was often vague about his comings and goings. She was about to pry a little more, but instead, he became the questioner.

"Why'd you call?" he asked, his eyes innocent. "Something bothering you?"

"Well, there's lots to be bothered about. Louisa's in the hospital, and Dylan Hastings is hovering over her like a vulture. She's in a rotten mood, which won't help her recovery."

"You've got a point. Plenty to be bothered about." But then he brightened. "And here comes Mrs. Tidwell. Mrs. Tidwell, I swear that blue is your color. Indeed, it is."

Mrs. Tidwell smiled girlishly. "Reynard, you're a total rascal."

He smiled up at her. "That I am, love. That I am."

The woman took their orders and left. She returned in a moment and brought their drinks. Reynard quaffed deeply.

He wiped his mouth and then stared affectionately into Marie's eyes. "You saw Andrew today again?"

"What?" She recoiled in surprise.

"He borrowed the cook's truck," Reynard said, as if he read her mind. "I didn't ask why, but I wondered. And soon I knew."

She was speechless and her face heated with a blush.

"I was driving to pick up some lumber," he said casually. "Just happened to take that road that bends where the old girl's property meets the late Sam's. Saw that truck parked in the grove. And way back, where I could hardly see it, your bike."

She tried to look righteous. "I met him because he said maybe he could help Louisa."

"For this you had to disappear into the woods?"

"I didn't want to be seen with him," she retorted. "D'Angelo doesn't want any of us talking with the Prestons. He's right, and I don't intend to—make a practice of it."

Reynard leaned across the table. "You'd be better off intending never to do it again. But my curiosity is tweaked. Did he really know any way to help the old girl?"

Marie, conflicted, wasn't sure if she should answer. But she said, "Nothing concrete.

"Just a theory that Tyler's fire might be more than just a simple arson. That it might be part of a bigger plot. One involving some kind of land grab in Hunter Valley."

"Hmm. Interesting," was all Reynard said. He changed the subject. "I hear that the old girl's great-niece and -nephew are staying on. Odd that they should grow fond of her so fast."

"Rennie, don't be cynical. Megan seems truly concerned about Louisa. Patrick, I'm not so sure. But she's one of their last links to their mother."

"And," he added smoothly, "she's one of your last links to *your* mother. When the old girl's better, you'll need to make your move. So those two don't muscle you out of your rights."

"I don't know that I have any rights," Marie objected.

He drew on his cigarette and exhaled. Through the shifting smoke, he regarded her with his lazy-lidded gaze. "Don't worry, love," he murmured. "You may soon. Trust your Uncle Rennie."

Chapter Ten

Marie drew back and stared at him in disbelief. "What do you mean?" she demanded.

Rennie shrugged. "I mean trust my instincts. Be optimistic, that's all. You've come to believe it yourself, haven't you? That the old girl is Colette's mother? And your grandmother?"

"I—I almost believe it," she admitted. "I don't know if I'd ever act on it. But how can you say I could prove it?"

He cocked his head and took another sip from his schooner. "My sister didn't have a great deal of education. But she was bright. The DNA, love. The DNA will prove it, I'm sure."

"It won't reach that stage," Marie said firmly. "*She* certainly wouldn't want tests. And I don't, either. I'm sick of this mess. Let Louisa leave her money to the relatives she knows. I'll stay around until she's well. Then I'm going back to Darwin."

"What if she doesn't get well?" Reynard said. "I mean, just suppose she died? Wouldn't you stand up for your share of the estate? Wouldn't you take it to court?"

"No. I haven't got the stomach for it. It's too mercenary.

Besides, it would cost a fortune to go to court. I haven't got the money—or the inclination."

He shrugged. "A sharp lawyer might do it for a percentage of your settlement."

"No. I *mean* it."

He acted as if he didn't hear her, but looked up and beamed. "Ah, here's the estimable Mrs. Tidwell with our supper. You're a delivering angel. I see you've got a new bartender. I hope he won't take my place in your affections, duck."

"You're a caution, Rennie," the woman said, with a coy smile.

When the woman left, Marie stared at Reynard tucking into his lamb chops. She thought, *Rennie, sometimes I don't feel like I really know you. Who are you? What are you? What are you trying to make me into? And why?*

The next day Marie realized she couldn't leave Hunter Valley as soon as she'd wanted.

The hospital would hold Louisa longer than originally thought; Dr. Burgess wanted to keep her under observation. She was so nervous and irritable that he insisted on strictly monitoring her medications and testing her. But rumors buzzed that she was being held by the hospital to keep Hastings from taking her into custody.

Louisa hated the hospital; she annoyed the nurses and was blatantly rude to Burgess. She welcomed only the visitors who came from Fairchild Acres, and she impulsively declared it was not that ignorant jackass Dr. Burgess who'd saved her life, but Marie and her edible food and tolerable beverages.

In the meantime, Detective Dylan Hastings, hanging on to the case like a pit bull, wanted a bedside hearing for Louisa as soon as possible. The thought sickened Marie.

That night, at precisely nine o'clock, Marie's phone rang. She answered and blinked hard when she heard Andrew's voice.

"Marie? I'm sorry I didn't call sooner. I've had a real break. One of the big equine societies in Brisbane is renting me a private plane for the rest of the campaign, for almost nothing. And a pilot. A guy named Ollie Millwhit. This is going to make traveling a lot easier—and less expensive."

"A private plane?" she echoed, realizing that talking to him made her tremulous.

"Yeah. A little jet. Darci says it'll be a huge help. She helped arrange it. Her dad used to be president of the ITRF."

A private jet, she thought, and once again the differences in their backgrounds seemed like a chasm gaping between them, vast and unbridgeable.

But she said, "I'm glad. That's wonderful."

"It is," he said. "And isn't. Darci's booking me into more appearances, arranging more rallies. So I'll be gone more."

Perhaps that was good, she thought, but it didn't make her feel good. He'd be far away, and she remembered him being near, very near. Yesterday came flashing back to her, the strength of his arms around her, and hardness of his chest against her breasts. The warmth of his lips and tongue, the scent and taste of him had made desire flicker through her mind and body, cascading sparks of fireworks.

With a sigh he said, "I *can't* see you. But I'd like to call you every night. Even if we can't see each other, we can get to know each other better. Tell me about yourself. I know your mother's gone, and Rennie said she was extraordinary. A great cook and a woman of enormous sweetness, that's what he said."

"She was." Marie thought, *She was illegitimate, too—just like me. Rennie is, too. Are you sure you want to know me? You're a blue-blooded Preston. I belong to the Bastard Nation. You work with the rich and the powerful. I work in a kitchen. Should we even be this involved?*

"I called a detective in Sydney today," he said. "I gave him the basic information. I'll be in Sydney in a couple of days if all goes well, see him in person. He's interested. He's already got people sniffing around like hound dogs."

"Andrew?"

"What, honey?"

She thought that a man with a deep voice and a Southern accent saying "honey" to a woman ought to be classified as a genuine aphrodisiac. "I like your funny accent," she said.

"And I like yours. It's even funnier," he teased.

But she felt the familiar tension climbing her spine. "Going to a detective—could that, well, put you in danger of any kind?"

"Hardly anybody knows about it. You, Tyler, Darci. I keep thinking about yesterday and you. Maybe it's good I'll be far away. It'll be easier for me to be a gentleman. You're very kissable, you know?" He laughed. "Somehow, I bet you don't know. You're one of a kind."

She felt herself blushing. "Should you say things like that on a phone?" she asked. "I mean, you were concerned about being watched. What if—what if somebody put a tap on your phone?"

Oh, good grief, she thought. *I'm starting to sound like Bindy. Conspiracy around every corner. Intrigue and paranoia everywhere.*

He laughed. "You can't tap a cell phone. Well, if you have zillions of dollars, you could. Only governments can afford that kind of equipment. I don't think Australia's interested in a horsey ol' boy from Kentucky like me."

"You're sure?" she asked.

"Trust me. I've asked about taps. You can't tap a cell phone. So I can say it all I want—your lips are kissable, kissable, kissable."

"Stop," she ordered, but in a soft voice, because she liked hearing him say it. It made her think again of his mouth, so firm, yet sensitive on her own.

"Then talk to me. Tell me about your day."

"Well," she said wryly, "Fairchild Acres is at sixes and sevens. Louisa is *not* a model patient. Dylan Hastings wants a bedside hearing—how morbid can you get? And Louisa's lawyer wants Hastings's head on a stake, but he's trapped in Sydney."

"And what about you?"

She took a deep breath and felt a bit desperate about how this "getting acquainted" was going to work out. But she'd prepared herself, just in case.

"I'd rather hear about you. I—I found a sort of quiz in a magazine Megan left on the kitchen table. It's supposed to tell a lot about a person. Should I ask you the questions?"

He gave a low laugh. "Sure."

"It's called the Proust Questionnaire. Like what's your worst fear?"

"Losing someone I love," he answered without hesitation.

"What's your favorite way to spend time?"

"With the people I love. But tell me how *you'd* answer those two questions before you go on. Fair enough?"

"Fair enough," she said.

Before she realized it, they'd talked for an hour and a half.

At last he said, "Oops, I hear Ollie coming back from the bar. I'll call you tomorrow from Geelong."

"Okay, I suppose…"

"I'll call you two nights from now. When I'm in Melbourne. All right?"

"All right," she said. And when she hung up the phone she was happy, in some strange way that she couldn't understand or analyze.

During the next few days, the household staff was wild with gossip. Rumors flew that Louisa's lawyer would have an injunction for Dylan Hastings that would end Hastings's career.

And Monday, word came Louisa would be spirited back from the hospital that night, a good sixteen hours earlier than the press expected.

D'Angelo had made it back from Sydney, and he didn't want a media circus at Louisa's expense. Her early release had to be kept completely secret. Marie knew she couldn't tell Andrew.

Another secret to be kept. But at least this one would be short-term.

He called at nine o'clock sharp. "How are things? I hear there're still fire watches on. I'm coming back tomorrow, but I'm not ready to face another fire."

"I don't want to face one, either," she said with feeling. "Tell me how the campaign's going."

He told her it was going fairly well, but Jacko didn't want to talk issues. He was in full personal attack mode. "Let's not dwell on that. I finally saw the detective, Gerhart. He says Jacko's connections to any sort of crime group seem tenuous. But he also says he's sure there's more there than meets the eye. He quoted that line about following the money. He said it would be a twisting trail, but it might lead to some surprising destinations."

"Nothing more specific," she asked.

"Not yet. As soon as I know anything, you'll know it. But we've got personal things to talk about. Don't you still have some questions left on your trusty questionnaire? Hit me with one."

This time they talked an hour and twenty minutes, and when Marie hung up she felt that same happiness again. She felt as if she was genuinely getting to know him. And, for one of the few times in her life, she was allowing someone to know her.

Andrew had told Marie he'd be back the next morning.

On the way from the airport to Lochlain, Tyler phoned him.

"Listen," Tyler said. "Things are happening fast. Word is they're releasing Louisa from the hospital today. Dylan Hastings is ready to pounce on her. But it sounds as if Louisa's lawyer's going to slap an injunction on him. I need to be there. I mean, it was my barn that burned, my horses that were damaged, and my property where Sam was killed."

"I'll join you," Andrew said.

"Good," Tyler told him. "Because somebody's got to make a speech. It isn't going to be me, mate. You're the one with practice."

"Yeah," Andrew replied grimly. "I've had lots of practice all right. But I'll have to write it in my head as I go along."

"Darci's going to be there and some of the Fairchild Acres staff. The press will be out in full force. Including Jacko's hyenas."

Andrew swore inwardly. He'd have to watch every word he said or Bullock's media monster would devour him. "Okay," he said, sounding more confident than he felt. "See you shortly. I'm about twenty minutes away."

"Perfect," said Tyler.

When Andrew reached Pepper Flats and approached the hospital, his innards knotted. The parking lot was full, crowded not only with Lochlain and Fairchild Acres vehicles, but dozens of press vans and cars. Paparazzi swarmed around the front stairs and wheelchair ramp, snapping pictures and thrusting microphones at people.

Andrew parked a block away and, striding swiftly, reached the stairs. Although the press immediately surrounded him, he plowed through until he was with the familiar crowd at the top, outside the doors.

Tyler was there with his arm around Darci Parnell. Dan Whittleson, Sam's son, looking stormy, stood beside his wife. Andrew recognized grooms and stable workers from Fairchild Acres and some from Lochlain and some from Whittleson Stud.

Megan Stafford pressed near Mrs. Lipton, but there was no sign of Patrick Stafford.

And, making Andrew's heart spin, Marie was there, slightly apart from the others. She wore her usual uniform of navy shorts and a white T-shirt, but she held herself straight, her chin high, set in determination, and she had one hand on her hip. The sun made her hair gleam like a golden helmet.

Andrew walked over to her. "What's been happening?"

"Dylan Hastings is coming to arrest Louisa," she whispered. "He doesn't know she's already gone to Fairchild Acres."

He stared at her in disbelief. "We heard the press would be here," she said. "We came to show our support, that's all. But the media wants a statement. Can you give one?"

"I can try." He nodded solemnly to her, his eyes lingering on hers. Then he went to stand next to Tyler.

"Preston!" cried a reporter. "Andrew Preston! Why're you here? Louisa Fairchild supports your opponent."

Microphones waved in his direction. He prayed for the words to come.

And they did.

He wasn't dressed to make a speech, he hadn't planned on this, Marie could tell. He wore boots, jeans and a chambray shirt, opened at the collar so she could see the cord of his wooden charm. His hair was rumpled, and there was no slickness in the way he looked or the way he moved.

Marie could see the strain in his face. But he spoke clearly, firmly and with a fierce conviction.

"Louisa Fairchild is a vital member of this country's strong and proud legacy…" he began. "I want to say—" he nodded to Tyler and Megan "—that we *all* stand by and believe implicitly in Louisa Fairchild's innocence." The word *innocence* rang out as sonorously as the roll of a cathedral bell.

He was an intriguing paradox: a firebrand who was perfectly controlled. And the crowd must have sensed both his staunchness and his strong sense of right and wrong. They listened.

He pledged his full support for Louisa and her family. "They've been victims of police ineptitude, deprived of justice because of this current state of emergency."

Marie noticed that Dylan Hastings had appeared on the outskirts of the crowd, leaning against a jacaranda tree. He looked as if Andrew had struck him. He turned and abruptly left.

If Andrew noticed, it didn't slow him. "I'll work with the Fairchild legal team to ensure that the people who've caused her this distress are held responsible for their actions."

The little knot of people around him all nodded in agreement, and Louisa's biggest groom crossed his arms over his massive chest, as if daring anyone to jeer.

"That's all I have to say," Andrew said. "Except that I know that all the folks up here—and a lot of you out there—agree. Thank you."

Many in the crowd at the foot of the stairs applauded. And some did not.

He stepped away from the microphones and began to make his way back down the steps, but the press swarmed him. Marie flinched as they closed in, but he kept moving. He was a tall and powerful man, and he stayed steadily on his path.

But when he reached the sidewalk, one of Jacko Bullock's reporters planted himself in front of Andrew. "Did you come here to get into Louisa Fairchild's good graces?" the man demanded. "To try to gain her support?"

"Louisa Fairchild can support who she wants," Andrew shot back. "I'm here because I don't like seeing people railroaded." He frowned. "Or being tried by the media. Courts should try people, not the press. My family had trouble once, and you all know *that* story—the media piled on us, saying we lied about Leopold's Legacy's bloodlines."

His lip curled in disdain, he glowered at the reporter. "We were proven innocent. But not before the media wanted to lead a lynch mob—and some are still trying to do just that. I don't like lynch mobs. Period. Not for me. Not for Louisa Fairchild. Not for anybody."

But the reporter stood his ground. He was a squarely built man, almost as wide as he was tall. "Come clean, Preston. Why are you really here today? For the big photo op?"

"I've got a better question for you," Andrew said, his eyes narrowing dangerously. "How come Jacko Bullock *isn't* here? Louisa Fairchild's been loyal to him for years. She's poured thousands into his campaign. But I don't see him. Do you? And I haven't heard him say a word in her defense. Have you? I'd think her 'good friend' Jacko would be here with Louisa's other allies. But he's not. He's conspicuously absent. Conspicuously."

With that, Andrew shoved his way past the man and stalked back to his car. This time, the reporters let him go. They fanned out and began questioning others, Tyler, Daniel Whittleson, people in the crowd. Once again Daniel angrily insisted Louisa should be arrested.

Marie saw Andrew stride alone down the street, jerk open the door of his car and get inside. She wanted to run after him, to tell him how proud she was of him, but she knew better. There were far too many reporters. She hoped with all her heart he'd call tonight.

And she guessed that there, on the hospital steps, as she watched him rebuke Jacko Bullock's lackey, it had finally happened.

She'd realized that this was a man she could love.

"So Andrew Preston stuck up for me!" Louisa said, nearly cackling. "I adore it. Or maybe he's trying to suck up to me. Either way he did a good job, by God. And he's right. Where was Jacko? Oh, he sent a fancy bouquet, but he kept his distance. Afraid my criminal reputation might rub off on him?"

But then she started to cough. "Megan—my cough medicine," she said between the hacking sounds. "Marie, please make me a cup of strong tea."

Megan folded her hands primly and said, "Dr. Burgess prescribed new medications for you. And you're not to have more than one cup of caffeinated tea a day."

"Oh, damn," Louisa said in disgust. "Marie—go make the tea. Do you have my new prescriptions, Megan?"

"I have."

"Well, *get* them," Louisa ordered. "Marie—*strong* decaffeinated tea."

"Fine," Megan said with resignation. She and Marie exited the room together, shutting the door behind them.

Marie gestured helplessly. "I thought this experience might change her. Mellow her."

"She has mellowed a bit, I think," Megan said, but looked pensive.

Marie sighed. "I need to go to Branxton to some of the gourmet shops. It's going to be hard to keep Louisa happy on a limited diet."

Megan nodded. "It's just hard to keep Louisa happy period. But she's had a difficult life. More difficult than I'd ever imagined. She has demons to fight. Awesome demons."

Marie cocked her head in curiosity. "Really?" she asked. "What?"

Megan only shrugged and gave her the guilty smile of a person who knew she'd accidentally said too much. "Never mind," she said. "There's a storm coming. I hope it doesn't bring lightning. More fires could start."

"This community can't take another fire," Marie said. "Everybody says so."

And what, Megan, do you mean about awesome demons?

Andrew called her before the usual time, at about a quarter to eight. "There's too much lightning, too many spot fires, and the wind's blowing in your direction. You'll need extra hands."

Marie could see the fires from the kitchen window, and they

were moving closer fast. If the separate blazes met, they could form an inferno.

"I can see them coming. They look bad."

"They are bad. When they started up in Koongorra, they were contained. But if they join, and the wind doesn't shift, they could jump the Hunter River."

"Good grief, Andrew. Is Lochlain safe? Are we? Should people be evacuating?"

"Louisa's place looks like the first that would be hit. Tyler's sending a few men over to help wet things down and dig firebreaks. Rennie and I'll be with them."

"You?" she asked. "You shouldn't put yourself in danger. Help your cousin. Louisa doesn't fully appreciate what you did today. I'm sorry, because I thought you were wonderful."

"I didn't expect her to appreciate it. And Tyler wants to try to mend fences. She didn't help him when he needed it most. But he won't, in conscience, do the same to her. She's old and ill and erratic."

"That's very good of him," she replied. "And you, too."

"We'll leave in a few minutes. But talk to me a little, okay? I heard Dylan Hastings is going to lose his badge. How do you feel about that?"

She hesitated then said, "I don't like the pigheaded way he handled Louisa—like she was the only possible suspect. It never made sense. But I also feel sorry for him. God knows he's shorthanded. It has to be terrible on him."

She changed the subject. "Let's not talk about him. Tell me about you. Your campaign. How's it going?"

"Fairly well. I'm waiting for Jacko to use his death ray on me at the last minute. Pull out his dirtiest tactics. Tell me about you. Everything you've done and thought and said."

"Nothing important. I fed Louisa, I fed the staff. And now— I'm glad you're back."

"It's good to be back. I missed you."

Did he mean it? Did she dare to say it back to him? Instead she said, "You were great today. Especially with that goon of Jacko's. And I was proud of you."

"I probably shot myself in the foot," he said, his tone sardonic. "But it doesn't matter. I said what I thought."

And let your anger show, thought Marie. *You weren't the cool Mr. McPerfect today. You were a human, passionately defending another human. And you were wonderful.*

"Uh-oh," he said. "They're loading up. I need to go."

"Be careful—please," she said. "And watch out for Rennie. He's still nursing those cracked ribs. I think he was hurt worse than he ever admitted."

"Will do, honey. Take care of yourself."

He hung up. She sat on the bed in her Spartan little room.

Why is he so kind to me? she wondered. *He acts as if he really cares. But how can I know for sure?*

Ten minutes later word came that the fires had joined. Marie heard sirens, and even inside the house the acrid scent of smoke hung in the air. Louisa ordered every able-bodied member of the staff to help with hoses and move the horses to a safe place.

Louisa herself turned on the vast sprinkler system to wet the lawn.

Marie, Bindi, Helena and some of the stronger maids worked with the stable boys to lug the heavy hoses to the property's edge. The hoses were as big around as Marie's wrists, and though she was strong, the things coiled and knotted and tangled in the shrubs, and when the water was turned on, she felt she was fighting a water-spewing anaconda.

The most experienced men, grooms and trainers, got the horses out of the stables and into the far paddocks by the lake. They were waiting to turn on the sprinkler systems in the stables until it was absolutely necessary. Then they came and relieved the women handling the hoses.

Bindi backed off a few steps, then sank to the muddy ground, crying with fatigue. Helena knelt beside her, trying to comfort her. Marie, exhausted, managed to run, gasping, back to her bungalow. She was filthy, but she snatched up her cell phone, took it back outside and tried to dial Andrew. In the chaos, she hadn't seen him or Rennie or any of the other men from Lochlain.

No answer. She dialed Reynard's cell phone, and she heard his voice, his breath heaving in thick gasps. "Where are you?" she demanded. "Are you and the others all right?"

"Bit of a close call," Reynard panted. "The wind blew a burning branch to the edge of Lake Dingo. Fire sprang up and threatened to ring the whole lake. We beat most of it out, almost got it. Gotta go, love."

"Wait! Where at Lake Dingo?"

"Near that big boulder shaped like an arrowhead. Gotta go, love. Stay safe."

She ran to her room and jerked two blankets off the closet shelf. Then she set off, fast as she could toward the lake.

At the edge of Hunter River, she could see a hellish and sickening conflagration. Most of the fire trucks were there, and some men had come staggering back, choking from smoke, their faces sooty and their clothes blackened.

She tried to run toward the lake, but a policeman seized her by the arm. "Who are you? What do you want?"

Breathless, her throat burning from the smoke, she told him her name and that she wanted to make sure her uncle, Reynard Lafayette, was all right, that a fire had broken out at the lake's edge.

Roughly, he told her to go back; the site could be highly dangerous, she wasn't needed and would only create more confusion. She jerked free and headed again toward the lake. The policeman shouted he'd arrest her, but then someone on the lawn screamed for help, and he turned and lumbered off in the opposite direction.

She ran until she saw a tall figure looming out of the smoke. He took Marie's arm far more gently than the policeman had. Behind him she could see small tongues of flame flickering through the haze. It took her a moment to recognize Andrew. He was so dirtied by smoke, his shirt ripped half-open, his hair wildly tumbled and hanging in his eyes.

He leaned closer to her. "You shouldn't be here. It's dangerous."

"I had to know if you and Rennie were safe," she said, and the scene was so surreal, so close to violent destruction that she felt the two of them stood in the pit of hell itself.

"He's safe, but he strained his ribs," Andrew said, pulling her closer. "He won't stop fighting the fire, though."

"Still fighting?" she cried, tears welling in her eyes and spilling down her cheeks. "Do I need to get him to an ambulance?"

"I don't think you could. He's a stubborn old coot—and fearless. You need to get back. This is still a hot spot. Get to a safer place. We called. There's a pumper truck coming as soon as they can spare one."

She looked and saw Rennie, hunched with pain, beating at the fire with a wet horse blanket. The big man named Winkler fought beside him, his face red from firelight and black from smoke. Two other men helped, but she didn't recognize them.

She couldn't go back. She shook her head, squinting her eyes against the sting of smoke. "No. I'll help you fight it. I brought blankets I can wet. I'll work with you."

"Marie…" Andrew said, trying to caution her.

"I'm not going," she told him, "so get to work. If Reynard can do it, so can I."

"Good lord," he said and reluctantly released her.

The next twenty minutes seemed like a marathon, soaking a blanket, slapping it against the smoldering grass with all her might, then soaking it again, and then again. At last the pumper truck came down the slope, and Marie, exhausted and aching, stared numbly at it.

Reynard sat down on the wet ashes, hugging himself, his face blackened by smoke, holes burned into his shirt and jeans. Marie stared at him. She didn't know he had such raw courage, and it made her want to cry harder.

"Rennie?" she said, her voice quavering. "Are you all right?" She started to move toward him. He waved her away. "A stitch in my side is all. I'll be fine. Just leave me be for a minute to get my breath."

Marie's knees started to go weak, partly from relief that it was ending, partly from dizzying fatigue. She'd been going on sheer adrenaline, but the adrenaline was gone now. Completely. She felt faint and swayed slightly. She gave a broken little sob.

Andrew stepped to her side and took her into his arms. "It's going to be fine, Marie. And Rennie's going to be fine. Don't cry. Please don't."

She pulled back slightly, staring up at him. "And you? Are you all right?"

In the flickering gloom, she saw his expression change. "Yes. Don't worry. But you need to go back. This is no place for you. Be careful, for God's sake. I wish I could take you back, but—"

"But they'll still need you here," she said tightly. "Oh, be careful…" Her voice broke.

"Don't cry, Marie," he said, his voice low. "I'll watch out for Rennie."

Suddenly he bent and kissed her, almost desperately, holding her tightly, his hands exploring the planes of her back, his lips pressing hungrily against hers. She didn't resist. She couldn't. She kissed him back with the same wild need.

Amid so much ruin, she needed something that promised life, a rebirth, a rising out of the ashes. Perhaps he felt the same primal urge. They tried to lose themselves in each other, to transcend the danger and the loss. For a long moment she felt they couldn't stop, to stop would be a surrender to the darkness.

But at last she broke the kiss, and they both drew back, staring at each other with something like incomprehension. She felt dizzy and unreal. "Be careful," she said. "Please."

"You, too."

Her heart pounding, she started toward the house. She cast one last glance back at Andrew. Against the dying glare of embers and the murk of smoke, he stood very straight, watching after her, a dark silhouette like a man standing on the brink of hell.

When she made her way back to the lawn, the fire along the river seemed under control. She limped to her room and took a twenty-minute shower, using up a whole bar of soap. She was too tired and confused to think straight.

Reynard was hurt again. She'd never seen so many flames, fires burning so widely and wildly. And Andrew had kissed her.

That part seemed dreamlike, impossible to her. The kiss was different from before. She didn't understand. But she felt different. As if something within her had changed.

Changed forever.

Chapter Eleven

It was shortly before midnight.

In Scone, Feeney sat alone in his tatty little rented apartment, his headquarters for this operation. He'd told the apartment manager that he was a designer of computer games, tired of living in the city. Electronic devices crammed the apartment, and he had a crate of mobile phones. He used them and disposed of them like tissues.

Feeney was a rather nondescript man of middle height, middle age. His hair was brownish, his eyes were grayish, and the only noticeable things about him were his extraordinary pallor and his rasping, ragged voice.

But he noticed things about other people. He noticed all sorts of details. And he had an almost infallible eye for people who were corrupt or corruptible. He put this talent to excellent use.

Tonight he relaxed by watching a telly program about a little old English lady who solved fiendishly complicated murders. He loved this program because it was so utterly, perfectly, flawlessly stupid.

He half wanted the old English lady to adopt him and half wanted to put a bullet in her forehead.

He reached for his glass of absinthe. The liquor was one of his few cosmopolitan indulgences. He made it the old-fashioned way, and even had an antique slotted spoon to sift the sugar into the emerald drink and change its color to a swirly yellowish green.

He liked absinthe's reputation—the most beautiful and degenerating drink in the world. The favorite tipple of the wicked. It was known as "the green goddess" and "the green fairy," and it was rumored to drive those who loved it mad.

This, of course, was rubbish. Sugared, in the old-fashioned way, it was both bitter and sweet to Feeney's jaded tongue; it numbed his ever-aching throat, and soothed his pinched stomach.

Absinthe gave some people a mere alcoholic fuzzy buzz. But Feeney was one of the lucky ones. A few sips and he felt his mind being lifted into an intense clarity, certainty and elevation of thought. This could last as long as twenty or thirty minutes at a time and made him feel nearly invulnerable.

He liked it, and he liked to do it several times after a hard day.

Today had been a hard day. He'd had to arrange—perfectly— two hits in Sydney, a pair of double-dealing loan sharks who'd gotten cute with the Granger gang. The Grangers didn't like being stiffed. That's why they'd thrown in on the murder of Sam Whittleson, who'd run up big debts but hadn't paid them.

Shame on Sam for being so dangerously, so foolishly in hock. Still, it had made him the perfect sacrificial lamb for the other business, the business with Jacko. His death satisfied both parties.

But Lord, the complexity of setting such things up just *so*.

Feeney took his first sip of the green goddess, and was savoring its anesthetic effect on his throat, when his cell phone rang. He swore and answered it. He recognized the voice: one of his people in Hunter Valley. This particular foot soldier was not bright, which was unfortunate, but he was brutal, which was always helpful.

"Feeney," Chalk said, "Preston's got a woman. I saw him snogging her like he'd take her in front of me and everybody else."

"Did you get a picture?" Feeney asked, already knowing the answer.

"Hell, no. You know how stupid that question is?"

Do you know how stupid that answer is? Feeney thought, piqued. *One word from me and tomorrow morning you could be shark kibble.*

"But," Chalk said, pride in his voice, "there's others that saw. He was all over her. And I know who she is."

So do I, you Neanderthal. I've known for days. I'm already working on it. That's why I'm where I am, and you're where you are. But he pretended. "And this woman is…?"

"Some sort of cook at Fairchild Acres. A looker. A little bit of a thing. I seen her around before. Marie Lafayette."

Feeney restrained himself from yawning. He knew what Jacko wanted to do to her, and Feeney'd already started doing it, long-distance. His business was to help Jacko.

In turn, Jacko's business would help Feeney's people. But Jacko was far from subtle. He was furious at Andrew Preston and wanted something truly horrifying to engulf Preston.

What Jacko wanted, Jacko got.

"Marie Lafayette," Feeney repeated, as if just familiarizing himself with the name. "Tell me. You say she's young, good-looking, little?"

"Absolutely. A nice piece of spunk."

"I see. But could you hurt her if you had to? Really hurt her?"

The other man didn't hesitate, for in this business, loyalty was all. "Do it in a minute," he said. "Wouldn't think twice about it."

Wouldn't think. That was a given. Feeney said. "Consider yourself on call."

"You let the people higher up know I'm the one found this out?" the other man asked, almost pathetically eager. "Found out who she is?"

"Of course," lied Feeney. "I need to ring off now. Get this news out."

He hung up without saying goodbye.

It was past midnight now. He threw his cell phone into the nearby wastebasket. He reached for his absinthe and let it cool and numb his throat. Clear and sharpen his thoughts.

Marie slept uneasily and rose late, still feeling dazed.

The others in the kitchen were up and agog over the latest news.

Mrs. Lipton cried, "Marie! Last night Sergeant Hastings found evidence that clears Miss Louisa! Imagine that! *Dylan Hastings* helped her. She had him in for a brandy."

Marie blinked in astonishment. "He did? She did?"

The older woman nodded. "He's found a clue that might help prove Miss Fairchild innocent. The case could be solved—and he'd be reinstated—so there's cause for celebration all around."

Marie stared at her, stunned, unable to take in this sudden change. And since she couldn't get her mind around it, she asked what had dominated her thoughts since she'd awakened. "Some of Tyler Preston's men came from Lochlain last night to help. Did Miss give them any recognition?"

Mrs. Lipton's smile faded. "She had Helena and I feed them all breakfast. She told me she'd thank them later—and give them a reward—and Tyler, too. She was exhausted, poor creature. Keeping to her room this morning. She's grateful, but after so much destruction last night, so much excitement…well, she needs some peace." She cocked a brow wryly. "After all she's been through, I'm sure she'll be in a state. She's gone through both good and bad, and we'll have a bumpy ride for a while."

Marie nodded, knowing that the old woman could be as quicksilvery as mercury itself. But she remembered Megan's mysterious words: *"It's just hard to keep Louisa happy period. But she's had a difficult life. More difficult than I'd ever imagined. She has demons to fight. Awesome demons."*

How did Megan know this? Had she had discovered something, some key to Louisa's character? And if so, what?

The next morning, Reynard appeared at the kitchen door with eggs. He looked a bit scruffy, not fully recovered from fighting the bushfire. Still, he had a knowing twinkle in his eyes, a mischievous smile playing at the corners of his mouth.

"Here," he said, handing her the basket of eggs. "Two dozen fresh ones. The hens were off their laying right after the fire. But they're back at work, making fresh cackleberries."

His spirits seemed high, even though he limped worse than before, and his voice was still hoarse from smoke. Marie knew he was in pain and also knew if she asked him, he'd deny it like crazy.

Mrs. Lipton beamed at him and said, "I'm *so* glad to see *you* up and around again."

"They taped my ribs again, even better than before. Quite comfy, in fact. Too many snootfuls of smoke, though. I haven't wanted a ciggie for two days."

Mrs. Lipton smiled. "Do sit down and have tea. Yesterday I made fresh brandy snaps—I must have sensed you'd show up."

"Well, then sit down with me, the both of you. For I come bearing more than eggs. I bring good news."

Mrs. Lipton set the teapot and cups on the smallest kitchen table. She opened the tin of brandy snaps and sat down. Marie sat, too, looking at Reynard with curiosity. "Well—" Mrs. Lipton nodded "—news? What sort?"

He put an elbow on the table, seeming pleased with himself. "Lochlain got a call from the police station about an hour ago. They have Sandy Sanford in custody. He was supposed to have left the morning before the fire."

"Sandy Sanford?" Marie asked. "The carpenter from Sam's place?"

"I heard that boy left because his mother was ill," Mrs. Lipton said.

Reynard shrugged. "That was his story. But the night of the bushfire, Dylan Hastings found Sanford's ditched ute—and the missing security CD-ROM. It shows that Sanford shot Sam Whittleson and started the fires. The last thing on the CD is him reaching up to snatch the disk out of the camera."

"Sandy Sanford did it all?" Marie asked. "So Louisa really *is* cleared?"

"Completely. The state police caught Sanford early this morning. Got him at Tweed Heads, going north into Queensland."

"God in heaven," breathed Mrs. Lipton. "Did he confess?"

"Indeed," said Reynard. "As soon as he heard about the disk, he admitted it. But he won't say why. Shut up tight as a clam. Afraid to talk, I'll wager."

Marie jumped up so fast she almost spilled her tea. She grabbed Reynard and threw her arms around his neck. "Rennie, I love you! This is the best news we could get! I've got to tell Louisa immediately. The nightmare's really over."

She dashed out the door and up the stairs. She nearly collided with Bindy, who was in the upstairs hall, coming out of Megan's room.

"Marie," she said, looking a bit guilty, "I've got something to confess—"

"Not right now, Bindy," Marie said with a grin. "I've got big news for Louisa."

"What?" Bindy asked apprehensively.

"Go to the kitchen. Rennie'll tell you. Oh, this is fantastic."

Bindy descended the stairs with seeming reluctance, and Marie pounded on Louisa's door like a madwoman. Louisa's voice was sharp with irritation. "What? What? Can't a body have a moment's rest? Come in before you smash down the door!"

Marie barged in, mindless of decorum. "Miss! Rennie just came from Lochlain. They've caught the arsonist. Sandy Sanford— Sam's carpenter. Somehow he lured Sam to Lochlain and shot him. They told him about the security disk, and he confessed."

Louisa's hand flew to her heart. She sat at her small desk and stared at Marie in shock.

Marie could barely contain herself. "You're cleared! They can never hold this over you again. The police finally have the real killer."

To her amazement, Louisa burst into tears. She buried her face in her hands. "Oh, my God," she kept saying. "Oh, my God."

She wept so violently that Marie, without thinking, went to her, bent and took the old woman in her arms. Louisa laid her cheek against Marie's shoulder and sobbed like a child.

Marie felt pity and relief for her.

"There, there," she said, holding Louisa more tightly. "It's over. It's really over, and you're safe, and Fairchild Acres is safe, and you've got your good name back."

At last Louisa stopped crying. She pushed Marie away and reached for a tissue to wipe her eyes and dab at her nose. "I'm sorry for his display. It's not like me. Now I *do* need to be alone. To think. To sort things out. Come back in an hour."

"Yes, Miss. Of course." Marie turned and left the suite, stunned by Louisa's show of emotion. She made her way downstairs, and when she entered the kitchen, she felt as if she walked into an unreal world, a strange, dreamlike loop incoherently repeating itself.

Now it was Bindy, sobbing uncontrollably against Mrs. Lipton's ample bosom. "What's this?" Marie asked, bewildered.

Bindy turned her face so that Marie couldn't see it.

"Be still, dear," Mrs. Lipton said to the girl. "You didn't know. How could you?"

Marie looked at Reynard, and he shook his head unhappily.

"She was seeing Sandy Sanford," he said in his rasping voice. "The bugger that burned the barn. He'd come around here, and sometimes she'd get called out of the kitchen. He must have poked about and taken the gun. She met him the night before he left. He told her he had to go see his mother, that she was sick, and he needed money. He took all she had."

"Miss will never forgive me," Bindy wept. "She'll sack me for certain."

And Marie looked at her sadly, knowing it was true. Bindy had been a fool for love.

At last Bindy could cry no more. Reynard awkwardly patted the girl on the back and wished her luck. He had to get back to Lochlain.

Mrs. Lipton sat Bindy down at the table and poured her tea. "Bindy," she said, "I'm sure the police will want to talk to you. Don't be frightened. Just tell them the truth."

"Will they tell Miss Fairchild?" Bindy asked, sniffling.

"No," Mrs. Lipton said gently. "I'll tell her. I'm the one who hired you, and it's my responsibility. I'll go now and let her know. I don't want you to be in the house. Why don't you go to the bungalow? I'll call you afterward."

"But she will fire me, won't she?" Bindy asked, her voice shaking. "What you're saying is go pack, isn't it?"

"I just want you out of range of her temper," Mrs. Lipton said. "And I suggest you think about calling the police yourself. I believe they'll treat you more kindly if you do. Now be off with you, dear."

Mrs. Lipton left the kitchen, looking grim. Bindy hid her face in her hands. "How could he do this to me? I *loved* him."

"I'm sorry," Marie said softly. "But she's right, Bindy. Let's get you out of here. I'll walk you to the bungalow."

"I'll go by myself. I know I'm through here. I know it, and I'm going to need to be alone."

"Are you sure?" Marie asked, putting her hand on the girl's arm.

Bindy wiped the tears from her cheeks with the back of her hand. "I'm sure." She rose and faced Marie, her expressions uncertain.

"Marie, I want to tell you something. I saw the niece, Miss Stafford, take a box of Miss's private papers to her room while Miss was in the hospital. She brought them from a barn where they were stored—because of the office being done over, you know? I—I was curious."

Bindy wiped her eyes again. "I never trusted Miss Stafford. She was fooling around with Dylan Hastings, and everybody knew. I thought maybe she was trying to get something against Miss for him, why else go through her private papers? So I...decided to play detective."

The young woman took a deep breath. "Miss Stafford's gone this morning. I looked in her room. The box was there. It was full of letters. I read some. I was gobsmacked...."

"The letters were old, the 1940s. No stamps. Not sealed. But addressed. Miss Louisa was writing to somebody named Kent Oxford. She was in a home for unwed mothers. She hated it. She wanted him to come take her away. But she must never have sent it. And later she wrote him a long, sad letter about how her baby girl lived only a day, and the doctor said she could never have another child."

Shaking her head, she murmured. "I hope Miss Stafford hasn't got them for blackmail or something. Do you think so? Should Miss Louisa know? It does make Miss Louisa easier to understand, everything she went through and all. And I'm so sorry for what I done to her, about Sandy and...all..."

She drew away from Marie, hiding her quivering mouth with her hand. "I loved working with you, Marie. Maybe I'll see you again sometime."

She rose, took off her apron, set it on the counter, and then pushed the back door open.

She turned to face Marie. She took a deep breath. "At least, I'm not pregnant. I know that for certain. At least he didn't do that to me, as well."

"I'm glad, Bindy. I'm relieved for you."

Bindy just shook her head, looked out toward the paddocks, and walked out the door.

Marie, numbed, sat down at the table, not wanting to watch her go. Poor, naive Bindy, always so excited about her "beau," her "boyfriend," her "sweetheart."

But she was stunned by what Bindy had said.

Louisa *had* given birth to a daughter out of wedlock. In the 1940s. And she believed the child had died.

And Kent Oxford was the man Louisa's *sister* had married. He was Megan and Patrick Stafford's grandfather. And if he was the father of Louisa's baby, then he was most likely Marie's grandfather, as well.

That baby hadn't died, Marie thought, stunned. The home must have lied to Louisa. Perhaps her parents had arranged for such a lie, thinking she'd put the experience behind her, never have to wonder if she had a child somewhere.

Marie felt faint, as if she couldn't stand up if she tried.

How would Louisa feel if she learned that her daughter had lived? And *how* her daughter had lived, without money or privilege or security—and how she'd died?

"This is impossible," Marie whispered to herself. Perhaps Louisa should never know the truth. Ever.

* * *

Louisa, of course, fired Bindy as soon as she heard of the affair with Sandy Sanford. Mrs. Lipton came downstairs blinking back tears. She said that Louisa wanted Bindy off the property as soon as possible. She'd written the girl's last paycheck and sealed it in an envelope for Mrs. Lipton to deliver.

"So deliver it I must," said Mrs. Lipton, straightening her spine. "And now, Miss wishes to see you."

Marie nodded. She climbed the stairs to Louisa's suite, her pulse drumming with anxiety, for Louisa might be even more overwrought now. And for the first time, Marie would face her knowing that Louisa very well might be her grandmother.

She tried to calm herself as she rapped at the door. "Come in," Louisa answered, her order as swift and sharp as a rifle shot.

Marie pushed open the door. This time Louisa was standing, her fists on her hips. "Well," she said. "Doesn't that bugger all? Silly little Bindy let a *murderer* in my house. The lout stole my gun and framed me and nearly killed me. Because of *her*. I hope a snake bites her."

"I—I'm sure she had no intention of mischief," Marie said. "She had no idea that he—"

"Don't defend her," Louisa snapped. "She wasn't malicious, I'm certain. But she's a fool, and that's just as bad. It led to the same end—death, destruction, arrest, illness. She's not just an idiot, she's the tritest sort of idiot, a silly girl letting a man turn her head. Bah! The oldest trap in the world."

"Many a smarter woman's fallen into the same trap," Marie retorted, and then thought *What have I said? Louisa herself made that mistake.*

Louisa looked at her coldly. "On any other day I'd give you a tongue-lashing. But I have more important things to think of. I've phoned my lawyer to make sure all action is dropped against Dylan Hastings. I want his slate wiped clean."

Marie could say nothing. She stood with her mouth open in surprise.

"I am not a forgiving person," Louisa said. "I haven't been for decades. But lying in a hospital bed, listening to my very old heart go 'beep' on a machine was sobering. Very sobering. So I may as well make up with Hastings. I know that he and my great-niece are attracted to each other. They didn't do a very good job of hiding it."

Marie made herself close her mouth. She'd had no idea that Louisa knew about Megan and Dylan. She, too, had been aware of their attraction and wondered why Megan, an attorney herself, so blithely ignored the advice of Robert D'Angelo to avoid police and other suspects.

Louisa must have noticed her expression. "Of course, I knew about them. I have eyes in my head. He'll probably be part of the family, so we'd better bury the hatchet. I'll be having dinner with Mr. D'Angelo tonight. He likes steak. See if you can do something clever with it. We'll dine at eight—privately. Feed Megan and Patrick separately."

"Yes, ma'am," Marie said, trying to hide her agitation at all she'd learned this morning.

"I wish to renew my ties to Lochlain Racing," Louisa said, gazing out the window at the paddocks and the burned land beyond. "For starters, I'll send a check to each man who came to help and an extra-large one for your uncle. I heard he hurt himself again. Is he better?"

"That would be a lovely gesture, Miss. And yes, he's better. He's a survivor."

"But as for Andrew Preston, I'm not sure. He's behaved very decently toward me lately. I heard that he fought right beside your uncle."

He behaved more than decently, Marie thought, *He behaved like a hero. They all did.*

"But I can't support two candidates," Louisa muttered. "Still, I don't wish to seem ungrateful to the man." She paused. "So I'll probably send him a check, as well, but make it clear it's not a campaign donation. If he doesn't want it, he can donate it to one of his everlasting causes."

Marie fought back a sigh. On the hospital stairs, Andrew had put his political reputation at stake; he'd faced a raging fire for her, and she would send him a check that would be nothing compared to all she'd done for Bullock.

"Hmm," Louisa said, studying her. "I can see by your face, you don't approve. I often see that look on your face. It makes you seem so virtuous. But I'm old and opinionated—and I've seen much of the world. Someday you may be the same and then you'll better understand me."

Louisa laid her finger against her cheek thoughtfully. The pose gave her an almost girlish air. "You're bright, my girl. You've risen to the occasion better than I could have imagined. You've been doing the work of two cooks and doing it well. I have good news for you. Mrs. Lipton found a French chef. He'll be joining the staff soon. Your workload will be easier."

"I appreciate that, Miss."

"We'll have to replace Bindy, too, of course. That'll be a bother. But that's Mrs. Lipton's problem."

She moved to the chaise lounge and sat down. "I want to reward my staff, too, for helping keep Fairchild Acres safe. So, perhaps a barbecue for them. How does that strike you?"

"Very thoughtful, Miss. It's a terrifying thing, facing a fire."

"There are many terrifying things in life to face," Louisa said, her expression unreadable. "I heard you worked beside the men from Lochlain. Not many women would have such guts. You're full of surprises, you are. I wonder about you. Oh, yes. But I'll do that in private. You may go."

Marie went back to the kitchen, shaken. She couldn't let Reynard know of Bindy's story about the letters—not yet. It would only fire his zeal to have her reveal herself to Louisa, and she couldn't face that.

In her room that night, she was stripping down to put on her pajamas when the phone rang. Wearing only her shorts and bra, she grabbed the receiver and said, "Hello?"

It was Andrew calling from Melbourne. "How are things? I heard about Bindy. I'm sorry."

"So am I," she said. "She took it hard. But she shouldn't have let that man inside the house. She knew it was wrong."

"It must have been upsetting for everybody. Are you okay?"

No, I'm not, she wanted to say. *Today I found out Louisa may well be my mother's mother. But I can't bring myself to face her. I feel like an interloper, a sneak.*

Instead, she said. "Well, it's been quite a day."

"How's Louisa doing?"

"She's wildly relieved that she's been cleared of murder. And I'm afraid to say this," she admitted, "but she seems a little mellower since she left the hospital. You know what? Mrs. Lipton said she not only gave Bindy her pay, but two weeks severance pay, as well. Plus fifty dollars to help tide her over—along with a terse note warning her about smooth-talking men."

Andrew laughed, a low chuckle that made her stomach feel quivery. "Maybe it took a near-death experience to shake up her outlook. Let's hope it lasts."

Her heart beat harder. "And how about you?" she asked.

"I get back on the plane tomorrow," he said, regret in his voice. "Another trip to the Western Territory. And I haven't seen you since the night of the fire. It was only a short while ago, but it seems like a thousand years."

"I know," she whispered.

"Do you think since Louisa's cleared, I could take you out? That Robert D'Angelo can stop playing Gestapo?"

She closed her eyes, wishing. "I think so. And Louisa even said nice things about you. She admired you for fighting the fire."

"Then I'll keep calling you until I get back. And I'll think about you all the time…wonder about you. What kind of little kid you were…"

"Willful," she said, "but friendly. And too curious. I'd stick forks into electrical outlets, fall out of windows, eat bugs. Once I ate a stinkbug. That was a real mistake. What were you like as a boy?"

"McPerfect, of course," he laughed. "A straight arrow. My mother said I was 'intense.' That I really concentrated on things—a book, a toy, a story on TV."

"Good grades," she teased.

"All A's," he said. "Start to finish."

"A Boy Scout?" she asked with a smile.

"Of course. Eagle Scout."

"Campus politics?" she prodded.

"President of my senior class. And the student council."

"Oh, you're designed to make everybody in the world feel inferior," she joked. "No wonder some people think you're a robot."

"You know I'm not," he said, his voice seductive.

"Yes. I know." Too well she knew.

They talked until nearly midnight. They spoke of ordinary things, but beneath the surface of their conversation thrummed a strong current of sexual attraction, of growing desire.

When they had to hang up, Marie closed the phone reluctantly, smiling to herself. She felt warm and tingling all over, almost as if she glowed with a kind of happiness she'd never before known.

She told herself she was not another Bindy, blinded by love, no longer able to see reality.

And she hoped it was true. But as much as she loved talking to Andrew, she wanted to see him again.

Not only to see him, but to drink him in with all her senses, to hear his deep voice, to smell the scent of his aftershave, to feel his long, strong body against her small one, to press her lips to his again, to explore his tongue with her own, to taste the salt on his skin, to...

The images were becoming too vivid, too sensual. Instead of putting on her pajamas, she shed her clothes and took a long, icy shower.

She was all too conscious that she still had a virgin's body. And she wanted that to change. For Andrew to change it—and her.

Marie awoke early. The cold shower had cooled her body last night, but not her imagination. Her dreams had wakened her because they embarrassed her. She had dreamed of being naked with Andrew, and of them doing things to each other she'd only read about in books.

I'm twenty-five years old, she thought with chagrin, *and I just reached puberty.*

Physical activity was what she needed, and lots of it. Though the sun had barely risen, she quickly dressed and took her bike for a ride over the estate's dirt roads.

She enjoyed the coolness of the morning, even though the tang of smoke still touched the breeze. Birds were awakening, chirping, whistling, cawing. She turned to go toward the eastern pastureland, when she saw a figure in the distance. With a shock, she realized it was Megan Stafford, carrying a cardboard box.

Marie stopped and watched. Megan's back was to her, and she entered one of the outbuildings, a barn, and disappeared. Marie turned around and sped back to where the road forked. She stopped, dismounted, and acted as if she was inspecting her rear tire.

She saw Megan leave the barn and begin to walk back. Marie toyed with her bicycle wheel until she could see Megan more clearly. The box was gone. She'd left it in the building.

Marie remounted her bike, waved amiably at Megan, and Megan raised a hand, returning the greeting. Then Marie took off, legs working madly, mind working just as fast, wondering about the significance of what she'd seen.

She'd known she could never search Megan's room for Louisa's letters; it seemed too much like burglary. But now the letters might be sitting in an unlocked barn.

Did that change matters? She didn't have to tell Reynard about them. She could simply go see for herself.

If she looked at them, was that another morally compromising act? Or would the letters change her mind about leaving the valley without telling Louisa about Colette?

To read them? Or not?

It was, Marie decided, too big a decision to make on impulse. She must think and think hard.

The idea of the letters haunted Marie all morning, but she did nothing about them. Then, after morning tea, Mrs. Lipton said Louisa wanted to see Marie. She did not say why.

Marie went to the suite in apprehension. When she entered,

Louisa was in her riding costume, sitting in the chaise lounge, looking displeased.

"You wanted to see me, Miss?" Marie asked.

Louisa nodded, "I went riding this morning. It wasn't as easy for me as it was before my spell. The doctor told me not to, but I did, anyway. I intend to inspect my property to the end—even if I'm reduced to the indignity of riding in a golf cart."

Marie said nothing. Louisa raised an eyebrow and said, "This morning I found one of my outbuilding's unlocked. The barn in the eastern pasture. I was appalled. I'm keeping some private papers in there until the office is remodeled. What dunderhead left it unlocked? Here. Take this padlock and lock that door tight. I don't want anyone snooping in my personal correspondence."

She held out a large, solid-looking padlock. "Do as I say, my girl. You can ride over there on your bicycle."

Marie took the padlock, her mind whirling. Why was Louisa giving this job to her?

"Go," Louisa said with a shooing motion. "Just go. Zip on over, then zip back. It's easier than sending one of the men."

"Of course, Miss." Marie held the heavy padlock in her hand. She nodded and left the room. She went to the bungalow and got her bike, the lock a weight in her pocket.

She rode to the outbuilding and tested the door. It opened easily. She peered inside.

Everything seemed orderly, except for a rumpled horse blanket on the floor, flecked with straw. She didn't touch it. She didn't touch anything. But she cast a longing glance at the stacks of boxes.

She closed the door, put the padlock in place and snapped it shut firmly. She tested it, and it was sound. Nobody would be able to get inside the building again without the key.

And that included her.

Wasn't it better this way? Let Louisa keep her secrets. And Marie would keep hers.

PART THREE

Australia, The Hunter Valley
April

Chapter Twelve

The week passed peacefully for a change.

A new woman, Bronwyn Davis, came to replace Bindy. She was a tall, lovely widow with auburn hair and a ten-year-old son named Wesley. Bindy's and Millie's rooms were being refurbished the day Bronwyn arrived, so she and Wesley were given a temporary set of rooms in the house.

Wesley was a sweet and unaffected child, obviously still getting over his father's recent death. He became a favorite of the staff, and surprisingly of Louisa's. The old woman *was* growing mellower. Perhaps her hospitalization and close brush with the law had given her a new and kinder perspective on life.

And perhaps her growing rapport with Patrick and Megan was also responsible for her better temper. Megan was now living half-time in Sydney and half-time with Dylan Hastings, but Patrick had stayed on, working from Louisa's house.

The French chef, Francois, arrived, a large jolly man who reminded Marie a bit of the late Pavarotti, the legendary opera tenor. He was a most charming man, but oddly, he didn't charm

Louisa. She frequently found fault with his cooking, which annoyed him immensely.

Obviously Louisa hadn't mellowed completely.

Andrew, still on the campaign trail, called almost every night. Talking to him was the high point of Marie's day. The sexual attraction seemed to grow between them, so strong she felt endangered by it, yet she had never felt so fully alive.

But Andrew was no longer simply a sexy and handsome man, he was becoming a friend. They were getting to know each other more deeply than they might have in an ordinary relationshiop—and she realized that besides the desire they felt for each other, there was also a growing fondness, a true affection.

They knew each other's earliest memories, their proudest moments and their most painful. They knew small things, like the names of each other's favorite pets and their most liked—and disliked—subjects in elementary school. He talked about having two brothers and a sister. She talked about being an only child.

He told of his first love, Kellie Maguire, who'd said that there was a door in the moon. If you could find it and open it, you'd see the future. "She was young and beautiful and smart and independent, and she died in a stupid accident that never should have happened." Marie could hear the emotion in his voice. Then, abruptly, he changed the subject.

He confessed that Jacko Bullock had been quiet lately, and that disturbed him. Something must be up.

Marie said, "Maybe he's worried about a federal investigation. Patrick says they think Sandy was part of a bigger operation. Organized crime, like you said. And maybe he'll talk if he can get something out of it."

"Could be." Andrew didn't sound convinced. "But given Jacko's reputation, the longer he lies low, the nastier the surprise he'll spring. And he can strike as fast as a snake."

"You're stronger than he is," she told him. "I know you are."

"Thanks, beautiful," he would say in that low, lazy Southern voice she loved. He was the only man who'd ever called her beautiful and made it sound like a compliment, not a come-on.

She felt safe enough to tell him her worries about Reynard.

"He seems on tenterhooks. He's uneasy at The Secret Heiress. He won't sit at the same table twice in a row. And he's drinking much more than he used to. He'll take me out and drink his schooner or two. But then he drops me off and goes to the Crook Scale. Some nights, he disappears altogether. And doesn't say where he's been."

"Maybe he's found a lady fair," Andrew suggested, a smile in his voice.

"He'll always be able to find a lady fair," she said. "When he brings the eggs, even Louisa makes sure she's in the kitchen when he arrives. He's one of the few people who can actually make her laugh. But when I'm alone with him, he's not in his usual high spirits."

"I'm sorry. But if he's drinking, maybe when I get back I can get him talking and find out what the problem is."

"I feel guilty," she said. "You shouldn't have to take on my family problems."

"You listen to me bitch and moan about the campaign. You help keep me from imploding. When I ask your opinion, you're honest. When you give advice, it's good. I mean it."

She smiled with pleasure. Then his tone changed. "I miss you," he told her. "I think about you all the time."

"And I miss you," she said, and it was a daring statement for her to make. "And think about you."

"One of these days, I'm going to talk to you face-to-face again. I hope."

"I hope so, too," she said.

"And more than face-to-face. I want to hold you again."

Her body tingled, remembering his touch. "Maybe it'll be easier when the election's over."

"It should be," he said. "But, of course, Louisa may want to shoot me if I win."

She gave a mock moan. "*Please* don't talk about her shooting anybody! I swear Wesley, the little boy here, is softening her. He's a darling little boy. His mother, Bronwyn, the one who replaced Bindy? It turns out that she's the widow of a man named Ari Theodoros. He was imprisoned for—"

"I know what he was imprisoned for," Andrew said, his tone suddenly hardening. "Doping horses. He was up to his neck in racing scams. And Louisa's letting his widow work at her place? Has she gone soft in the head?"

"No," Marie replied. "But maybe soft in the heart. She's quite taken by the little boy. And she seems to have a strange sympathy for Bronwyn. I get the feeling that Bronwyn and Patrick used to know each other. It's odd, but I have to wonder if—"

"My God," Andrew exclaimed. "Do you have your TV on? Something's happening."

"What?" she asked in confusion. "What's going on?"

"Let me listen a sec." There was a long pause and she could hear the sound of the television, a vague mumble in the background.

Then Andrew spoke again. "Marie? This isn't good. Sandy Sanford was shot to death tonight. They're not saying how it happened, only that it's under investigation."

Sam's killer shot? But he was in custody. It made no sense to Marie. It didn't seem possible.

"Dead?" she echoed in disbelief. "But how…"

"They may not want to say more. Damn! Dead! He was the one possible link to a syndicate connection, and he's gone. How in hell did this happen?"

"Oh, Andrew," she said, truly upset. "Do you still have that detective you hired?"

"I've got him working on the syndicate or gang connection, but so far the feds aren't sharing their info. That's the big problem. I'll light a fire under him. This can't be a coincidence."

"Andrew," she said, "please be careful. First Sam's dead, now Sandy. This is scary."

"Don't worry about me. I can take care of myself. Remember me? The Yank? From the rough-and-ready land of Dirty Harry? Oh, hell, somebody's beating on my door. Bet it's Ollie, come to tell me about Sanford. Talk to you tomorrow, beautiful. Sweet dreams."

"Sweet dreams," she repeated mechanically. But how could any dreams be sweet tonight with another death connected to Hunter Valley?

* * *

The next morning, Louisa sat in the kitchen, grumbling. Marie guessed that she was impatiently waiting for Reynard so she could ask him what the hell he thought was going on with the death of Sandy Sanford.

Marie busied herself making the staff breakfast, bangers and mash. The normally genial Francois bent frowning over a skillet, scrambling egg whites and vegetarian sausages for Louisa. "I did not study the great cuisine of France," he muttered, "to make pabulum. This will have all the flavor of paste."

"Oh, be quiet," snapped Louisa. "*I'm* the one who has to eat it. Ask my two culinary consciences here." She glanced at Marie and Bronwyn.

Bronwyn had studied nutrition in college and was one hundred per cent committed to Louisa eating healthy foods. But this morning, Bronwyn looked wan and uneasy.

Helena was in the staff dining room, laying the table. Louisa perked up when Reynard's truck drove up and he came to the door with his basket of eggs.

"Hello, Reynard," Louisa said crisply. "Come in. Sit with me. Mrs. Lipton, get him some of those sweets he likes and a cuppa. Reynard, you heard the news about Sandy Sanford?"

He looked his usual alert and irreverent self. "I have—and I'll gladly join you," Reynard said. "Yes, Sandy's croaking's the talk of Lochlain."

Reynard settled into a chair. Louisa said, "I read on the Internet they were transferring him to the jail in St. Heliers, and he was shot getting out of the police car. How could such a thing happen? At a *jail?* Surrounded by the bloody *police?*"

He shrugged. "Word of his transfer must have leaked."

"Leaked?" Her nostrils pinched in distaste. "How could it be leaked?"

"There's corruption everywhere, Miss. Even the police force isn't perfect. Policemen have been known to be bribed and bought. And somebody, or some group, probably didn't want Sandy talking."

"Group? As in organized crime?" Louisa demanded. Mrs.

Lipton looked suddenly alarmed as she gave Reynard his brandy snaps and tea.

"Probably," he said.

"And the killer got away?" she said in disbelief. "With the police right there? How?"

"The shot came from an abandoned building," Reynard said. "A cop was hit, too. Whoever did the shooting set the building afire. He raised enough confusion to escape."

Marie felt sickened. Louisa bent closer to Reynard and peered in his eyes. "But the police will find him?"

He gave her a crooked grin. "I'd say they're motivated. Wouldn't you be? But if I was the shooter, I'd be out of the country by now. Long gone."

"You seem to know a lot about criminal acts," Louisa said, her eyes still on his.

He gave her his lazy, heavy-lidded look. "I read the papers. Sanford's not the first man to be killed in custody. Nor will he be the last."

"I don't feel very good," Bronwyn said suddenly. "I need some air." She opened the back door and fled outside.

Reynard and Marie exchanged glances. Bronwyn's husband had also died in police custody. Had too many painful memories overwhelmed her?

"Humph," was Louisa's only comment. "Why was Sanford moved?"

"He was charged with murder. He was desperate. They probably thought he'd try to escape. Orders to move him had to come from higher up."

"And how do *you* know?" Louisa wheedled.

"Good deal of jaw-jaw about it in the bunkhouse last night," he said. "That's what folks were saying, is all."

He turned to Marie. "Marie, love, this has shaken everyone up. Want to have a glass of wine at The Secret Heiress tonight?"

Marie nodded silently.

"Good. I have to get back now, sorry to say." He got to his feet and smiled at Mrs. Lipton. "Mrs. Lipton, when you get to heaven, St. Peter will ask, 'Did you bring the brandy snaps?' And if you have, you'll make him a very happy saint."

"And what," Louisa asked, looking up at him archly, "shall St. Peter ask me when I arrive?"

"He won't ask anything. He'll say, 'At last someone to get the celestial stables in shape.' There have to be horses in heaven, or you wouldn't go, would you, Miss?"

"Indeed, I would not," said Louisa, smiling in spite of herself. With a wave, Rennie strode out the door.

Louisa, too, rose from the table. "Have the new girl bring me my breakfast, as usual," she told Mrs. Lipton. On the way out, she peered into Francois's pan. "Don't overcook my eggs again," she said rather testily.

When she left, Francois said a very bad word in French. Marie understood it perfectly and knew he was both hurt and angry. She put her hand on his shoulder. "Don't let her get to you. She likes to goad people. Especially at first. She's a bit temperamental sometimes."

"I am a chef, and *I* am temperamental," he growled. "We will see who is best at it."

Marie shook her head in resignation and went out to see how Bronwyn was. She stood by a jacaranda tree staring out at the stables.

"Are you all right?" Marie asked.

"No," Bronwyn said. "Marie, you know what happened to my husband, to Ari…"

"Yes. I know."

"He was a criminal. I never knew until he was arrested. He was in prison for doping horses. Two men, first Ari, now Sandy, connected to horse racing crimes—both killed while they were in custody." Bronwyn's voice was shaky. "That's too much of a coincidence, don't you think? And it's frightening. And after what's happened in Hunter Valley—and to Louisa? These deaths and all this violence connected with racing? I wonder if Wesley and I are safe here."

"You told me before you never knew Ari was into doping.

Nobody has reason to harm you or Wesley. Ari's the one they wanted to silence, and now he's gone. You shouldn't worry."

Bronwyn tried to smile but wasn't completely successful. "Thanks," she murmured.

Marie smiled back, but she thought of what Andrew had said at the Hermit's Cave, that there could very well be a plot to get the main Thoroughbred properties in this part of the valley. Back then, the idea seemed overly dramatic. Now it seemed too real.

Would there be more deaths? And who would be on the hit list?

Marie honestly didn't think Bronwyn and Wesley would be in danger. But some malign force, some unknown persons had nearly killed Louisa. Would they move against her again?

And Andrew? *They would want to get rid of Andrew. He was against everything they represented, the fraud, the greed, the conspiracies.*

Wouldn't they want to stop him however they could?

Hans Gerhart was the senior partner of the Gerhart and Phelps Agency. His office seemed better suited to a stock broker or an insurance executive than a detective. It was modern, with sleek furniture and only a single picture, a black-and-white photograph, on the walls.

Andrew found this photograph, a portrait, infinitely distracting. It was of a young woman from another era, and she was heartbreakingly beautiful. She had a delicate, almost perfect face, and dark blond bobbed hair. She reminded him, almost viscerally, of Marie.

He tried not to stare, to concentrate on Gerhart instead. The detective was a trim man in his late fifties with a bony face. His blue eyes were pale and mild.

He was casually dressed in black slacks and a pale gray polo shirt that matched his hair. He looked as if he could be a professional golfer, but he was one of the highest priced investigators in Sydney.

He sat at a plain walnut desk, the surface clear except for one folder. Tapping the folder, he said, "The Whittleson murder case was botched."

Andrew straightened in his chair, dark brows drawing into a frown. "Botched? I know that. Everybody knows it."

"There was too much going on here with the APEC violence. We had over forty deaths here. Hunter Valley had one. So your Sandy Sanford fell through the cracks. The state police had other priorities."

Andrew heaved himself out of his chair and began to pace the gray carpet. "And when will they pry him out of the cracks? All they ever got were a few basic facts. He'd followed the racing trade. He'd been questioned about betting fraud—but released."

Andrew leaned with both hands on Gerhart's desk and looked the man in the eye. "That's it? The guy lured Sam to Lochlain, shot him, set a fire and framed Louisa Fairchild. Why? What was his motive? For doing *any* of it, for God's sake?"

"Calm down," Gerhart said, his voice as unemotional as a robot's. "The state police and feds are still sorting out the bombings and other violence. And the usual crime rate didn't drop. There's a huge backlog. The police system's jammed."

Andrew opened his mouth to damn the whole Australian legal process, but Gerhart raised a hand to silence him. "Phelps and I aren't *in* the police system. You pay us to find out something? We find it out—with or without their cooperation. It just takes longer without."

He pulled open a desk drawer. "Sanford's killing? We're on it. And we already have info on Sam Whittleson."

He drew out another folder and set it on his desk. "Whittleson was up to his neck in gambling debts. He'd borrowed money from some real sharks. Guys you don't stiff. But Sam couldn't pay. That may be why he was killed."

Andrew straightened up, tensing with curiosity. "Are these guys organized? Like in a syndicate?"

"The Grangers? Affirmative by rumor. Hard proof? These people always work in the shadows—proof's difficult to find. But we'll find it. We're not under the same constraints as the police. But we do have to get solid evidence. Understand?"

Andrew nodded. Gerhart and his people could work in ways

that the law couldn't. He said, "It has to be organized crime. It has to be. Too much has happened in the Valley."

"I don't deny it," Gerhart said in his bland way. "But we've got to connect the dots carefully and completely. That's why you pay us. Don't *you* try it. You—or anybody close to you. You could get hurt."

Andrew couldn't help himself. He looked at the photograph of the beautiful girl with the bobbed hair. And it seemed that, across the years, some ghostly ancestor of Marie stared back at him—a lovely girl, both strong and vulnerable.

Studying her, remembering Marie, he felt his groin tighten and his heart fill with yearning. "I don't want any more people hurt," he said.

"You keep looking at that portrait," Gerhart said without emotion. "Do you know who she is?"

Yes. She's the image of the woman I can't get out of my mind. "No," he said gruffly. "No idea."

Gerhart almost smiled. "Louise Brooks. A girl who came out of nowhere. Maybe the greatest silent screen beauty ever. That's one of the few pictures of her looking blond. It's from *The Canary Murder Case.* She was actually a brunette. Men used to take one look at her and fall in love. Can you imagine that?"

Yeah. I can imagine that. He remembered a face just as unforgettable, drawing close to his. He remembered kissing lips even more desirable. He remembered touching flesh that was real and soft and fragrant and more stirring than any image.

He dragged himself back to reality. "You think Jacko Bullock's mixed up in this?" he asked Gerhart.

Gerhart's eyes told him nothing. "People who orchestrate things like this, they're very good at staying invisible, Mr. Preston. That's how they survive. My advice to you? Watch your back. You don't know what such people might use as weapons. Be very careful."

Andrew thanked him but didn't quite believe him. He *had* been careful. He'd walked the line since being in Australia, and he'd walked it straight and narrow. He was bewitched by Marie, but he hadn't compromised her or himself.

What could Jacko or anybody else have on him?

Nothing.

But, against his will, he looked up at that haunting photograph again. And the woman from the distant past seemed to convey a message: *You're not as safe as you think. Nobody is.*

When lunch was over, Marie took a break and rode her bike, glad to have a few hours to herself. She rode aimlessly but tried to avoid a route that would take her past too much of the Koongorra fire damage.

She found herself on the curve in the road by Lake Dingo, where Louisa's land met Sam's. The grove where she'd met Andrew still stood, tall, rustling and untouched by the fire.

On impulse she dismounted the bike and chained it out of sight, behind a blackberry thicket.

She made her way down the slope and to the Hermit's Cave. She sat in the same spot where she and Andrew had rested on the checkered picnic cloth.

She vividly remembered how he'd looked that day: tall, lean, and broad-shouldered. His usual blue chambray shirt, faded jeans, well-worn boots. He looked more like a cowboy than a rising star in the Sport of Kings.

His air, sexy and electric, had warred with the impression he gave of total self-discipline. He'd radiated conflict, honor wrestling with desire.

The memory gave her a shiver deep in her stomach, and she had to admit she'd found herself the same conflict. For the first time in her life, she'd felt almost helpless with sexual longing. It had been the forbidden delight that she'd never wanted to experience, never wanted to admit was real.

But it was real, and ultimately it frightened her. Why? As long as she could remember she'd been disciplined, cautious, temperate, even puritanical. Would Andrew break all those defenses down the next time he took her in his arms?

He could. For he had truly courted her, but it was almost all by words, not touching. He'd drawn her inextricably into his mind, his emotions, his life. He treated her with more respect than any man who'd ever pursued her. He was gentle, he was attentive, and he took his time. And she felt she was learning to know him better than she had ever known another human being—except for Colette.

Chapter Thirteen

That night Andrew called Marie from his hotel room. She didn't pick up at nine or nine-thirty, so he tried again at ten. He was about to give up when she answered. "Andrew? Hi—I was just getting out of the shower when the phone rang."

He tried not to think of her stepping from the shower, naked, glistening, water sliding between her breasts and gleaming on the nipples of her pert breasts. He tried not to think of a towel wrapped around her waist, or her toned legs spangled with droplets.

"Oh," he said and thought about all those arousing images anyway.

"It's okay," she said. "I jumped into my sleeping uniform."

She'd used this phrase before, and he knew it meant sensible pajamas. He hoped the bottoms were short, showing off her legs. He hoped the top had buttons that weren't all done up, revealing a bit of cleavage. And he hoped someday to have her in no uniform at all, just her silky skin, in his arms and in his bed.

"Were you out?" he asked, his throat tight with imagining her.

"I went to The Secret Heiress with Rennie. I—well, I learned something today. I wanted to talk to him about it."

He tried to push lust out of his mind while he lay back against the pillows of the hotel bed. "Can you tell me?"

"If you'll keep it to yourself," she said. "The new woman—Bronwyn? I sort of identify with her."

"And why would that be?" he asked.

"She grew up poor. Even poorer than me. And she had only her mother. But hers wasn't as strong as mine. Bronwyn married a man named Ari Theodoros for security—or so she thought. She didn't know he was into crime until he was arrested."

"Right," Andrew said. She'd told him the bare bones of this story before, and she wasn't the kind to repeat herself without reason. "So now what's happened?"

She paused. He could almost see her thinking, the golden brows drawn together, the pretty mouth worried. "Bronwyn says she and Patrick Stafford were a couple for a long time. But he never seemed serious about making a living. So she married Ari instead."

Andrew was a bit surprised. Patrick didn't strike him as the "couple" sort. He seemed a man born to play the field. But an old flame had flickered back into his neighborhood?

"So maybe she's there to reignite the old spark?" Andrew said with a frown. "That may put him off. Theodoros lost everything when he was convicted, right? But Patrick's in line to inherit a big chunk of Louisa's estate. Look, I know you like her. But if I were him I'd be suspicious."

"I understand. But suppose she has a different motive? And it's not to marry Patrick."

Andrew smiled. Marie was acting so feminine, so caught up in the emotions of her friends. He thought it was sweet of her, and he was curious about why she sounded perplexed.

"So what *is* her motive?" he asked almost jokingly. "Just to apologize for dumping him?"

"No," Marie said in a careful voice. "She wants Patrick to acknowledge that the little boy is his son, not Ari's."

He sat up straight in bed. "Marie, doesn't that immediately

get down to money? Does she want child support? Or some kind of annuity? A permanent home at Fairchild?"

"No," she answered. "She just wants Patrick to recognize the boy. Wesley loved Ari—but now he's ashamed. Ari wasn't just arrested, he was *murdered*. She thinks it'd help her son to know the full truth, and for Patrick to take an interest in him."

Andrew was skeptical. "What does she want you to do? Plead her case to Louisa? So Patrick gets cornered into doing what Bronwyn wants? How can he even know it's his child?"

Marie's voice went cool and deliberate. "The boy's the image of Patrick. I've seen pictures of Theodoros. Short, stocky, a bulbous nose. Wesley doesn't look like him at all."

"Honey," he said, "I asked you a question. What's Bronwyn want *you* to do?"

"She just wants a confidante, that's all," Marie said defensively. "Are all men programmed alike? You're saying the same things Rennie said."

He sighed. She was smart, but even smart women could be manipulated when little kids were concerned. He pushed his forelock back from his brow. "You're right. I'm acting preprogrammed. Let's talk about something else."

"Fine," she said almost airily. "You saw your detective today. What did he say?"

"Not enough. Nobody knows what Sandy's motive was for murder and arson. But if he did it on somebody's orders, that's probably why he got killed. To keep him quiet."

"The detective—did he warn *you* to be careful?" He thought he heard fear in her question.

"Yes, honey, he did. And the same goes for anybody I care about. That means *you*. We've tried to stay under the radar. But be cautious, Marie. I don't want anything happening to you. I couldn't take it."

She said nothing in reply, and he supposed he'd startled her, filled her with foreboding.

"So," he said, keeping his tone steady, almost light, "you take care and so will I, okay?"

"Okay," she said in a small voice.

"Let's start this conversation over. What did you do today? Anything special?"

"I went back to the Hermit's Cave. I climbed down there and sat for a while. Just looking at the trees and the birds and... thinking."

"Thinking about what?" he asked.

"You. Me. Us."

His heart went into a long, uncertain tailspin. "And what did you think—about us?"

He remembered the cave, and kissing her, holding her, drawing her closer and closer—and then going too far. Which was why he'd spent the last weeks on the phone with her. And why now they were like two Victorian lovers, communicating very politely, while inside, both were afire with passion.

"I think," she said, "that we're doing the right thing. And I'm grateful to you, Andrew. For not pushing me or laying down ultimatums. For giving me some space. I think we know each other a lot better than if we—you know."

He knew. If he'd had his way and made love to her at the cave, a furtive act in a hidden place, it would have been a lust too easily satisfied with a woman he hadn't really known. And if she'd been like that, maybe he wouldn't have wanted to know much more.

"But," she said, surprising him, "I want to be with you again. Soon. Maybe not alone, yet, but at least in the open. Maybe we could start slowly. You could meet with Rennie and me at The Secret Heiress. You know, very casual."

If I'm in the same room with you, at the same table, within touching distance of you, I will not feel casual, he thought. I will feel crazy with wanting you.

"I'm seriously thinking of going back to Darwin," she said. "I told that to Reynard, but he doesn't want to accept it."

He got up and began to pace the floor, just as he'd done in Hans Gerhart's office. "I don't want you to go, either. I want to be as close to you as possible."

"We talk on a phone now. We can do that if I'm in Darwin. And you said you'd come to see me in Darwin. Or didn't you mean it?"

"Of course, I meant it," he said with feeling. "But Darwin's a long way off. At least in Hunter Valley we're only a few miles from each other. And I don't think Louisa'd have any objection to me seeing you."

"She appreciates what you've done. Even though she's pledged her support to Bullock."

She sighed, but he smiled. The old girl had sent him a fat check after the bushfire with a brusque note that it *wasn't* a campaign donation. He'd donated the money to the Laminitis Research Fund. But he suspected he'd won her acceptance of him, if not her support.

"I've actually gotten to like Louisa," Marie said with a little laugh. "She *has* gotten much less prickly since she went through all those troubles. She almost dotes on Wesley. But I know that now she's on the mend, I need to go back to my own life."

"Marie," he said, a knot in his throat, "don't rush into this. Think about it. We've had so little time together."

She was silent a moment, then said, "When *will* you be back? Soon, I hope."

"I could make it there in three days and stay maybe two nights. My schedule's getting crazier all the time, but Lord knows I want to see you."

"Yes," she said shakily. "This is getting hard to bear."

"I think of you all the time," he said earnestly. "Not just because you're beautiful. Not just because you're smart and talented and spirited. You're moral and honest and stand up for what you believe in. And I admire all those things in you."

He thought he heard her catch her breath, as if she choked back a small sob. "Hey," he teased gently. "Now it's your turn to say something nice about me."

"Okay," she said. "I'll try. You're patient and kind. You always seem to protect the people you care about. You can admit you're wrong, and you can apologize. You don't back down from your beliefs and show no fear. You face setbacks squarely, and you go on. You keep your word."

She paused and then finished. "I believe in you. And I want to keep believing in you…is that enough?"

He thought it more than enough, and it brought a great jolt of anticipation. He thought of the feel of her perfect body in his arms once again, under his hands. He thought of burying his face in the fragrant golden silk of her hair. He thought of the words she'd just said, and hope and desire flooded him.

"I think that's about as good as I could ever ask for and more than I deserve," he said, his voice low. "Sweet dreams, love. I'll come home to you soon as I can."

He hung up. She couldn't speak. She hugged her phone to her chest a moment. He'd called her "love." He'd said "I'll come back home to you."

But he'd also said she was moral and honest. She hadn't felt moral and honest since she'd arrived in Hunter Valley. The truth assailed her: he didn't really know her.

And maybe, in some terrible, cowardly way, she didn't want him to know the truth. If he discovered why she'd come to Fairchild Acres, he'd think she was greedy and deceitful, a scheming sneak. Why, oh, why, had she let Reynard talk her into this?

She needed to go back to Darwin before her impersonation was exposed. She needed to reclaim her soul and her self-respect.

Would Andrew really come to her there? If he knew the truth?

The kitchen staff was gearing up for the gala, and Francois was clearly vexed at Louisa's constant supervision—and her criticisms. Just as clearly, she was anxious about the gala; she wanted it to be perfect, and she didn't care if she achieved perfection by dancing on the aching heads of her staff.

Then, suddenly, two days before the gala, she disappeared from the kitchen, apparently distracted by something else. Francois loudly thanked God and at least half a dozen saints for keeping her away.

And Bronwyn whispered to Marie just exactly what had torn Louisa's attention from Jacko Bullock's Glorious Gala. Marie stared at her, eyes wide with shock. "How'd she take it?" she asked Bronwyn.

Bronwyn grinned. "I think she's actually happy..." then leaned and whispered in Marie's ear again.

That night, Marie went with Reynard to The Secret Heiress. They sat in the dimly lit room, and light from the candle on the table flickered over his face, making it seem changeable and phantomlike.

"Rennie," she said, "remember how I said Bronwyn told me that Wesley is Patrick Stafford's son?"

Reynard looked skeptical. "Women often pop up and make such claims when the 'father's' got money. Or, like Patrick, is *about* to get it."

"Don't be so cynical," Marie told him. "The child looks just like him. And today, Louisa found out. And she intends to recognize the boy as her great-great nephew."

Reynard swore and smacked the table so hard that his beer nearly spilled. "The Old Girl's got one foot in the grave and now heirs are coming out of the woodwork—like a swarm of bleedin' greedy termites!"

He swore again and glowered. "*You're* her only direct descendent. Who are these Johnny-come-latelys?"

Marie eyed him with mixed calm and distaste. "They're her *legitimate* heirs, Rennie."

"The kid's not," he snapped. "He's a right little bastard. If she's going to recognize any bastards, it ought to be your mother and you."

She felt her expression go cold. "That's not funny and not called for. And remember you're a member of the club yourself."

He squared his shoulders and stared at her in determination. "I talked you into coming here because it was maybe the one significant thing I'd ever be able to do for you. You've got to make your move soon. You'd best speak the truth. Before another six battalions of descendents march in."

"Oh, cool off, Rennie. I can't prove I'm related to her. And I've waited too long to speak up."

"You know about those letters she wrote from the home for unwed mothers," he challenged.

"They're locked away," she shot back. "And she may

destroy them at any time. She may not want Patrick and Megan ever to know."

"I'm so angry I could eat my own head," he grumped. "But we can't give up. I want you to get your rightful share. I owe it to my sis to see you do."

"I don't want it," Marie said, and she meant it. "I want to go home. I'll give Louisa two weeks notice—"

"And then quit? Just quit? Trot off like a scared sheep? A lily-livered coward?"

She refused to rise to the bait. "You call it cowardice. I call it conscience. As soon as the gala's over, I give my notice."

He squinted at her, his expression hard. "You may think differently by then. If you've any sense, you will." He sipped his beer, his eyes still on hers.

"I'm sorry," she told him. "I know you had my welfare in mind. But I was brought up to take care of myself. And I will."

"Ah," Rennie said sarcastically. "You see how far that's gotten me in life."

"I'm sorry," Marie repeated, and patted his rough hand. But she knew she wouldn't stake any claim about being related to Louisa. Louisa belonged only to the family she knew as hers. She was happy.

Let her be.

By the next evening, Marie didn't feel so forgiving toward Reynard. He took her, as usual, to go to The Secret Heiress, but absolutely refused to let Andrew join them when he came back

"He's bad luck on two legs," he grumbled. "Maybe you're right. Just get yourself back to Darwin and sling hash."

He got up and limped toward the restroom, muttering under his breath.

She quickly called Andrew at Lochlain to tell him Reynard was being contrary. Just the sound of his voice made her feel the prickle of magnetism between them.

He said, "It's still early. Have Reynard bring you back. We could meet later, by the gate. We'd have until midnight, at least. Is that so much to ask?"

She thought about it. He'd kept his word for weeks now. She felt closer to him than she would have believed possible. How could she refuse him such a simple request? "I'll meet you," she said.

"Then I'll be there, darlin'. In front of God and everybody."

She loved it when he sounded Southern. "I'll be there, too," she vowed.

Reynard took her home, and at precisely nine-thirty, Marie met Andrew. He drove up to the gates, got out, opened the door of Tyler's Jeep, and helped her into the passenger seat. The guard stood impassively, as if he saw nothing, but glancing back, Marie saw him pick up the phone.

Was he going to tell someone she'd gone off with Andrew? *Let him,* she thought rebelliously, her heart banging against her breastbone.

Andrew glanced in his rearview mirror. "Is he phoning somebody?"

"I think so," she said.

"Do you suppose it's about us?" he asked.

"I don't know."

He put his warm hand over her cold one. "Would it bother you?"

"I don't know that, either," she said, clutching his fingers as if they gave her strength. "Andrew...where are we going?"

"Where do you want to go? Back to The Secret Heiress?"

No, no, she thought, resisting pressing her other hand to her temple, where a vein throbbed with tension. Mrs. Tidwell would see them, and soon the whole shire would know about it, including Reynard.

"Somewhere more private," she managed to say. "Secluded."

He tossed her a smile. The moon was nearly full and silvered his features. "Still not ready to be seen in public with me?" he teased.

"Rennie's being strange," she said, holding more tightly to his hand. She told him some—but not all—of Reynard's warnings.

The smile faded and his chiseled features turned stern. "Maybe he's right."

"Let's just go someplace where we can be alone," she said. "Just you and me. That can't hurt anything."

Can it? she thought. Just a few hours with him? Alone…

He didn't speak for a moment. Then he said, "I know a place…an isolated one…"

The isolated place was on a much-neglected back road on Tyler's property. The Jeep rolled over the ruts of a cresting hill to a small promontory overlooking the Hunter River. On the edge of the promontory stood the strangest little building Marie had ever seen.

It struck her as some sort of small, wondrous ruin from another, more ancient and possibly enchanted, world. At its center was a stone arch that opened to the river and the night sky. On one side was a sort of buttress of the same stone, and on the other, what seemed to be the crumbling remains of a roofless round tower, half its second story broken away. Round windows, like empty antique portholes, punctuated the tower's crumbling first story.

The whole, unlikely structure was no wider than a fair-sized cottage, the tower too small to be lived in except by the most abstemious hermit. It was all built of some gray stone that looked like aged pewter in the moonlight.

"Wh-what is this?" she asked, turning to Andrew.

He grinned. "It goes back to the early settlements in Australia. It's a copy of what the British called a 'folly,' an imitation ruin, a decoration, pure and simple. Aristocrats had them. So did a few would-be aristocratic colonists. This is one. Come on. Take a look."

He got out, helped her from the car, and led her to the arch. She looked across the river at the land, half-ravaged by fire, beyond. She put a hand against the stone, which still held the warmth of the vanished sun.

"I've never seen such a thing," she breathed. "What's it for?"

"Amusement. Fantasy. Pleasure. And 'folly' doesn't mean something foolish, only something to make you feel happy."

She looked more closely. The tower's remaining windows were barred. She turned to Andrew questioningly.

"To keep out drifters, bushrangers," he said. "And just plain old party types."

"You can't get in?" she said in disappointment.

"No. But you can hide in its shadows."

Gently he steered her toward the central stony face of the buttress and put a hand against the wall on either side of her head. He leaned nearer and kissed her on the mouth. She felt as if she were somehow falling upward, spinning toward the stars.

His mouth was firm, hungry and seeking. Her lips parted. He raised his hands to frame her face, bringing it closer to his, deepening the kiss. Her stomach fluttered tipsily, and heat invaded her body, a heat that was powerful and tingling.

So this is what all the songs and stories are about, she thought in wonder. This *is why people in love go a little crazy.* She felt ringed round with happiness, and at its center was Andrew, touching her, his lips searching hers.

He drew back and she looked at him. The light of the moon shone on his hair, cast his face into a work of silver and shadows. His breath, coming fast, tickled her mouth.

"I was afraid you wouldn't really meet me," he said.

"I was afraid I wouldn't, either." Her voice trembled. "I wasn't sure…"

But she'd had to see him; she hadn't been able to resist. It was as if the moon and stars and darkness had drawn her here to be with him. And it felt so good, so *right,* being with him. But it also frightened her. All of heaven could look down on them, nothing hid them but the shadow of one whimsical building. They were otherwise completely in the open, vulnerable and, yes, more than a little reckless.

"If anyone comes down that road…"

He stroked her cheek with his thumb. "I doubt anyone will. And we'd hear them from far off."

"But—"

"Maybe it's time to stop worrying so much about being seen," he whispered. "I think people are starting to realize how I feel about you. And there's nothing shameful in it."

"I'm not so sure," she said, gripping his biceps more tightly. "Your campaign..."

"I can't stop being a human because of the campaign," he said, bending nearer. "I want you to be protected. But I want to be with you, too. I care about you. So much. So much."

He lowered his head and kissed her again. This time his tongue delicately explored her lips, her mouth, and her own hesitant tongue. She loved the sensations he made pulse through her, but as her desire quickened, so did her anxiety. She pulled back, and he lowered his hands, gripping her shoulders to keep her from moving away from him.

"I care for you, too," she admitted. "But what if Jacko Bullock finds out about this and uses it against you somehow? Uses it to hurt you."

"Marie, we've been discreet. More than discreet. Why not just admit we're a couple? Be open about it? It's probably *safer* to do that. If people discover we have a secret relationship, it'll seem much more suspicious. And we have so few opportunities to be together. I have to leave again tomorrow."

A knot formed in her throat, and her muscles went taut. "Just for now let's keep it secret," she whispered. "It won't be long until the campaign's over. Please. It'll be easier on *both* of us in the long run. If people know about us now, the press will go snooping. They'll find out I'm illegitimate and so was my mother. It'll be all over Jacko's papers. I don't want that for either of us."

She was pleading with him with all her might, and she felt tears stinging her eyes.

But what terrified her most was that someone would somehow discover—and make public the reason she'd come to the valley in the first place.

If that came out, she would seem deceitful and scheming, and Andrew would seem too gullible to deserve the presidency. And Louisa would again find herself and her home the object of gossip.

Confused, conflicted, she said, "Sometimes I wish I'd never come here."

"If you hadn't, I wouldn't have found you again."

He lowered his head to kiss her once more, but she turned her face away. "Being here like this is too—too difficult."

"For now, maybe. But someday, it won't be. And we'll be together. Like normal couples."

She shook her head. "We're not a normal couple."

"We will be. We'll make it happen. I'll find a way. *We'll* find a way. We'll escape."

"We can't," she said. "That's like trying to escape reality. Your campaign exists. You could compromise your whole future."

"It's not a future I want if you're not in it."

Did he mean that? Could she believe such an extravagant statement? She searched for words, but imagined that she heard a car rounding the curve and flinched.

"I don't feel safe here," she said, trying to pull away. "I'd better get back. Take me back. Please."

"Wait," he begged, not letting go. He bent to kiss her hard and with a barely restrained desperation. "One last time," he whispered. "And don't worry about the campaign—"

They stood in the untamed landscape, the strange ruin and the running river bathed in the ghostly luminescence of the moon. And his lips took hers one last, tormented time.

Chapter Fourteen

The next day was wildly hectic, the whole kitchen hustling to prepare for the night's gala for Jacko Bullock.

A caterer would arrive from Newcastle to provide and serve the main menu, but Francois was in charge of appetizers and Marie was to make the desserts, which included three varieties of Louisa's beloved Pavlovas, lime cheesecakes, lemon bites and bread pudding with a sauce of berries and rum.

Francois grumbled that he had not become a chef to play second fiddle to some ridiculous rural catering company. But although in ill humor, he labored to make the appetizers, outdoing himself with crab cakes, lobster rolls, grilled squabs, and figs stuffed with goat cheese.

"I will upstage these farmers," he muttered. "The guests will feast on my appetizers until they have no appetite for the main courses."

The party rental people had swarmed over the front lawn, setting up tents, tables, chairs, accessories, and even a stage.

Twelve huge inflated kangaroos in digger hats were staked,

massively bobbing, on either side of the drive. Twelve poles flew the flags of the Australian states and territories.

"I've never seen so much fuss," Marie said, shaking her head.

"She used to do things even more elaborately," said Mrs. Lipton. "And she'd arrive in a gloriously colored hot air balloon—'descending like a goddess from the sky,' she liked to say."

Marie sighed. She and the rest of the kitchen staff would have to stand by during the gala, just in case there was a missing server, or an emergency of any sort.

She had to admit the gala would be impressive, but it also struck her as a tremendous expenditure for such a dubious guest of honor.

The evening was nearly half over, but people kept revisiting the dessert buffet. Mrs. Lipton asked Marie to get the last two Pavlovas out of the fridge. "Your work is a great success," she whispered to Marie. "Miss will be pleased."

On the stage, a group of musicians played old standards, and the moon had risen and seemed suspended over their heads as if it were a prop. Marie got out the last of the Pavlovas and set them on the buffet table, then took the emptied serving dishes to return to the kitchen.

She had sidestep a clown passing out buttons and balloons that said Jacko For President. A group of laughing people made her detour again, until she felt boxed in between the champagne tent and the wine tent.

"Ha," a hearty voice boomed in her ear. "Louisa told me that you're the little sheila who made these desserts. Fair dinkum! I ought to steal you for my own. How about it, blondie?"

"No," Marie said without looking at him. She smelled gin on his breath and felt him moving close to her, far too close.

"Oh, don't get uppity," he laughed. "I know more about you than you think. Used to work at the Scepter, didn't you? Heard you came down this way. Got a boyfriend?"

He patted her bottom and gave one hip a squeeze.

Marie was tired, she had serious matters on her mind, and she didn't tolerate men grabbing her. She reacted automatically and turned, bringing down her foot as hard as she could on the man's instep.

"Keep your hands to yourself," she ordered from between clenched teeth.

People nearby gasped. She looked up at the man and realized with horror that he was Jacko Bullock. He was a big man, widely built and elegantly dressed. But no fine clothing could disguise his basic coarseness. Or his anger.

His faced reddened in rage and pain. "Who do you think you are?" he demanded and called her a nasty name.

It was a name so vulgar that her temper rose again, eclipsing any chance that she'd apologize. "And who do you think *you* are?" she shot back.

A woman's voice, shrill and sharp, rang out. "Marie!"

Marie blinked and saw Louisa coming toward them. Obviously, she'd witnessed the whole sorry scene. "Marie," she said again, "get back to the kitchen—now!"

Jacko looked at Louisa and gave her a boyish smile. "I just complimented her. Gave her a little pat of appreciation. She misinterpreted it."

"I did *not*," Marie retorted, inflamed by his lie.

"Marie, I told you to go," Louisa said fiercely.

As Marie stalked away, she heard Jacko say, "I shouldn't have tried to be nice to the little skank. I hear she's had half the blokes in Darwin."

Her face burned at the accusation and her temper flared.

What's he mean? she wondered in panic. *Half the blokes in Darwin—what a filthy thing to say.* She moved fast, and the music and the murmur of the crowd drowned out any more of the conversation. But gossip moved faster than she did. By the time she made her way to the kitchen, the story of her outburst had already reached Mrs. Lipton.

She seized Marie by the arm, her eyes wide. "I just heard that you stamped on Jacko Bullock's foot," she said. "Is it true?"

"Well…yes," Marie managed to say. "But I didn't know it was his foot. A man grabbed me and I just…reacted. Louisa saw. I'll probably lose my job."

What, she wondered again, had Jacko meant about "half of Darwin" having had her? How could he even remember a nobody like her from the Scepter? Was it because she'd rebuffed him before? The night she'd been tempted to pour the drink on his head?

She remembered how powerful Jacko was. And although the night was warm, she shivered.

When the evening was over, the staff was exhausted and Francois was still fuming.

"I hope Miss is happy," Marie said. "She honored Bullock as if he were a king. I don't know why she thinks so much of him."

"I'm not sure that she does anymore," Mrs. Lipton said, grim-faced. "She's been increasingly disillusioned by him."

Marie blinked in surprise. "She has?"

"He's taken her too much for granted. And Miss doesn't like it that he never spoke up for her when she was in the hospital. All he said was 'Unlike Andrew Preston, I'm not going to use Miss Fairchild's misfortune for publicity. The law will equitably solve the problem, and I have word her condition is excellent.'"

"That's *all he said?*" Marie asked in disbelief. "Why didn't she cancel the gala?"

"Perhaps she didn't want to go back on a promise. Perhaps she hated to admit she was wrong about him. Perhaps she was giving him one last chance. Who knows?"

Marie shook her head in confusion. "This situation gets too tangled for me. I keep thinking I ought to resign and go home."

"Not right now," said Mrs. Lipton, her smile vanishing. "She's going to want you around for a while. Francois just went to his room to pack. He's leaving. She hurt his pride."

"Francois? No!" Marie exclaimed, her hand flying to her mouth in shock.

"Yes. I'm sorry, too. But Miss will want you to stay. At least until she can find a satisfactory replacement. Which will be difficult, my dear. Very difficult indeed. For I've heard her say myself that you're irreplaceable."

"Me?" Marie asked in disbelief. "She said that about *me?*"

Mrs. Lipton nodded and smiled. "I think she'd like to keep you on for good."

Marie was flooded by confused emotions. Louisa had come to like her? How surprising. How strangely touching. And how ironic. They were becoming attached to each other.

All the more reason to leave. Soon.

Feeney sat on his bed, half watching a horror movie on television while he filed the serial number off a gun.

The move was a silly thing about mutant venomous spiders taking over an American town and killing just about everybody. The spiders would bite their prey by hiding in ingenious places like football helmets and toilet bowls. Feeney admired their inventiveness.

His phone rang and he sighed. He stopped the TV with the remote and answered. The caller ID said simply Unknown.

"Feeney here," he said without enthusiasm.

"This is Henry Tudor," said Jacko. He thought by using the names of different kings of England, he would throw off anyone eavesdropping.

Feeney sighed. He knew the conversation couldn't be taped. "Are you still in Hunter Valley?"

"No," Jacko said, his voice sullen. "I flew back to Sydney. I left the old bat's party early."

"I thought it was for you," Feeney said out of the side of his mouth. He lit a cigarette.

"Her idea of a party and mine are different. Besides, somebody tried to cause a scene." There was a pause, then Jacko said, "Is Andrew Preston still interested in that tart from Darwin? That Lafayette tart?"

Feeney sat up straighter. "Affirmative. But he ain't getting any."

"Would he like to?"

"Of course." Feeney laughed his scratchy laugh.

"He sees her, though?" Jacko persisted.

"Not often. For a little while tonight. It's heating up, though, I can tell."

"I'm tired of waiting," Jacko said, sounding petulant. "Take him down."

"Take. Him. Down," repeated Feeney, slowly and sarcastically. "All we have are a few pictures."

"Take him down, dammit," Jacko ordered. "And use her. Do you know when they're going to see each other next?"

"Yeah. If they arrange it by phone. But what exactly do you mean, use *her?*"

"The extreme method. Like we talked about. She slips out to meet him, slips back in, right? Next time she does—be there."

Feeney paused. "You-know-who won't like it."

"Won't like it? So what's he gonna do? Anybody can be made dead, and he knows it," growled Jacko. "I mean it. I want the Preston bastard ruined. Use her. I want them both taken down. ASAP. Got it?"

"Got it," Feeney said, stifling a sigh.

"You have that man in Darwin working on some testimonials for me?" Jacko asked. "Like you said?"

"Talked to him an hour ago. He's probably got enough. Eight. I'd like a few more. He can get them in another day or two."

"Eight's plenty. Go with eight if a chance comes up. I'm tired of waiting."

Then Jacko hung up. Feeney swore. He turned his movie back on and considered making himself a glass of absinthe. Why was Jacko suddenly so hot to get the little blond cook? She must have gotten Jacko's goat somehow.

Shame. She was a right pretty little thing. Oh, well. It had to be some woman, somewhere.

Why not her?

He blew a smoke ring.

PART FOUR

**Australia, The Hunter Valley
May**

Chapter Fifteen

The next morning, Louisa called Marie to her sitting room. The old woman was in a lovely dressing gown, her hair pulled back into its usual bun, but she looked worn from the long night at the gala.

"Sit down, my girl," she said with a restless gesture. Her breakfast, untouched, still sat on the coffee table.

Marie did as she asked. "Your breakfast didn't suit you, Miss?"

"Nothing suits me," Louisa said. "And I suppose you've heard Francois left, the pompous ass. I'm temporarily promoting you to head cook. If your work is satisfactory, the position will be yours permanently."

Panic swept Marie. "I can't stay on permanently," she said. "I want to go back to Darwin soon. A new semester's starting. And I miss home."

Louisa eyed her balefully. "I haven't mentioned your salary." Then she named a monthly sum that Marie found astonishing. It was three times what she earned with tips at the Scepter. *And* her room and board here were free.

"Don't argue with me," Louisa said wearily. "I'm sick of conflict and disappointment. Jacko Bullock hardly raised a finger in my defense. I kept my word to him last night, and now he's slobbering on me like a fawning dog. Promising all sorts of things. Surprising information. Revelations. Assurances that he kept quiet on purpose—for my best interests."

Marie's nerves vibrated. *Revelations? Surprises? Did that mean things damaging to Andrew?* But she said nothing.

Louisa shot her a measuring glance. "But what are my best interests at this point? I'm tired of power games. I thought I never would be—they were fun. But I am. Tired, tired, tired. And I have a bit of a family now. Megan, Patrick, little Wesley. I have my home and my horses and my dogs. Perhaps that's enough."

Marie stared at her, wondering if Louisa meant it. "It sounds as if it should be enough," she murmured.

Louisa raised a thin eyebrow. "Should it? And you'll oblige an old woman by staying for a while? To tide me over in this most troublesome time? Till the end of May, at least? Would you?"

Marie swallowed hard. "Three or four weeks more, Miss? I—I suppose. Yes. And I really don't want to seem ungrateful to you. But then I *must* be back in Darwin."

Louisa gave a harsh sigh. "As you wish, Marie. You're a very stubborn girl, aren't you?"

Marie couldn't restrain a one-cornered smile. "It runs in the family, Miss."

Louisa smiled wryly in return. "Does it? Oh, one more thing. About Jacko Bullock's foot?"

Marie stiffened, suddenly wary. "Yes, Miss?"

"You should have stomped harder. Broken the bastard's arch. You lack true wrath. Work on it. You might need it some day. You may go now, my girl."

Andrew phoned that night from Adelaide. "I've got good news and bad news. The good news is that Darci's found a weak spot in Bullock's strategy. He's not going to Singapore, Malaysia, or New Zealand at all—he's blowing them off completely. He's convinced they're not important enough. He's sure that Australia alone will decide the election."

"Do they vote the same day?" Marie asked, still bewildered by the complexity of an international election.

"Yes. The bad news is Darci's arranged for me to head that way pronto. Leaving tomorrow. I'll be gone at least a week and a half. But then I'll be back, concentrating on Hunter Valley. I'll be near you again."

Her stomach knotted in conflict. She didn't want him to go away for another long stint. But when he was away, so was temptation. She wouldn't let herself be lured to do something foolish. She *wanted* to fall into his arms again—but only when he was free from the election.

And when she was free of Hunter Valley and the long shadow of Louisa Fairchild.

Marie blinked hard. "Come back soon," she said in a shaky voice.

"I will," he promised. "I'll come back. And we'll find a place where we can just be two people in love. Because I do love you, Marie."

"I—love you, too," she managed to say.

To be able to say such a thing seemed truly a miracle, a gift from heaven.

Andrew phoned her every night. Their talks were growing more intimate, and he made more allusions about life together after the election. Every day, he sent her notes with news, jokes, reminiscences, musings—and endearments.

"I should warn you," he wrote in one. "My great-grandfather raised horses in Ireland. But he also—I did warn you—wrote poetry. He published a volume. A woman in London read it and wrote to him. He wrote back. It got intense. He proposed by mail. She accepted by mail. She came to Ireland with everything she could pack in two suitcases.

"He was waiting for her at the train station. He already had the wedding license in his pocket. He'd got it an hour before he ever saw her face. They were happy together for sixty-two years.

"Sixty-two years," he repeated. "If you ever have any doubts, think of that. And believe."

* * *

She kept musing on this, and later asked Bronwyn, "Do you think people can fall in love long distance?"

Bronwyn laughed. "Oh, Marie, get real—look at all the Internet romances in the world! Think of the people who used to fall in love just by exchanging letters—it happens all the time."

"I—I'm not so sure," Marie mused.

"Look," Bronwyn told her. "Somebody said that in love there are two things, bodies and words. Too many people forget about the words. Without the words, you've only got lust."

Hmm, thought Marie, maybe. Just maybe.

But then, Bronwyn had become an optimist. She had a new job as fitness director for Fairchild Acres. More importantly, she and Patrick had fallen in love again, he loved and accepted Wesley as his child, a marriage was in the offing, and Louisa's little family was becoming more tightly knit. Louisa herself seemed happier, although her attitude could still be critical, her tongue sharp.

But with Andrew gone, Marie's days were focused mostly on his calls and e-mails. He made her smile, laugh, and often he made her think.

"Jacko's philosophy is that he wants no change at all," he told her. "I'm with the philosopher who said, 'Everything flows and nothing stays… You can't step twice into the same river.' The need for change is rustling through Australia, through the world. And if we don't apply new remedies, we have to expect new evils.

"As for you, my honey child, my darlin' and my dear, I'm *east* of you right now, and it's drizzling and gray in Auckland. But I found a poem that made me think of you. Here goes—

"Western Wind, when wilt thou blow?
The small rain down can rain,
But, oh! That my love were in my arms
And I in my bed again."

Marie's heart jumped in both excitement and fear. He'd never said anything so explicit before… *That my love were in my arms/And I in my bed again.*

Andrew had laughed and said, "Tomorrow Ollie and I ride the western wind back to you. You won't make my poetic hopes crash and burn will you? Not after I went to all the work to memorize four whole lines…"

Marie shook her head in wonder. A kind, idealistic, thinking man who could quote poetry and crack jokes—and who looked good with his shirt off. Could she ask for more?

She ached to be with him.

"I'll be back in Lochlain tomorrow evening," he said. "I'd love to see you, be with you."

"I'm not sure that's wise at this point," she hedged.

"Will you at least consider it?" he asked. "There's a place I'd like to take you. Just the two of us. Say you'll at least think about it."

"I—I'll think about it," she said, her throat tight.

"Promise?" he teased.

"I promise to *think* about it," she said.

She wanted with all her being to be with him, to be in his arms, to shut out the rest of the world except for the two of them. But not here. Not tomorrow.

Soon the election would be over and she would be home again in Darwin. They would be free to be themselves again. Would she ever tell him about Louisa?

She knew that she must, to be honest. And that would be the hardest thing—telling him what had made her come here.

All that could save her sense of honor was that someday—far distant from here and now, she'd find the courage to tell him the facts—she owed him that. He deserved the truth.

Louisa, though, was different. The best gift Marie could give Louisa was to leave her in peace, satisfied with the family she'd finally gathered around her.

Marie could go back to her own world, having learned her grandmother, for all her prickliness, was a decent woman. Louisa had finally given Marie respect for who and what she was, not for her bloodlines, not her kinship.

And Louisa's respect, to Marie, was worth far more than Louisa's money.

As for Andrew, she must be honest. If he could not forgive her, it would be the price she'd pay.

Marie felt at peace with her decision until the next day. Reynard called unexpectedly right before luncheon.

"Are you alone?" he asked.

She glanced about the kitchen. Helena was mopping the counters, while the new clean-up girl, Fiona, rinsed the cooking utensils.

"I'll step outside." She slipped out the back door and stood staring at the stables and the sleek horses in the nearest paddock. She saw Louisa introducing Wesley to a new filly, Looking for Trouble.

"Yes?" Marie said.

"I need to see you tonight." Reynard's voice was tight with tension. "I'll pick you up at seven-thirty. And we *won't* go to The Secret Heiress. There's a pub outside Pepper Flats called Walkabout."

"Rennie, what's this about?"

"Something's wrong. Somebody's watching you. They're onto something. I've got a plane ticket waiting for you at the airport in Newcastle. You need to get out of here. You go first thing tomorrow."

The world seemed to go dim and sway before Marie's eyes. The sky turned from blue to gray, the horses lost their sheen, and Wesley and Louisa turned into monochromatic, shimmering figures.

"Reynard," she said in disbelief, "what's happening? I can't just up and leave. I promised Louisa—"

"It doesn't bloody matter what you promised," he retorted. "Do as I say, for once. You're about to get into big trouble, so for your own damned good get ready to disappear—fast."

She couldn't reply. Her voice choked in her throat as she struggled to grasp what he said. Did somebody suspect her relationship to Louisa? "What kind of trouble—" she began.

He cut her off. "This may blow the whole Louisa scheme to hell, but there's no choice."

"Scheme?" she echoed, repelled. "It's a *scheme* now, is it? No more high-minded talk about a quest for truth for Mama's sake or healing the past or—"

"I'll pick you up at seven-thirty," he told her. "Maybe it's still possible to repair this. Maybe. But you have to do what I say. Don't argue."

She shook her head, trying to clear her confusion. "You want me to go back to Darwin?"

"No. I'll tell you where to go."

"But why should I—"

"Don't ask questions," he snapped. "And as for Andrew Preston? I heard he'll be back in town tonight. I've warned you and warned you to stay clear of him. Don't even think about talking to him. That's an order."

"Rennie, this is intolera—"

"Don't argue," he said, interrupting. "I'll give you your instructions tonight. After that, just do the hell what I say."

Never before had he spoken to her this way. He no longer sounded like the Rennie she knew and loved. He seemed a stranger—a bullying, dangerous stranger.

"Rennie," she said, ready to argue with him, but he interrupted her again.

"Seven-thirty," he said. "And do *exactly* as I say."

Before she could protest again, he hung up.

Marie felt queasy as she stepped back into the kitchen. What was wrong, and why was Reynard acting this way? Leave Fairchild Acres? As fast as possible? Did he expect her to run away without explanation? It would make her seem like a fugitive, fleeing in guilt. But she'd done nothing wrong. Not really—or had she? She'd come here without telling the full truth.

A small, cold voice inside reminded her that Louisa was not just wealthy, but fabulously wealthy. Could someone suspect Marie of trying to exploit an old woman by fraud or blackmail or extortion?

Helena looked up. "Are you all right, Marie? You're pale. Are you coming down with something?"

"I—I don't feel too well," Marie stammered. It wasn't a lie. "If you don't mind, I'd like to go to my room for a while. Don't worry. I'll be back to help with supper."

"Don't push yourself," Helena warned. "You really do look shaky."

Shaky didn't begin to describe it. Her knees felt like jelly beneath her, and when Wesley and Louisa waved at her, she forced herself to wave back, but the motion was automatic, almost without her volition or even awareness.

She went to her room and sat, stunned, on the narrow bed. Somebody *watching* her? Who? Reynard wanted to send her away as fast as possible, but not to Darwin? Then where? And why?

And Reynard demanded that she not so much as talk to Andrew. Did whoever was watching her know about Andrew, too?

But she *had* to speak to him—she couldn't just disappear without a word.

What if somebody actually did expose her relationship to Louisa? And in exposing her made Andrew seem a dolt, caught in the snares of a backwater con artist? It would deal his campaign a terrible blow. He'd seem rash, easily fooled, a man of inexperience and flawed judgement.

And what would he think of her when he knew? Only one thing—that she was a plotting, opportunistic little hustler, lying to Louisa, lying to him, playing on both of them for her own gain. He'd despise her.

And then it struck her that no matter what Reynard said, at least she could see Andrew one more time. She could have one last meeting with him before everything went wrong. She glanced at her watch. He was due back at Lochlain this evening.

Her mind raced. Perhaps she'd never had a chance with him, but now she was certain to lose him forever. And she knew what she wanted to do. It was wrong, but she'd been so disciplined, so restrained for such a long time. She would never have another chance.

Her hands unsteady, she took her phone from her pocket and

dialed his number, her heart beating so wildly that her whole body shook. She got only a recording inviting her to leave a message.

She fought to keep her voice normal. "Andrew, I—I've changed my mind about some things. I need to talk to you as soon as possible. I have to meet Rennie at seven-thirty, but afterward, well, we can see…if you want…because…"

She couldn't go on. Did she suddenly seem too eager? Too erratic and flighty and unpredictable? Did she sound like a temptress, issuing a clear invitation? Or a tease playing games? Or a naive dunce?

"Anyway," she finished lamely, "I'd appreciate it if you'd call. I won't have my phone on while I'm with Rennie. But afterward…if you want…to talk? Or…meet…"

She hung up, feeling foolish, frightened and out of her depth.

Reynard took her to a small, dingy tavern outside of Pepper Flats. They sat at the farthest corner of the bar. His mood was dark, and hers was bleak.

"All right. Tell me what's happening," Marie said. "Explain. *Please.*" She let her wine sit, untouched.

Reynard hunched more crankily over his schooner of beer. "I can't explain it. Not yet. But it's true. You're being watched. *Investigated.* Somebody's gathering information on you. Not all of it true information, either."

Her stomach twisted in anxiety. "Me? Why? How do you know?"

"I was told."

She stared at him dazedly. "Who told you?"

"It doesn't matter. Tomorrow, I'm picking you up at six in the morning. I'll take you to the Newcastle airport. I've got a ticket reserved for you. To Perth."

Her jaw dropped. "Perth? That's the other side of the *continent.* I don't know anyone in Perth. Wh-what am I supposed to do in Perth, for God's sake?"

"A bloke'll meet you there. His name is Jermaine Kopu. He's a Maori, very tall with a moko—a tattoo on his face. A kind of blue swirl near his right eye. He's missing the little finger on his left hand. He's a good man. He'll take you someplace safe. Until it's all right to go back to Darwin."

A feeling of unreality engulfed her. "Someplace safe? Until it's all right to go back? What are you *talking* about?"

"Here," he said, handing her a folded sheet of paper. "It came this morning."

She opened it and saw a letter, a computer printout. It had no date and no return address and no signature. Silently, her chest tight, she read it:

We know about you and your niece and Louisa Fairchild. Also your niece's messing with Andrew Preston. You're playing a dangerous game, and it's going to blow up in your faces.

Get her out of Hunter Valley and keep her out. You're going to get her hurt. Better move along yourself. Your welcome's worn out, bugger.

She gazed at him in numb disbelief. "Who sent this? And why? If they're planning something, why warn us? And why send it to *you?* What's going on here?"

"Who? I don't know," Reynard said in disgust. "Why? I don't know. Why me? I don't know that, either. I suspect that new bartender at The Secret Heiress. I was leery of him from the start."

"But why would anybody threaten *me?*" she demanded.

"Louisa's money?" he challenged sarcastically. "Maybe somebody doesn't want another heir showing up."

"Like who?"

He cocked his head and looked cynical. "Megan Stafford? Her brother? Your good friend Bronwyn, wanting her kid to get his full share? The woman was *married* to a criminal. Don't tell me she doesn't have a crooked friend or two."

"I can't believe that," she retorted.

"Then don't," Reynard shot back. "Or maybe it's about Preston. His people protecting him. I don't know. But I *always* warned you to stay away from him. I told you he could hurt you.

He only wants one thing from you, and if he gets it, he'll paint you as the bloody little tart."

She glared at him in angry incomprehension.

"Marie, I've tried to help you. With all my heart I have. But we've got to pull back. You need to go. Leave a note for Louisa— tell her something, anything. Except the truth. And in the name of all that's holy, stay away from Preston. I'll soon be on my way, too, and in touch later through Jermaine."

She held his stare, defiance in her eyes. "I was a fool to let you get me into this," she said bitterly.

"Yes," he said, his expression turning cold. "You were. And so was I, to think you could handle it. But it's almost over. Maybe completely. Maybe not. We'll see."

He drove her back to Fairchild Acres. She couldn't bring herself to speak to him except to ask him to stop at a pharmacy so she could buy a bottle of aspirin. He did so, looking both resentful and righteous.

He let her out at the gate to Fairchild Acres. "I've done everything out of love for you," he said in a harsh, low voice. "Maybe eventually you can approach Louisa, humble and contrite like. Work out a story. Be able to come up with answers to what she might ask."

"I'll answer to my own conscience and nothing else," she said coolly. She got out and slammed the door.

"I'm the best friend you've got in the world, Marie," he called after her.

She didn't answer him.

She walked into her room, turned her mobile phone back on, and it rang, almost immediately.

"Marie," said Andrew. "I've been trying to get you. God, it's good to be back, to be near you again."

In truth, he sounded happy, and suddenly she was, too, even though she knew the emotion couldn't last. His voice dropped, sounding more Southern than usual.

"Did you think about it?" he asked. "About tonight? About being together?"

"Yes." The word came out almost as a whisper. "It seems so long since I've seen you."

Since I've touched you, she thought. She could think of nothing more to say except, "That is, if—if you want to."

For an interminable few seconds, he was silent. Had she been too forward? And had she any right to ask this of him?

But when he spoke, he said, "There's nothing I'd want more. Nothing. But I can't believe it. Don't, whatever you do, change your mind."

"I won't," she promised. *Right or wrong, I won't.*

They made arrangements to meet at nine-thirty, near the grove by the Hermit's Cave.

She wanted to tell him about Louisa. But not tonight. She wanted to be with him just this one night, without worrying endlessly about the mistakes of the past or the uncertainty of the future.

Feeney had switched on the recording device as soon as the buzz and the flashing green light indicated that Preston was calling. He had to turn off his video again, put the listening device in his ear.

He almost smiled. It was Preston, all right, calling the blonde. Making plans to meet. They said when. They said where. She'd promised to come. He listened to their goodbyes and smiled bitterly. He watched the red light that said the machine was recording it all.

And when they were through, he switched it off. He looked around this cramped, claustrophobic little room in the middle of nowhere and thought, *I'm gonna be out of here finally. Goodbye and good riddance.*

He flipped open his mobile phone and dialed a number. "Chalk," he said. "It's going to happen tonight. They're meeting. She'll go out. She won't come back. Get your mate. Do it."

He listened a moment, his face impassive. "If that happens, kill him, too, but make it seem he just disappeared. Call when you're finished."

Almost over. Almost free. He reached for the absinthe bottle.

Chapter Sixteen

A half hour after Marie had said goodbye to Andrew, she was dressed and feeling reckless and desperate. She wore her green outfit from the thrift store in Scone, the shimmering green top and shorts. She put her black pumps into her backpack along with the folded green skirt that matched her outfit.

She felt like a foolish-looking Martian, green and sparkly and helmeted, wearing her old sneakers, slipping across the grounds until she could mount her bike and speed over the road through the pastureland. When she saw the white fence near the grove, her pulse sped wildly, and her conscience warned her that she shouldn't do this.

But she was shaken and felt as if part of her life was ending forever. If she did not spend one night—one short night—with Andrew, then someday she would be sitting in a nursing home, and her greatest regret would be never having been with him, even once.

He was waiting for her. He crossed the road as she took off her helmet. He leaned over the fence, pulled her to him and kissed her so long and hard that he dazzled her senses, made her see drunkenly dancing stars. "Lord, it's good to hold you," he said against her lips. "I've dreamed of this."

She raised her hands to frame his face. "Andrew, I'm scared, but I want to be with you. And I want to go out of town. Can we? Please?"

"Of course, whatever you want. Come on, let me get the bike over the fence. And then we'll get you through."

She slipped through the fence and they ran across the road to a truck she thought belonged to Daniel Whittleson. "You borrowed a different truck?"

"Yes," he said. I thought we could stay under the radar better. He hoisted the bike into the truck bed. "Ready?"

"Almost." She'd opened her backpack, and was fastening the green skirt around her waist. She slipped off her shorts and tennis shoes and put on her black pumps. She slung the backpack onto the floor of the front seat. "Ready," she said.

He stared at her, as if fascinated. "Did you just turn into Cinderella?"

"No. I guess this is my Going Out uniform. It's new. New to me anyway. So I'll call it my Going Out Uniform."

He shook his head and smiled. "You're either the strangest woman I've ever met. Or the most sensible. Or maybe both. You're certainly unique."

He helped her into the truck, and her elbow tingled where he touched her. He got in beside her. "There's a nice little inn, very private over at Banksia Springs. A good restaurant. Want to go there?"

An inn, she thought. *Yes. That's what I want. God forgive me, but that's what I want.*

"Sounds perfect," she said. "Now tell me about Singapore and Malaysia and New Zealand."

"I had to have a translator in Singapore and Malaysia. I wish you'd been there. You can speak the languages, can't you?"

"Yes. Enough to get by." Darwin was the most multicultural city in Australia. She could speak French, Chinese, several Southeast Asian languages, Spanish and a bit of Korean.

Perhaps the language she could no longer speak was the truth.

She stared at his profile. "How did the trips go?"

"Well, I think. Especially New Zealand. I can't believe Jacko's ignoring it. Maybe he's so arrogant he thinks he's got it tied up. And maybe he's right. But they seemed receptive."

All the way to Banksia Springs, she kept the conversation focused on his travels. When they arrived, the restaurant was brightly lit, the inn nearly dark. He parked the truck.

"Have you eaten? Darci forced a shark fillet and yams down me. How about a glass of wine and whatever you want? I think I'll just have a drink and a light dessert."

"Me, too," she said, then paused. "And then—I'd like to check into the inn."

His expression went blank, and he studied her by the golden light radiating from the building. At last he said, "Do you mean that? You're sure?"

"Yes. I mean it. I've thought hard about it. I'm sure. I want to be with you—that way."

He shook his head in wonder. "But I thought—"

"I turn in my notice tomorrow. I need to leave. It's time."

He frowned. "I thought Louisa wanted you to stay longer. That *you* wanted to stay longer. Tomorrow?"

"Yes. It's time for me to go."

"Back to Darwin?"

She said nothing. She made a motion something like a nod. How could she explain about Perth when she couldn't understand it herself?

"Why?" he asked with feeling. "Why so suddenly? I don't understand. I don't think I've ever understood what's going on between you and Louisa."

"I don't completely understand it myself," she said. "If it bothers you, my leaving so suddenly, and you don't want to do this, be with me…" she began.

He leaned nearer. He kissed her. "I want this. More than anything in the world. But I need to drive back, get a condom…. I would never want you to—you know."

"I bought a package," she said, hoping he couldn't see her blush. She hadn't bought aspirin when Reynard stopped at the pharmacy.

She took a deep breath. "I don't want to be a third generation unwed mother. And I have to warn you. I'm not very experienced. I—well, I'm just not."

He leaned near again, took her chin between his thumb and forefinger. "You're the most mysterious creature in the world. I'll be careful with you, Marie. I'll be gentle. I promise."

"I know you will," she said, looking into his eyes. "And now I think that maybe I don't need the wine."

"I don't want any, either," he said. "I'll check us in. You stay here. I don't think anybody's around who could see us, but we'll just park in back and go straight to the room."

"Maybe that would be safest," she said, her voice almost a whisper.

He left and she sat alone, the restaurant's windows glowing with amber in the vast darkness surrounding it. *We should be safe here,* she thought. *I wouldn't put him at risk for anything. I love him. And this may be the last night that he'll ever think that he loves me.*

Was this how Louisa had felt all those years ago, yielding? How her mother had felt?

Lost in her own thoughts, she did not notice they had been followed, stealthily and expertly. Two men were parked too far away for her to see. But they saw her. And they'd seen Andrew get out and go inside.

Their cameras were already snapping.

Once inside their room, she and Andrew stood for a moment, staring at each other. He looked her up and down, then his gaze fastened on hers. "You're more beautiful than I've ever seen you."

He paused but kept staring at her as if hypnotized. "You look like a girl in a dream. A very beautiful dream."

She raised her eyes to his, too filled with emotion to speak.

He took a step closer to her. "You were right about me. I was trying so hard to be flawless I was coming across like a robot to some people. But you made me feel human again. I've felt different since knowing you. I've acted different. Like speaking out for Louisa. Being more open. Maybe that sounds crazy, but it's true."

"If I helped at all, I'm glad," she said. She was so tense that every muscle in her body felt taut. She didn't know what she was supposed to say or do now that they were in this room with its large, satin-quilted bed.

It wasn't simply a large bed; it was immense. The moss-colored quilt and pale yellow sheets were turned down, ready for them. Only two small lamps were on, sitting at each end of the dresser. Their glass was amber colored and knobby, and they cast a softly dappled gold light in the dim room.

He moved closer still. "Why am I talking like a political nerd? I liked you the first time I saw you. When you stamped that lout's foot. I thought, She's beautiful and fearless, the kind of woman I always wanted to find. And then you showed up at Fairchild Acres. It seemed like a sign."

He put his hands on her shoulders, firmly, possessively. "I lost the charm. You found it. That seemed like another sign. I found out what the charm is," he said, his voice lower, softer. "A man in the airport in Sydney told me. This morning, in fact. He's an art professor. It's a love charm. I got it about eight hours before I saw you at the Scepter. And that seems like the most important sign of all."

He reached inside the open collar of his blue shirt and drew it out. "Here," he murmured. "Will you wear it for me?"

"I shouldn't," she tried to protest. But he took it and placed it over her head so the wooden bird lay between her breasts. He bent and kissed her until she felt her will power go winging out of her body as if the bird bore it away.

Again, she knew that what she was doing was wrong, but she couldn't stop herself. She rose up on her toes to kiss him back— he was so deliciously tall—and she wrapped her arms around his neck to bring his face closer to hers, to press their mouths into the most intimate union possible.

Their lips demanded, they tempted and teased. Andrew and she took turns searching, caressing, nuzzling and ravaging. Marie felt faint with wanting him.

He seemed as swept away as she did. He scooped her up so swiftly that she lost a shoe, and then kicked the other off. He carried her to the bed and stood her beside it. "Can I undress you?" he asked, his voice uneven.

She nodded, closing her eyes to keep from swaying at his touch. He undid the skirt, and it floated silkily down past her knees. Urgent yet gentle, he undid the green buttons of her blouse, and it, too, fell away, soft as gossamer.

She shivered as he undid her bra, and shivered harder as he eased it from her body and the room's cool air touched her breasts.

He stood back and admired her, a dazed half smile on his face. "No surprise. You're loveliest with no uniform at all. Undo my shirt, Marie."

With trembling fingers she unbuttoned the blue shirt until a long, vertical strip of his bronzed torso was visible. He, too, kicked off his shoes, snatched off his socks. He straightened up and said, "Unbuckle my belt—please."

She could already see the bulge of his arousal, and taking a deep breath, she undid the brass buckle. He took her hand and guided it to his zipper. None of this now seemed unnatural to her. One act flowed into the next, propelled by the most ancient of needs, the strongest of urges.

He stepped out of his slacks and she saw he had no underwear on. She looked at him in surprise, but also in pleasure. He was excited and erect—for her. He leaned and kissed her breasts, and at the same time placed her hand around his upright member. It was both hard and soft, the tip of it like damp velvet.

He drew away a moment to ease down her panties and let her step out of them. He began touching her where no man had touched her before. He kissed and suckled her nipples. He drew her to the bed, lay down with her and kissed and caressed her most secret places.

Something like liquid fire flowed through her system, and suddenly there was no such thing as wrong. There was only Andrew.

As he entered her he said, "I love you, Marie."

"I love you, too," she breathed. And then they ceased being two people and became one complete being.

In the early-morning hours, she awakened, drowsily happily. They slept curled together, one of Andrew's arms draped over her. She felt the reassuring hardness of his muscles, the warmth of his long body. He smelled of cologne, fresh sweat and sex, and next to her ear, his breath was soft and even.

So this is what it's like, she thought, nestling closer to him. *This is how it can be for people...*

She wanted to turn and kiss him, to make love with him again, but a grim realization pierced her rush of affection for him. This was also how it would never be again between them.

Last night he'd said he loved her. He'd been innocent of knowing who she really was and why she'd come to the Valley.

Once, she'd hoped that he would understand. Now she wasn't so sure. She'd hidden the truth from him so long and was still hiding it. He was a man in the public eye, and she was a woman who'd compromised herself repeatedly.

She fingered the charm around her neck. If the truth about her came out, rumors would sprout and grow like a tangle of malevolent vines. Her head and heart ached at the thought of what people would say about all of it.

She'd be seen as a gold digger twice over, after Louisa's money and Andrew's, too. She'd allowed herself one night with Andrew—a night still cloaked in half-truths and secret motives.

She shouldn't have done this, and she prayed their one night together wouldn't be discovered. Too nervous and guilty to go back to sleep, she wanted only to escape the scene of her crime— not theirs, but *hers.*

She woke Andrew and told him they needed to get back before it began to grow light. He tried to take her into his arms again, but she slipped out of bed. She felt unclean and she yearned for a shower. But there wasn't time. She was starting to panic.

She wanted to be back at Fairchild Acres. There, she would pack her things and write a note to Louisa saying she was leaving—no two weeks' notice, no noble excuses. She would just escape as quickly and cleanly as possible.

Andrew sensed her distress. "Marie? What's wrong? Do you have regrets? Are you sorry this happened?"

"I just don't want us to be caught—it might hurt you in the election," she said. "Jacko will smear you all he can. As for me, I just want out of here. The situation between Louisa and me's becoming too difficult."

"I don't want you to go," he said. "I love you. But if you have to leave, I'll come to you in Darwin, I swear."

You won't want to when you know the truth about me, she thought. *And I won't be in Darwin. I don't know where I'll end up.*

But she said, "Any place would be better than here. And after the election would be better than now. It was crazy dangerous to do this. And it was my fault. All mine."

He rose, still naked, and grasped her shoulders. "No. I've wanted you from the moment you gave me back the charm. And we touched. I never believed in charms and such things. But it happened. I wanted you, and I came after you. If what we did was wrong, I'm to blame, too. You never acted like a seductress, you know."

I did last night, she thought, but said nothing. She started putting on her clothes. When she got to the bungalow, she'd throw the green outfit in the incinerator. She never wanted to see it again.

He frowned. "Marie? You want to go back right now? Don't you want to even take a shower? I mean—"

"I want to go now," she said unhappily. "I'm getting a bad feeling about being here. I don't care about a shower. I just want *out* of here before it's light."

Looking perplexed and disbelieving, he followed her lead and began to dress. "If you regret this, I'm sorry, but—"

"I don't," she replied. "I wanted it to happen. But I should be back on the grounds without anyone seeing me. It's best to go now. Please." She was nearly in tears. He held her a long moment.

"Please," she whispered again, her cheek against his chest where his charm used to rest. "Please."

When they stepped outside, the sky was still dark. She had been a virgin when she'd entered this room, but was one no longer. But she better understood now what had happened to Colette. And to Louisa.

She and Andrew talked little on the drive back. She knew that she seemed distant and moody and more than a little sad. The silence became harder to bear, so that almost a mile from the Fairchild Acres gates, where a road forked, she suddenly asked Andrew to stop. She'd bike the rest of the way.

He got the bike from the truck bed while she changed back into her tennis shoes and shorts. She folded up her skirt and tucked it into her backpack. Without waiting for Andrew's help, she got out of the truck and shouldered her pack into place.

She walked to the bike and took it by the handlebars. He looked down at her, his expression both puzzled and concerned. "I wish you wouldn't go everyplace on that rickety old bike."

"It gets me where I need to go," she said airily. "And I need to go back and start packing."

"I'll call you tonight," he said.

"Sure," she replied as casually as she could. "You can try. I may still be traveling. But I'll talk to you as soon as I can."

"When can I see you?" Andrew asked. "I have to see you again."

"If you want to, then you will," she said cryptically. She stood on her tiptoes and kissed his cheek. "Good luck in the election. And goodbye for now."

He seized her by the upper arms. "No goodbyes. I'll see you soon. Count on it."

He kissed her so thoroughly the world seemed to spin around her. In spite of his words, she knew that this really might be goodbye, final and complete.

But she pretended otherwise. He managed a weak smile.

"Until later then," she said, and mounted the bike. He stood and watched her go.

Both of them were too distraught to notice two men, barely visible on the hill behind them, watching. Their camera had clicked almost a dozen times. It clicked as Andrew got back into the truck and drove down a different fork than Marie had taken.

The men got back into their own truck. They drove to the same fork and went left, following Marie through the darkness.

Chapter Seventeen

Marie became aware of headlights approaching from behind. They lit the tree trunks and leaves in a dizzying kaleidoscope of shifting brightness and shadow.

In fact, the lights were approaching *too* fast—whoever was behind her was speeding, as well as weaving, because the light and darkness before her arced crazily. She glanced over her shoulder, and the headlights almost blinded her. They seemed to belong to a truck that veered back and forth on the road, gaining on her.

A drunk, she thought nervously and began to pull over to the side to get out of its erratic path. But a ditch ran beside the road, leaving her only a narrow margin to negotiate, and suddenly the truck was upon her, slowing now, keeping her in the beams of its headlights, and it seemed headed straight for her.

She struggled to keep the bike balanced in the long, dry, clutching grass. The brightening glare confused her, and the rumble of the engine filled her ears. The driver was bearing down on her, going more slowly, but she couldn't dodge out of his way.

He's doing this deliberately, she thought. Or he's completely out of control—and then she had no time to think, because the truck braked, hitting her back wheel, sending the bike spinning out of control and into the ditch. Somehow she swung herself free, but landed on it, a handlebar hitting her stomach, and her head striking the dirt. Pain flashed through her, and she couldn't get her breath.

Then she heard someone scrambling down the bank, but opening her eyes, could see only a man who seemed made of shadows. She struggled to get to her feet, but he was on her, pinioning her arms, and a rough hand clutched her throat.

An unshaven face scraped her cheek, and a hoarse voice whispered, "Don't worry, love." Stunned, flailing impotently, she felt herself hauled from the ditch and pushed into the back of a van.

Then a second man grasped her face and forced her head to tilt back. He pried open her jaws. She gathered her strength to try to fight back, but then she felt something warm and watery shoot down her throat. What? she thought in panic. Are they drugging me...?

The realization stumbled and swayed in her mind, and then it vanished. The world went dim, she could no longer think, and she collapsed limply on the backseat. She barely felt her hands being tied behind her, or the impact of her body being pushed to the floor, or the scratchiness of an old blanket spread over her motionless form.

She woke groggily to the distant sound of ranting galah birds. She heard wind and smelled dust and mustiness. Opening her eyes, she saw that she seemed to be in some small, nearly empty building of stone and weathered planks. An old shelter for a shepherd or stockman. Slices of sunlight beat through the missing split shingles of the roof.

She ached all over, her brain was muddled, and her mouth dry. It was also taped shut. Her hands, wrists scraped, were bound fast behind her back, and her feet tied together at the ankles. She lay on her side on a rough blanket on the dirt floor.

She stared at a stony wall with one old window frame, empty of glass.

And she knew she wasn't alone. The scent of tea hovered in the hot air and, oddly, peanut butter. A mumble of voices came from behind her, men playing cards. Their voices were low, their words indistinct because of music coming from a tinny-sounding radio.

She could see her green shorts and shirt, now torn, dirty and spotted with dried blood. Her thighs were criss-crossed with scratches, darkened by bruises. She wriggled, trying to ease the pain and cramping of her body.

"Oh, ho!" said a man. "Look who's awake. Wonder where you are, blondie?"

She tried to snap a sarcastic answer, but the tape muffled it. She heard the man rise and move heavily toward her. Then his hands were on her, harshly jerking her to lie nearly on her back. It hurt and she tried to grimace.

But when she saw his face up close, she forgot her pain and fought to wrest herself from his touch. He was large, fleshy, and his head was shaved. But she recognized him. It was the man called Winkler from Lochlain, Chalk Winkler, the one who'd seen Andrew snatch her out of reach of the snake, who'd been at the fire beside Reynard that night.

He must have seen the recognition in her eyes. His thick lips curved in a smile. "Ah, remember me, do you? I'll be one of the last things you'll remember. You're going to be a maggot farm—it happens fast here, y'know. Maggots and ants and the crows."

She tried not to flinch, but couldn't help herself.

He leaned closer. "Shame, you bein' so pretty. But I could have you first, blondie. Have you any way I want."

He seized her by the jaw and brought his big face close to hers.

The other man, his back to her, rose from the rickety table. "Leave her alone, Chalk. She just came from being with Preston. She's got traces of him all over her. Don't muddy the water, you great fool."

The words struck her like jolts from a stun gun. The voice was Reynard's—*Reynard* had betrayed her? He had stalked her, hurt her, kidnapped her, and now she was his prisoner? And he and this man planned to kill her. *Why? Why? Why?*

Tears of fury and helplessness filled her eyes. Reynard walked over and stared down at her. Laconically he said, "Sorry, love. I told you to stay away from Andrew Preston. I told you he's got enemies. You should have listened." He winked at her slyly. "Shouldn't you? Ahh, but it's too late now."

He hauled the other man to his feet. "Don't get ideas, Chalk. Your brain's not built for it. How long until we kill her? I'm ready for it to be over. And for us to be out of here."

Chalk, towering over Reynard, spoke between his teeth. "Feeney said we wait till the drug's out of her system. Another half hour at least. I told you twice already, you deaf old coot."

"I just wish it was over, is all," grumbled Reynard. "Sit down and deal, will you? I intend to take you for another fiver at least."

But Chalk hesitated a moment, looking down at Marie. "Know what we shot down your throat? A sedative. Ollie got it for us in Singapore. Feeney's got all *kinds* of people workin' for Jacko."

Ollie? Marie blinked, feeling even more sick and betrayed. *Ollie, Andrew's pilot? Him, too? And Reynard? And Sandy Sanford. And Chalk?*

It was, in truth, a conspiracy. But how big, how all-powerful was it?

At Lochlain, at exactly ten in the morning, Andrew sat moodily in the kitchen, drinking a cup of coffee. His phone rang again. Mechanically he answered, expecting it to be Darci with more campaign news.

But a strange voice said, "Andrew Preston? Candidate for the ITRF Presidency?"

"Yes?"

"This is Peter Topaz of ABC-TV, News Department. By e-mail our news department's received photos of you from a source we can't trace. They show you and a woman who's identified as Marie Lafayette, a cook at Fairchild Acres. They were taken with a camera with a date and time device. The two of you are shown entering a room at the Banksia Springs Inn at 8:37 last night and leaving at 4:27 a.m. Slightly later in the morning, you're shown kissing by the side of a road.

"There are other undated pictures of you holding her. You're shirtless and wearing an Aboriginal love charm around your neck. There's also a message that Miss Lafayette sometimes worked as a prostitute in Darwin. A prostitute with a penchant for blackmail. Whoever sent these says he has a list of eight men who'll testify to it. Mr. Preston, we've sent an attachment with these photos and the message to you and your campaign manager, Darci Parnell. We'd like your response to this material."

Stunned, disbelieving, Andrew managed to choke out "No comment" and end the call.

He immediately dialed Darci. "Listen," he said tersely. "I spent the night with Marie Lafayette in Banksia Springs. Somebody got photographs and sent them to ABC. They also got a message that Marie's a hooker. That there's a list of tricks, men she tried to blackmail."

"Oh, Andrew," Darci wailed. "What have you gotten yourself into? If ABC has them, all Jacko's media's going to have them, too. A hooker? Oh, my God."

"She's no hooker," he retorted angrily. "She's—she was a virgin."

"Then what's with the list?" Darci demanded.

"It's a damned smear is what it is," Andrew shot back. "You can pay flunkies to say anything. I'm calling my detective."

"Andrew," Darci warned, "this story will break. And it's going to deal this campaign a huge blow. Let me check this out. I'll call you back."

He didn't say goodbye. He could barely speak. He tasted a sourness rising in his throat and wondered if he was going to vomit up the coffee. He felt queasy and breathless. He knew she was a virgin. He *knew* that.

But had she set him up? He couldn't and wouldn't believe it. With an unsteady hand, he dialed her number. Nothing happened. Was her phone dead? Could she have turned it off?

What if she was already on her way back to Darwin? A throbbing hammered in his temples.

He looked up the Fairchild Acres number and dialed it. Mrs. Lipton answered, her voice shaking.

"Mrs. Lipton," he said. "This is Andrew Preston. I'm trying to reach Marie, but I couldn't get her. I wondered—"

"Oh, Mr. Preston," Mrs. Lipton said. "She's *gone*. The police were just here. They found her bicycle, wrecked, in a ditch beside the road. There was blood on the grass. There's no s-sign of her."

The woman started to sob.

Someone, Helena, perhaps, took the phone from her. "Mr. Preston? The local authorities notified the New South Wales police. They said they're doing all they can. I wish I could tell you more, but I can't. I'm very sorry. I—we'll keep you posted. We're all praying for her. Mr. Preston?"

"Thanks," he rasped, then shut the phone. Like an automaton he walked to his room and turned on his computer. He brought up his e-mail, opened the attachment, and stared numbly at the pictures.

The photos, though not explicit, clearly showed him and Marie, their arms around each other, standing on the tiny porch leading to their room. They were kissing. Neither had any luggage.

The next picture showed them pausing by the door to kiss again. In the next, they were leaving, Marie looking unhappy, but Andrew's arm was around her, his expression concerned. And then there were four photos of them kissing goodbye last night, and three of him holding her against his chest that day at Lochlain.

He swore and buried his face in his hands. Where was she? Was she all right? Had they both been set up?

His phone rang again. He snatched it up, hoping for news of Marie. But it was Darci again.

"I think I'm going to be sick," she said bitterly. "This is going to hit the news fast. We need a good response ready." The bitterness in her tone turned to disgust. "How could you do this to all of us? *How?* The vote's in three weeks. You had it in your grasp, and you've probably lost it for good."

Her tone turned militant. "I bet that girl set you up. That she's a plant."

"She's missing, dammit," he said angrily. "They found her bike wrecked and blood at the scene. For all I know she could be dead so just—"

"I hope she isn't. But if she is, tongues will wag. I know. I've been there, in the middle of a sex scandal. But I was a seventeen-year-old kid who knew *nothing*. You should know better. This raises all kinds of questions about you. People will ask if you had a lover's quarrel. Did she threaten to blackmail you? Did you follow her and—"

"Shut up!" Andrew barked, rubbing his forehead. "Don't waste your time on dirty scenarios. Find out what's going on here."

"What's going on, Andrew," Darci said, steel in her voice, "is that if this gets any uglier, your reputation's ruined. Probably for good."

Andrew hung up on her. He rammed the kitchen screen door open and marched to the Jeep. He was going to the police.

Chalk, Marie's burly captor, talked on his cell, then shut it off. "Feeney says ABC's got the message. He wagers the cops'll be looking at the stuff right now." He glanced at his watch. "It's almost time to waste the little sheila."

"I just wish it was over, is all," Reynard said loudly.

"You've said that half a dozen times," Chalk retorted. "You want me to do it? Her being your kin and all?"

Reynard went surly. "I'll do it because *I just wish it was over.* It's not that she means anything to me. I had her for a plant in the Fairchild house, that's all. But she should have stayed away from Preston. Can't say she wasn't warned. She should've listened."

He sighed tiredly. "She's no real kin to me. But she's a game little spunk. I'll be quick with her. I think you might enjoy it too much—and take too long."

"Cut her a bit for more bloodstains," Chalk said sullenly. "Then strangle her. Use gloves. Feeney knows what to do to get his man elected. El Presidente Jacko. Viva!"

Reynard spotted the leather thong around her neck and pulled the charm from under the neckline of her blouse. "Well, here's irony. The best incriminatin' evidence we got—Preston's famous charm. Marie, dear," he said, "roll over a bit. I've got to get this charm off and slide it under you. Like Preston dropped it. Very nice of him to let you have it."

He thrust the charm under her and released her. She glared at him.

He smiled down at her almost tenderly. "I wish it was over, but I'll try to make it painless as I can."

Surreally, Marie realized that Reynard would soon kill her. Why? It could only be to frame Andrew. She began to weep with anger and the pain of Reynard's treachery.

Reynard stooped over her. "I'll try to hurt you little as I can, love. There's nothin' personal here. Business is business." He winked at her again. "Just a little cut on the ankle, deary. And then one or two about the arms. Then I cut off your air. It'll be fast, my sweet. You want it over, and I wish it was over, too."

He barely pricked her ankle. He seemed to be trying to listen for something, something he could not hear. Dazed, she realized he'd cut the rope binding her feet.

He cut the ropes tying her wrists. "And a goodbye kiss from your Uncle Reynard, my chook." He put his face close to hers until their lips nearly touched. "If Chalk comes near you, kick him in the family jewels and keep kicking. Remember you're your mother's girl."

He put his gloved hands gently on her neck. "Oh, my poor dear," he said. "If only you'd listened…"

"What's takin' so long?" Chalk demanded. "I'm gonna do it meself. I thought you wanted it done fast."

"I do," Reynard admitted. *"I want it over right now!"*

"You crazy git," Chalk snarled. "Stop yelling!"

"I'm near deaf," Reynard shouted. "I can't always tell how loud I am. Don't pick on the disabled!"

"It's your head, not your ears what's disabled," sneered Chalk. "Gimme that. Why Feeney let you come along is beyond me." He shouldered Reynard aside and stooped over Marie as he pulled on his stretch vinyl gloves.

As he tugged at the right wrist, Marie kicked him in the groin with all the force she had. He doubled up in pain and she elbowed him in the face, then his throat, and kicked like a hellion.

Chalk staggered backward, reaching for the gun in his holster, but Reynard stabbed Chalk's hand clear through. He seized the gun and pistol-whipped him until the bigger man crumpled to the floor, unconscious.

"Land now!" he screamed in anger. "Will you bloody land, you bastards?"

Marie stared at him in incomprehension. He dropped to his knees and cradled her in his arms. He kept repeating "I'm sorry…I'm sorry…so sorry…"

His voice shaking, he tried to explain how he got trapped in this scenario.

In an almost dream state, Marie could not bring herself to hug him, but she found strange comfort in his sinewy arms, his apologetic endearments. Vaguely she realized that he was crying.

He cried, but strange sounds started to drown out his muffled voice. From overhead came an increasing clatter, and the distant sound of sirens. "Well," said Reynard, "New South Wales's finest is finally here. I'm an informer, dear. I been wearing a wire the whole time. They was supposed to close in as soon as I said I just wanted it over. How many times did I have to tell the stunned mullets? A hundred? Crikey!"

When the first of the NSW police burst in, Reynard chided them. "Where were you, you dipsticks? You know what you put this little girl through?"

A helicopter pilot eyed him malevolently. "Had to roadblock the local gendarmes before they came rip roaring down the road. Sorry. Bureaucratic screw-up."

"Imagine that," Reynard said sarcastically. He took the tape from Marie's mouth as gently as he could. To her he said, "I usually do drug cases. The cops sent me down here after somebody started threatening Tyler Preston. Because they had a tip somebody might try to sabotage Andrew Preston's campaign. And somebody did. My job? To ingratiate myself with any unsavory types. I overdid it. Come on, duck, let's get you outside into some fresh air."

He helped Marie to limp outside, and she leaned against the stone wall, her knees weak.

He looked into her eyes. "I suspected Sandy Sanford, but he wouldn't warm up to me. But another cove did. A plant straight from Jacko's connections. Chalk. We knew each other a bit from before. He let me know there'd be dirty business. I told him I was up for anything that paid a good price.

"Your Andrew was too smart, love. He'd figured it out. Bullock saw a way to get all that land if Sam and Tyler and Louisa were out of the way. With those three spreads, and the presidency of the Federation, he'd be the most powerful man in Australian racing. And he planned to bring Andrew down, even if murder was what it took. He used Feeney to arrange things, to keep his own hands clean."

She looked at him accusingly. "But why'd you help kidnap me?"

"It was the last thing I wanted," he said with intensity. "But conspiracy to murder should put Jacko away for life. Chalk trusted me from the old days, but he started getting suspicious because of you. He said I was to help do away with you. I knew it was a loyalty test. If I didn't seem to sell you out, he'd have killed me, then you. I had to say yes, if I was going to help you."

She shook her head wearily. "I still don't understand."

"It was Andrew's cell phone. It couldn't be tapped, but Ollie put a bug in Andrew's computer case. It was strong enough to transmit his calls to Feeney. All of them. Feeney knew Andrew was falling for you. He knew you'd be together last night as soon as you arranged it—I *warned* you not to talk to Preston, not to see him. I wanted you out of here for your own safety."

He paused and looked at her sadly. "You didn't listen. You agreed to meet him. And Feeney said it was the perfect time—Jacko wanted it to happen fast. It was only three weeks before the election. And you two were so careful. Who knew when there'd be another chance?"

She felt her face grow hot. He *had* warned her, repeatedly.

Headstrong, she'd defied him. And put his life, as well as her own in danger.

"Yes, you tried," she said. "But—but who sent you the letter? Who warned you?"

He put his hands on her arms, gripping her tightly. "Nobody sent it. I wrote it myself. To convince you to leave."

She blinked hard. "You said I was being investigated. That there was untrue information about me."

"It's truth. Feeney has people in Darwin. He had them bribe some blokes to swear they'd had their way with you, and that you tried to blackmail 'em. One of 'em had even worked with you. A busboy. So that was the scenario. That you'd try the same blackmail stunt on Andrew, and he'd do you in."

"And your bringing me to Louisa's in the first place?" she challenged.

"That truly was for you, love. I never dreamed you'd get mixed up with Preston. I only wanted you to get what was rightfully yours. If I'd known this would happen, I never would have let you come. I'm sorry, love. I am everlastingly sorry."

From a distance, she heard her name being called. The man's voice was raw with emotion. She looked and saw Andrew pounding down the road toward her. Right behind him was a Pepper Flats policeman. She turned and started toward Andrew.

"Just a minute, miss," cautioned an NSW officer stepping outside the building. "You're bruised and bleeding. We better take a look at you."

"Look while I'm running," she retorted and sprinted off with astonishing speed even though her gait was uneven.

"Is she always that stubborn?" asked the officer.

Reynard smiled ironically. "She gets it from her granny."

Andrew and Marie met with such force that they collided and fell, embracing and laughing and crying and kissing in the dusty road.

"Jacko Bullock had me kidnapped," she said in a rush. "He wanted me strangled and you framed. Look. They were even going to use this to help make it seem like you." She waggled the charm to show him.

Stunned, he stared at it. "They would have used that—good God."

"Reynard was the one who said he'd kill me. But he was a plant. He says he's some kind of informer or something—he cut my ropes. He saved me...."

"But he let all this happen to you?" Andrew demanded.

She glanced up the road and saw Reynard making his way toward them. "Yes, but he *saved* me. He was wearing a wire, and they've got evidence on tape that'll convict Jacko and his flunkies and probably bring down a whole bunch of people."

"I don't care," Andrew replied, rising grimly to his feet and drawing her up beside him.

Reynard reached them and extended his hand toward Andrew. "Marie had a few bad hours, mate, but everything's going to be fine. All's well that ends well."

"It will be shortly," said Andrew, and punched Reynard so hard he knocked him flat on his back. Marie clutched Andrew to keep him from further violence.

Reynard sat up and rubbed his jaw. "I suppose I deserve that. I suppose I do. Well, Andrew, you must have word of the pictures by now. The whole county will see them before all this comes out. Be sure of it." He gestured at the officers surrounding the shack and the men carrying a stretcher with Chalk strapped to it. "Hope I didn't kill him," he murmured almost to himself. "Gets messy, that."

He turned and squinted up at Andrew, rubbing his chin again. "Anyway, if you know about the pictures, there's something *I'd* like to know."

Andrew knotted his fist and growled, "What?"

"They show you smooching Marie up and going into the Whoops-A-Daisy Inn. Are you going to make an honest woman of my poor, disgraced niece?"

Andrew blinked at the words, looked at Marie and seized her possessively by the shoulders. "Want to be an honest woman?" he asked.

"Convince me," she said, winding her arms around his neck. He kissed her hungrily.

"I don't think much would get accomplished around here without me," sighed Reynard. "But what thanks do I get? I believe my tooth's cracked. This is how the crime fighter is paid for putting his life on the line? I despair of justice."

That evening, in Louisa's library, Andrew, Marie, Reynard and Hans Gerhart explained Jacko's plot to Louisa. She sat, queenlike, in an antique armchair. The four of them stood solemnly before her.

Shamefaced, hardly able to meet Louisa's eyes, Marie confessed about the letter from Willadene Gates.

"I shouldn't have come," she said. "Or I should have come to you and been honest from the start. I'm very ashamed. But I won't ever pursue this matter further. I ask nothing of you except your forgiveness, if you can find it in your heart. I'm going back to Darwin where I belong."

Louisa gripped the arms of her chair more tightly. She said nothing.

Reynard spoke up. "It was me that made her do it. It took everything I had to make her give it a try. The idea was mine, not hers. But I wanted, for once in her life, for her to have a break. For she's a good girl, she is. The finest. The best."

"And you," Louisa said, narrowing her eyes at him, "lie and sell information for a living. You pretend to be what you aren't. You beguile and flatter—and betray."

"Well, ma'am," said Gerhart, "he *does* do it for the authorities. And it's extremely dangerous work."

"I would have given anything if it hadn't gone as far as it did, madame. I will forever regret the deceit I inflicted on you, and the anguish I caused Marie."

Slowly Louisa rose from her chair. She stepped up and stared into Reynard's face. Then she drew back her arm and smashed the back of her hand as hard as she could across his mouth.

Marie gasped, Andrew put his hand on her shoulder, and Gerhart said nothing.

"That," said Louisa, "is for putting her in danger. You're lucky I don't have my riding crop, you glib bastard, or I'd whip you senseless."

"I have no doubt you would, Miss. And you would have every right. I *am* an insufferable knave."

Louisa glowered at him. "You could have gotten my granddaughter *killed.* And yourself, too, you fool. And you didn't deceive me. Not by a long shot."

She turned to Marie. "I suspected you were my daughter's daughter. I suspected from the first."

Marie's mouth dropped open, and Andrew blinked hard in surprise. Louisa glanced at Gerhart, and then stared at Andrew. "You're not the only person who can hire a detective, you know."

She paused and turned back to Marie. The strength that anger had given her suddenly drained from her. She sat down weakly in her chair and let her eyes drop to her gnarled hands.

"I had a child. I was told it died. I believed it. My parents told me it was for the best. That it was a mercy. I would never have to worry about its fate. Or anyone knowing the shameful thing I'd done. For in those days, it was very shameful."

She paused, knotting her fingers together tightly. "I was only…sixteen. Sixteen. And when I came home, the boy I'd loved no longer loved me. He'd married my sister. My very own sister."

She looked up, meeting Marie's eyes. "I felt betrayed. I was *glad* that I didn't have a baby by him. And he never knew. My parents would never speak of it, except once my mother told me that my sister Betty must never know. It was too scandalous. It would wound *her.*"

Louisa turned her gaze to the window as if staring back through the past. "I never felt the same about my family after that. Not for a long time. But after my parents died, I began to wonder if the hospital and my parents had told me the truth. If the child—the little girl—had lived."

She was silent a moment, then said, "It took me many years to work up my courage. But I consulted a detective, a very discreet detective. And he found that the little girl had lived. She'd been adopted by a family in Darwin. A family named Lafayette. My daughter was grown and had a daughter of her own.

"He gave me some photos he'd taken of her without her

knowledge. And of the place where she lived. And I knew she'd had a hard life. It showed. Oh, how it showed."

She raised her eyes to meet Marie's again. "And I was too *cowardly* to go to her, write to her. Until that moment, I'd never known I was a coward. But I was."

She shook her head and stared into her lap. "One hears stories of adopted children happily reunited with a birth parent. And one hears of reunions that are disastrous, full of disillusion and recriminations and resentment.

"Would she resent me? Hate me? She was poor, and I was rich. Would she pretend to like me for the money and secretly despise me? I visualized ghastly scenarios. Me—old, helpless, in her power, and her paying me back for everything I'd caused...

"And so, I did nothing. And I decided to seek out Betty's children instead. It was so much simpler."

She tossed Reynard a sharp look. "Reynard Lafayette? I never made a connection between you and Colette. Until you contacted Mrs. Lipton about Marie. Reynard, I always thought you a fast-talking rascal, the wheels in your head always turning. When you tried to finagle getting her into my house, I wondered if you and she had some sort of designs on me and my money. Perhaps Colette *had* known of me and wanted nothing to do with me. But Marie? Did she know?

"Marie, the instant Mrs. Lipton told me about you, I thought you must be Colette's daughter. When I saw you, I was almost certain. But you didn't tell me. I didn't know *what* you were up to. All along," she said, "we've played a game of cat and mouse. I sometimes wasn't sure which of us was the cat and which the mouse."

Louisa sat very straight again. "Marie, ten years ago I put a provision in my will for Colette and you. I could not face giving you myself. But I could give you money. I watched and provoked and tested you, trying to discover your motives. And to decide if I should write you out of the will for being a cunning little gold digger."

Marie's body tensed, and her heart thudded against her breastbone. "I didn't even know if you *were* my grandmother. Or if I wanted you to be, to tell the truth."

For the first time, Louisa smiled, wryly and knowingly. "Yes. That's what I finally realized. I was trying to see if you were worth recognizing. And you were doing the same damned thing to me. Oh, you've got more of me in you than you know, my girl."

Marie sucked in her breath in astonishment and could say nothing.

"You'll get your inheritance, my girl. More than the original amount. There's plenty for Megan and Patrick and Wesley—and my granddaughter. Come here, Marie, my kith and kin."

Marie moved toward her, Louisa rose, and the two women embraced. Louisa held her long and tightly. "Go back to Darwin if you must," Louisa said, her voice unsteady, "but if you do, come back here often to see an unpleasant old woman who's grown quite fond of you."

She looked over Marie's shoulder at Reynard. "As for your odious yet inventive uncle," Louisa said, "I'll send him to the United States to see if his tinnitus can be cured. It will, of course, be a waste of money, but I owe him something, I suppose. Including giving him a good whack on the skull with my stoutest walking stick."

"Use that heavy silver one," Andrew suggested.

"And you, I suppose," Louisa said to Andrew, "will be the president of the federation, and my grandson-in-law. I've seen the way you've been looking at her. Well, you come from a strong line and should sire some very handsome great-grandchildren for me, and I want *lots*. Hear me?"

Reynard gave Andrew a sideways look. "I suggest you follow her suggestion, mate."

"I hear, and I will obey," smiled Andrew, gazing at Marie.

Louisa drew back, but took Marie's face between her hands. "And if you choose to, you will always have a place here, a home. For I see you, indeed, as my Fair Child, miraculously restored to this Fairchild, who does not deserve you, but who is delighted to have found you."

The two women kissed, and Marie knew Louisa meant what she said. And she was flooded with happiness and a feeling of completion like none she'd ever known. She thought how bereft she'd been in February, consigning Colette's ashes to the blue waters of the harbor, how alone she'd felt.

Oh, Mama, she thought, *do you see this, know this? When you were gone, I thought everything was gone. But it wasn't. You told me where to look.*

You've given me a place to belong and people to care for, a whole new life.

Thank you, Mama. Thank you. I love you so much. And your brother, too. He got me here, Mama. You both got me here.

PART FIVE

Australia, The Hunter Valley
May and June

Epilogue

The story broke sensationally across Australia: Jacko Bullock had intricate ties to organized crime, and he used them to try to gain power and land in the Hunter Valley, and to destroy anyone who opposed him. He'd tried to throw blame on Louisa to keep anyone from suspecting an outsider of the crimes at Lochlain.

Federal investigators, state investigators and informants had enough evidence to swiftly arraign and indict him. And so, instead of vast tracts of land, Jacko found himself in a small, barren-looking cell.

His gang ties kept unraveling further and further, until the investigation turned into one of the largest in the history of Australian organized crime. Feeney, Chalk, Ollie and others were arrested, and more criminal links were uncovered each day.

The racing world was scandalized as the story grew bigger and reached ever further, even to corrupt law officers and politicians.

But the media made no mention of Reynard. Within a week he had disappeared from Hunter Valley without so much as a goodbye. *He's back at work,* Marie thought.

Andrew, now running unopposed, was a shoo-in, and when he made his acceptance speech after the election count, Marie was at his side. He lifted her hand high, announcing she'd consented to marry him. She wore a modest diamond engagement ring.

Andrew's inauguration ceremony took place two weeks later, with all the Preston family brought together for the first time in years. Louisa, of course, insisted on hosting a lavish celebration for the Prestons and friends from the Australian racing community.

And she was also determined to out-gala the gala she'd thrown for Jacko Bullock.

This time caterers came from both Newcastle and Sidney, and she somehow even enticed Francois back to do appetizers.

Once again the party rental people swarmed over the front lawn, setting up silky-looking white tents, tables covered with snow-white cloths and white wicker chairs. Florists placed bouquets on every table, and festooned the stage and each tent with garlands of tropical flowers flown in from Darwin.

This time there were only six enormous inflated kangaroos in digger hats staked to the ground, but there were also six inflated American eagles with Uncle Sam hats. Six white poles flew the Australian flag, six more the American flag, and also rippling in the breeze were the flags of New South Wales and Kentucky.

A playground was erected for the younger children—and there were many. For the first time, Marie met Andrew's fabled family, his grandfather Hugh, his parents, the sweet-faced Jenna and the sterner Thomas.

She was welcomed to the family enthusiastically by Andrew's younger sister, Melanie, and Marcus, her darkly handsome husband. She met Andrew's youngest brother, Robbie, his wife Amanda, and their two sons. And lastly she met the middle brother, the solemn-eyed Brent, his beautiful English wife, and their eight-year-old twin girls.

There were also cousins and second cousins and old friends, and an aunt and uncle, as well as Louisa's newly recognized family: Megan and Dylan Hastings, Patrick Stafford and Bronwyn and Wesley.

The evening's weather was perfect, the small orchestra onstage played everything from Bach to the latest love ballads, and Louisa had even hired a pair of brightly colored hot air balloons to take guests up to float nearer to the stars.

The elderly Hugh Preston seemed to find Louisa rather fetching, and flirted with her with verve, but she was not tempted. He was also interested in buying a share in her new favorite horse, Tons O' Trouble. And *that,* thought Louisa, might indeed be something to talk about with the feisty old fellow.

Andrew and Marie announced their wedding date and that the ceremony would take place at Fairchild Acres. There was a champagne toast to them, and Louisa had planned an elaborate fireworks display to mark the occasion.

But just when the cascading sparks and bright explosions were reaching their peak, Marie was overwhelmed and astonished to see Reynard.

He seemed to appear from nowhere as if he were a wizard who had just quietly teleported himself. He moved toward her, shaven, even wearing a starched white shirt with his jeans. He looked so wonderful to her that she no longer saw the fireworks, barely heard them.

He came to her, kissed her, and shook Andrew's hand, telling him to take care of "his love, Marie." He said he couldn't stay long, it might be dangerous, but he wanted to give them an engagement gift. He pressed a box into Marie's hand with an envelope. "I love you, chook," he whispered gruffly. He kissed her, then disappeared, again as if by magic, into the crowd.

Marie and Andrew drew off to the side by themselves and opened the letter from Reynard. He wrote that for his own protection, the NSW force was transferring him to another location far away, one that he could not reveal. He didn't know when, if ever, he might see them again, but he hoped that someday he would.

He apologized again for putting Marie in such a terrifying position, but said he had acted the scoundrel in order to catch greater scoundrels than himself. Still, putting her in danger was the greatest shame of his life. He hoped the truth that came to light from her jeopardy would make Australia a better place and racing more honest. Most of all, he hoped that she could forgive him.

And, he wrote, he really had wanted her to claim her legacy from Louisa Fairchild. He'd had no intention of getting her involved in any machinations of the syndicate. When she and Andrew became attracted to each other, he'd been arrogant enough to think he could keep her out of trouble. He'd been wrong.

As for me, I pray that a man may be a rogue, yet still have some decency in him. Set a crook to catch a crook, they say. I daresay I've done more in the cause of law and order than many an honest man, but then I'm a glib old rascal who always has an excuse, eh?

If you have kiddies and speak to them of me, please don't be too hard on your Uncle Reynard. Keep the item in the box for me. Next to you and Colette, it is what I am most proud of.

May your lives be long and beautiful and blessed.
Love always, Rennie

With trembling hands Marie opened the box. In the velvet interior rested the Australian Bravery Medal, a heavy bronze disk ensigned with the Crown of Saint Edward. Marie immediately recognized it. It was most prestigious medal the government could bestow on a civilian.

On a small piece of paper Reynard had written,

This was given to me in a private ceremony for certain work I did concerning breaking up a drug ring in Sydney. This was REALLY awarded to me and I did NOT buy it in a pawn shop. I had to get shot to get it. See my name engraved on the back, and the date, too.

Marie turned the medal over. Rennie's name was engraved on the award, and a date of three years ago.

"I remember," Marie said in a choked voice. "He was gone such a long time and we didn't hear from him. Then we heard he was in a hospital in Sydney, but he was always evasive about what was wrong. Shot! And the Bravery Medal. My mother would have been so proud."

Then she noticed a PS. "By the way, I have a touch of tinnitus, but my ears are better than a bat's. A great advantage in my line of work. It's amazing what people will say when they think a man's half-deaf."

Louisa appeared and said, "Did I see Reynard? I swore I did."

"He's gone," Marie replied. "He couldn't stay."

"Humph," grumped Louisa. "Didn't even say hello to me. What an impossible fellow."

She stared off into the distance. "I don't know if he was a good man with bad traits or a bad man with good traits, yet I rather liked him much of the time. She sighed. "Sometimes he made me wish I were thirty years younger...."

"Why?" Marie asked.

Louisa smiled almost to herself. "I think I would have tried to tame the creature. He needs a firm hand to bring out the best in him."

Andrew put one arm around Louisa, the other around Marie. He kissed Louisa's cheek. "You might have been just the gal to do it," he said.

The three of them stood together staring off silently in the direction Reynard had taken. Marie held the medal cradled in her hand, tears rising in her eyes, straining to see him. But he was gone. She held the medal more tightly and looked upward.

The last Roman candles flared, and the last showers of gold and silver and scarlet brightened the night and descended like falling stars.

* * * * *

Silhouette Desire kicks off 2009 with
MAN OF THE MONTH,
*a yearlong program featuring incredible
heroes by stellar authors.*

When Navy SEAL Hunter Cabot returns home for some
much-needed R & R, he discovers he's a married man.
There's just one problem: he's never met his "bride."

*Enjoy this sneak peek at Maureen Child's
AN OFFICER AND A MILLIONAIRE.
Available January 2009
from Silhouette Desire.*

One

Hunter Cabot, Navy SEAL, had a healing bullet wound in his side, thirty days' leave and, apparently, a wife he'd never met.

On the drive into his hometown of Springville, California, he stopped for gas at Charlie Evans's service station. That's where the trouble started.

"Hunter! Man, it's good to see you! Margie didn't tell us you were coming home."

"Margie?" Hunter leaned back against the front fender of his black pickup truck and winced as his side gave a small twinge of pain. Silently then, he watched as the man he'd known since high school filled his tank.

Charlie grinned, shook his head and pumped gas. "Guess your wife was lookin' for a little 'alone' time with you, huh?"

"My—" Hunter couldn't even say the word. *Wife?* He didn't have a wife. "Look, Charlie..."

"Don't blame her, of course," his friend said with a wink as he finished up and put the gas cap back on. "You being gone all the time with the SEALs must be hard on the ol' love life."

He'd never had any complaints, Hunter thought, frowning at the man still talking a mile a minute. "What're you—"

"Bet Margie's anxious to see you. She told us all about that R & R trip you two took to Bali." Charlie's dark brown eyebrows lifted and wiggled.

"Charlie..."

"Hey, it's okay, you don't have to say a thing, man."

What the hell could he say? Hunter shook his head, paid for his gas and as he left, told himself Charlie was just losing it. Maybe the guy had been smelling gas fumes too long.

But as it turned out, it wasn't just Charlie. Stopped at a red light on Main Street, Hunter glanced out his window to smile at Mrs. Harker, his second-grade teacher who was now at least a hundred years old. In the middle of the crosswalk, the old lady stopped and shouted, "Hunter Cabot, you've got yourself a wonderful wife. I hope you appreciate her."

Scowling now, he only nodded at the old woman—the only teacher who'd ever scared the crap out of him. What the hell was going on here? Was everyone but him nuts?

His temper beginning to boil, he put up with a few more comments about his "wife" on the drive through town before finally pulling into the wide, circular drive leading to the Cabot mansion. Hunter didn't have a clue what was going on, but he planned to get to the bottom of it. Fast.

He grabbed his duffel bag, stalked into the house and paid no attention to the housekeeper, who ran at him, fluttering both hands. "Mr. Hunter!"

"Sorry, Sophie," he called out over his shoulder as he took the stairs two at a time. "Need a shower, then we'll talk."

He marched down the long, carpeted hallway to the rooms that were always kept ready for him. In his suite, Hunter tossed the duffel down and stopped dead. The shower in his bathroom was running. His *wife?*

Anger and curiosity boiled in his gut, creating a churning mass that had him moving forward without even thinking about it. He opened the bathroom door to a wall of steam and the sound of a woman singing—off-key. Margie, no doubt.

Well, if she was his wife...Hunter walked across the room, yanked the shower door open and stared in at a curvy, naked, temptingly wet woman.

She whirled to face him, slapping her arms across her naked body while she gave a short, terrified scream.

Hunter smiled. "Hi, honey. I'm home."

* * * * *

Be sure to look for
AN OFFICER AND A MILLIONAIRE
by USA TODAY *bestselling author Maureen Child.*
Available January 2009 from Silhouette Desire.